SNAKE OIL: EASY PICKIN'S

SNAKE OIL: EASY PICKIN'S

MARCUS GALLOWAY

FIVE STAR

A part of Gale, a Cengage Company

GALE
A Cengage Company

Farmington Hills, Mich • San Francisco • New York • Waterville, Maine
Meriden, Conn • Mason, Ohio • Chicago

LIBRARY OF CONGRESS CATALOGING-IN-PUBLICATION DATA

Names: Galloway, Marcus, author.
Title: Snake oil : easy pickin's / Marcus Galloway.
Description: First edition. | Waterville, Maine : Five Star Publishing, a part of Cengage Learning, Inc., [2017] | Description based on print version record and CIP data provided by publisher; resource not viewed.
Identifiers: LCCN 2017004588 (print) | LCCN 2016058126 (ebook) | ISBN 9781432835019 (ebook) | ISBN 1432835017 (ebook) | ISBN 9781432832605 (ebook) | ISBN 1432832603 (ebook) | ISBN 9781432832636 (hardcover) | ISBN 1432832638 (hardcover)
Subjects: | BISAC: FICTION / Historical. | FICTION / Action & Adventure. | GSAFD: Western stories.
Classification: LCC PS3607.A4196 (print) | LCC PS3607.A4196 S63 2017 (ebook) | DDC 813/.6—dc23
LC record available at https://lccn.loc.gov/2017004588

First Edition. First Printing: June 2017
Find us on Facebook— https://www.facebook.com/FiveStarCengage
Visit our website— http://www.gale.cengage.com/fivestar/
Contact Five Star™ Publishing at FiveStar@cengage.com

Printed in the United States of America
1 2 3 4 5 6 7 21 20 19 18 17

SNAKE OIL: EASY PICKIN'S

CHAPTER ONE

Northern Kansas
1878

The road to Barbrady was every bit as scenic and interesting as the Rocky Mountains were flat. The young courier on that road at the moment was tempted to give his reins a flick, tie them off and take a nap. When Byron Keag had first pointed his cart toward the open Kansas expanse, he'd been genuinely excited to make the journey. Of course, that had been the better part of a week and several miles of flat trail ago. Now, his mind was muddied by the continuous sound of wooden wheels grinding against packed soil and the sight of open land splayed in front of him like a carcass that had long ago been picked clean. Although he fought the urge to doze off, he wasn't nearly alert enough to catch sight of a pair of gunmen approaching from the left side of the trail. By the time he did see them, it was too late for a damn thing to be done about it.

The riders swooped down on him from a low range of nearby hills like hawks converging on a mouse. Byron's hooded eyes snapped open and he braced his feet against the board separating his cart from the two horses pulling it. Gritting his teeth, the young man snapped his reins and prayed his team still had some fire in their bellies. Both horses whinnied loudly as leather cracked against their flanks. Despite the dust kicked up by their hooves, the cart wasn't about to make a magnificent escape anytime soon.

By the time the riders came up alongside of Byron, both were laughing. One of the men had skin resembling candle wax that had been melted and drizzled over his skull. A wiry beard jutted from his chin like thorns from a cactus.

The second rider was slightly bigger around the middle than the first with longer hair and a pug nose. One of his eyes was too lazy to look anywhere but down, making it difficult for Byron to notice much more about that man's face.

"Looks like yer horses need a rest," the man with the dark hair shouted while aiming his pistol at the animals hitched to Byron's cart. "You'd best oblige before I put them outta their misery."

Since his wheezing horses didn't inspire much hope of making a getaway, Byron pulled back on his reins.

Lazy Eye could see well enough to point his pistol at Byron while asking, "You want me to check what he's carrying, Sid?"

"Not if our friend here is neighborly enough to tell us on his own," Sid replied. "How about it, friend? You want to save us the trouble of rooting through that cart?"

"You . . . you're robbing me?" Byron gasped.

"Well, we sure as hell ain't about to ask you to dance!"

"All I'm doing is traveling into town on business," Byron explained. "All I've got is some clothes and . . . and such."

Extending his arm to aim his pistol squarely at Byron's head, Lazy Eye impatiently said, "Hand over everything you got or I'll shoot you and take it all myself."

"I don't have anything of value, I swear!"

"What about cash?" Lazy Eye asked.

"All I've got is a few dollars," Byron explained. "That's it!"

"Then you'd best hand over them dollars along with the rest of your valuables," Sid told him, "or we're likely to get impatient."

Byron dug through his pockets for the money. "There," he

said while handing over the little bit of cash that had been lining the inner folds of his dusty jacket.

Having jumped from his saddle, Lazy Eye went around to the back of the cart where he found a large carpetbag lashed in place by a rope looped through a set of iron rings screwed into the weathered wooden panel. "Hey," he shouted while pulling the carpetbag free and tossing it to the ground beside the front end of the cart. "Take a look at this." The bag landed near one of the horse's rear hooves, startling the animal enough for it to shift its weight and shake its head.

Byron sat in his seat, silver dollars still resting in the palm of one outstretched hand, as Sid moved his horse closer for a better look at the bag. It had opened when it hit the ground, allowing a good portion of the bag's contents to spill out. Sid leaned over in his saddle and after taking a lingering downward glance, shifted his eyes back to Byron.

"You got something else we want, mister," Sid said.

Ignoring the threat completely, Byron replied, "Here's your money. Take it and go."

"You must be a real successful businessman."

Lazy Eye ran over to the carpetbag. "I think I spotted some watches in there, too!"

"Forget the damn watches," Sid said in a slow drawl. "Because our friend here is holding something more valuable. Ain't that right?"

Byron shifted in his seat beneath the oppressive weight of Sid's squinting glare. He sucked in a few nervous breaths as Lazy Eye dug deeper into the carpetbag. "You're right," Byron sputtered. "There are some watches in there. Take them, too."

"Nobody gives a damn about no watches," Sid growled. "We're here for some documents."

"Why would you want documents?" Byron squeaked. The twitch at the corner of his mouth and the slow lowering of his head made it plain to see that he knew all too well he was digging a deeper hole for himself.

"Where are they?" Sid asked while moving close enough to the cart to pull open Byron's jacket. Instinctively, Byron recoiled from Sid's grasp. A fraction of a second later, the metallic click of a pistol being cocked rattled through the air.

Byron froze, his eyes fixed upon the weapon in Lazy Eye's grasp. Beads of sweat squeezed from Byron's forehead, trickling down his face.

Brushing past the interior pockets of Byron's jacket, Sid pulled the younger man's shirttail out from where it had been tucked. One more tug was all it took to reveal the wide belt strapped around Byron's stomach. Apparently, several pouches built into the belt showed some promise for the robber.

"Sid!" Lazy Eye said in an urgent tone that cracked like a whip. "Someone's coming."

Sid glanced over to his partner and then in the direction Lazy Eye was pointing. Keeping his pistol aimed at Byron, he muttered, "You stay put."

Byron held up his hands as the color drained from his face.

What had caught Lazy Eye's attention was a large wagon cresting one of the few hills in the vicinity. It ambled slowly toward them using a trail that was all but overgrown. The shoddy path came in from the southwest, circled Barbrady and entered town from a direction that would attract little to no attention. The only reason Byron knew about it at all was because he'd been warned to stay away from the trail by the man who'd sent him on his journey since the path was supposed to be frequented by an undesirable element.

Sid stood his ground as the wagon drew closer and Lazy Eye climbed back into his saddle so he could ride around the cart to keep his gun pointed at Byron's back.

"You make one wrong move and yer dead," Sid promised.

Byron nodded as if his head had been mounted on a spring.

The wagon approached slowly, pulled by a couple of horses that put Byron's to shame. One was the color of fresh coffee and the other had a dark gray coat with a few patches of black scattered along its left side. As attractive as the horses were, however, it would have taken a pair of elephants to draw attention away from the wagon itself.

In a former life, it may have once been a covered wagon but now it was so much more. The canvas top had been stripped off and replaced by a square wooden structure that looked more like a shack on wheels. Charms, chimes, bells and a few pans hung at varying intervals along the top of the wagon as if their sole purpose was to announce every bump in the trail with a loud mix of clangs and vaguely musical rattles.

Once it turned to merge with the main trail, the side of the wagon could be seen. It was covered with brightly colored letters and designs of all sorts. While some of the words were too small to be read from where Sid and Lazy Eye were keeping watch over Byron, the biggest and brightest letters could be seen from miles away.

PROFESSOR WHITEOAK'S TRAVELING
MEDICINAL EMPORIUM ELIXERS, TONICS,
SCIENTIFIC WONDERS AND OTHER ASSORTED
MIRACLES

GUARANTEED RESULTS

All three men strained their eyes to get a closer look at some of the smaller printing scrawled along the side of the approaching wagon as the man driving the garish vehicle stretched an arm out and waved it over his head. He was dressed in crisply ironed black pants held up by a pair of black and silver suspenders. A starched white shirt hung over a set of wide shoulders with sleeves rolled up to display a set of lightly muscled forearms. His face sprouted a light coat of whiskers and beamed with a wide smile. The voice that exploded from it couldn't have been louder if there were a dozen sets of bellows behind it.

"Hello there!" he boomed.

Now that he was closer to the waiting trio, the driver of the large wagon reined his team to a stop and reached down to pick up a black, wide-brimmed hat. After placing the hat carefully atop his head, the man propped a leg upon his footboard and set his reins down. "By the looks of it, there's a nice little gathering here," he announced. "You folks preparing to take Barbrady by storm or have you already left the place trembling in your wake?"

Lazy Eye stared at the well-dressed fellow as if he barely comprehended the words coming out of his mouth.

Byron did his best to keep still.

Sid, on the other hand, was downright amused. "Ain't none of your business, mister," he said through a light chuckle. "You can move along."

The fancy gentleman driving the wagon nodded. His grin faded a bit as he took in the sight of the men gathered around Byron's cart. In a cautious, yet prosaic tone, he said, "My name's Henry Whiteoak."

"Professor Whiteoak?" Sid asked.

"One and the same! You've heard of me?"

"No, but I can read."

"A genuine accomplishment, my fine sir," Whiteoak said without missing a beat. "Being a man of learning, you would most definitely be interested in my wares."

"Shit," Lazy Eye grunted. "Nothin' but a goddamn snake oil salesman."

Whiteoak dismissed that with a casual wave. "If, by that, you are implying my tonics aren't genuine, I can assure you no snakes were killed in the making of my oils." He smirked, saw his jest wasn't received well, and moved on. "Actually, I take that back. I do offer a certain vitamin syrup derived from an ancient Cherokee recipe using the rattler of a very rare reptile as a key ingredient. When added to your morning coffee every day for two weeks, it will make a man so light on his feet that he can practically—"

"Shut the hell up," Sid cut in.

Flinching in surprise, Whiteoak said, "Actually, I was going to say he can practically fly, but the practical applications of my tonics are, of course, up to whomever purchases them."

"No. I mean you. Shut the hell up. We're conducting our own business here."

"As am I and this is your lucky day. I'll be making a public presentation soon after I arrive in Barbrady and could use some friendly ears to hear me out." Smirking with a subtle shrug, Whiteoak added, "Due to some extended time I've spent in seclusion with a Mexican healer, my oratory skills might have gotten rusty of late and I could use a sounding board. If you'd all be so kind as to give me some honest opinions on my presentation, I'd be happy to show my appreciation with a discount on a tonic guaranteed to give your horses the speed of a bullet for a full day's ride."

"Horse tonic?"

Whiteoak nodded. "Something tells me that men like yourselves might need it."

"Men like us, huh?" Lazy Eye grunted. "And what the hell is that supposed to mean?"

"You are robbers, aren't you?" Whiteoak asked with an air of innocence. Pointing to the cart, he said, "Ahh! I can see by the look on that one's face that I've hit a nerve."

Sid immediately looked at Byron and found the cart's driver sitting in his seat, sweating profusely. "Tell you what, Professor," Sid growled as he turned to face Whiteoak again. "Since you didn't want to leave when you had the chance, how about you hand over that pistol?"

After a slight, cordial nod, Whiteoak picked up the shoulder rig that had been lying beside him on the seat. The holster dangled from his hand, a silver-handled .38 swinging like a pendulum. Sid rode up closer, snatched the holster from him and draped it over one shoulder before saying, "Now give us a look at what you're hauling in that wagon."

"Might I propose a simple wager?" Whiteoak countered. He climbed down from the wagon, careful to avoid wrinkling his trousers along the way. Once his highly polished boots hit the dirt, he removed a leather cord from around his neck and declared, "It's fairly obvious you men are out to rob the fellow driving that cart and me as well."

"Damn," Sid said dryly. "You really are a smart one, Professor."

Ignoring the snickering from two of the men in front of him, Whiteoak said, "Rather than risk a fight or any spilled blood that might follow, I propose we settle this like gentlemen."

"Too much talkin'," Lazy Eye sighed.

Sid nodded. "I'm inclined to agree. Where you headed with this, Professor?"

"With your permission," Whiteoak said, "I'd like to unlock my wagon. If you intend on relieving me of my valuables, we'd be doing that eventually anyway."

"Maybe."

"Well, that is where the lockbox is located . . . as I'm certain you've already guessed."

Both of the robbers looked at each other with the spark of shared greed flickering between them like static jumping from a brass door handle to a dry hand. Sid climbed down from his saddle and walked toward Whiteoak's wagon. His gun was held in a firm, steady grip which kept his aim locked on target. Without taking his eyes off the well-dressed man, Sid asked, "You got our friend covered back there?"

Having circled back around the cart, Lazy Eye straightened his arm to aim his pistol at Byron's forehead. Nodding, he said, "He ain't goin' nowhere."

"And neither are you, Professor," Sid growled as he stared a hole through the man in front of him. "Understand?"

"Oh, I certainly do," Whiteoak said.

"Now, what's your wager and why the hell should I care about it?"

"It's a simple affair, I assure you. May I?"

Seeing that Whiteoak was poised to open the wagon, Sid shook his head and pushed him away from the wooden structure. "What the hell you got in there?"

"Have a look for yourself."

In Whiteoak's hand, there was a small key. Sid's eyes narrowed as he studied the little piece of sculpted metal before snatching it away. Sid placed the key into the small, narrow door at the back of the wagon, turned it, and took a step back. As the door eased open, Sid watched the professor carefully. Nothing jumped out at him as he seemed to have expected and the only sound to be heard was the creaking of hinges.

Cautiously, Sid approached the wagon again. "You make one move and . . ."

"I know," Whiteoak said with hands held above his head. "I'm dead."

Inside, the wagon was big enough for a man to do a bit of pacing, but hardly enough for him to stand fully upright. One aisle cut straight down the middle of the interior and went all the way back. On both sides of that aisle were shelves, little square drawers, racks of bottles, water skins hanging from hooks, canteens, and a few cupboards attached directly behind the driver's seat.

"My wager is simple," Whiteoak said. "You win and I'll hand over my lockbox quickly and quietly."

"And if I don't?" Sid asked.

"Then we'll part ways with all belongings staying with their respective owners and call it a day."

"So you could head into town and tell the law about what happened here? Hell, I could just shoot you now and be done with it."

"Sure," Whiteoak said. "But they hang killers much swifter than they do robbers. And the commotion of all that gunfire so close to Barbrady will surely attract some unwanted attention. Besides, you can't honestly believe that a simple key or even a barrage of bullets will be enough to open my lockbox. That is, if you can even find it."

"We can sure as hell find it by tearing apart that god-awful wagon piece by piece," Lazy Eye threatened, spitting out every single word.

To that, Whiteoak merely shrugged. "You could certainly try, but I wouldn't advise it. If you push one lever that's meant to be pulled or touch one wrong item in there, several sticks of well-hidden dynamite will go off, turning that wagon into splinters. Most likely . . . very bloody splinters."

Glancing once more into the wagon, Sid found plenty of levers, handles and even a few large dials embedded within the cabinets and floor of the awkward structure. "Why the hell would you go through all that trouble? What the hell you got in there, anyway?"

"I'm a businessman," Whiteoak replied. "Much like you, I protect my assets. I'm also a gambler, so it's more amusing to settle matters through more sporting means than gunplay. What have you got to lose, anyway? From where I'm standing, not much."

Sid let out a haggard breath as his eyes drifted among all the intriguing bits and pieces stored within the wagon. "Just hand over the goddamn lockbox."

"I'm afraid I'll have to refuse."

"Do it!" Sid barked as he raised his pistol.

Whiteoak didn't flinch. "Kill me and you'll only draw attention. Also, there's the matter of finding my lockbox afterward. Even if you could find and defuse the explosive package, I doubt either of you two men have the time or patience to go through every last trap door you'll find in there. My methods were taught to me by a Gypsy princess who was very talented in the art of—"

"What's the wager?" Sid asked impatiently.

Stepping toward his wagon, Whiteoak asked, "May I?"

Sid nodded but kept his pistol aimed at the professor's head.

Slowly, Whiteoak reached inside the wagon for one of the racks close to the door. When he took one of several unlabeled bottles stored there, he was careful to show it to the other man. Inside was a cloudy white liquid that looked like watery milk. Stepping back again, Whiteoak held out the bottle and said, "I bet you can't hit the neck of this bottle when I toss it into the air."

"Just the neck?"

"Yes. You know . . . the skinny part."

"Yeah. I know the skinny part," Sid sneered. "That's it?"

Whiteoak nodded. "That's it. You hit it and you win."

Snatching the bottle from Whiteoak's hand, Sid tossed it into the air and bent his gun arm to fire a single shot.

Sid, Lazy Eye, and even Byron watched the bottle go up before the bullet from Sid's gun chipped a few shards of glass from the top of the bottle at the apex of its arc. With those men focused on that display of marksmanship, nobody noticed Whiteoak reach into the wagon for another bottle which he knocked against Sid's temple with a hard swing.

"What the hell?" Lazy Eye shouted. "You're—" Before he could finish, the robber was knocked from his saddle by the same bottle which Whiteoak tossed to hit squarely between his eyes.

"I know," Whiteoak said. "I'm dead."

For a moment, all Byron could do was look around to try and comprehend what he'd witnessed. Sid was still where he'd fallen and wasn't moving except for the occasional twitch. Lazy Eye was lying flat on the ground with a face covered in blood and spilt tonic.

"You just . . . those men were about to . . . how did you . . . ?" Byron stammered.

After reclaiming his gun and holster from Sid, Whiteoak said, "If you'd like to discuss the matter further, I suggest we do it away from here. Those two aren't likely to be very sociable when they wake up."

Still breathless, Byron leaned forward to offer his hand. "I owe you my life. How can I repay you?"

"Doing a good deed is payment enough, my good man." Wincing as he shook Byron's hand, Whiteoak added, "That's a mighty strong grip you have there. Might I suggest something to improve it further? I have a special blend that can make you strong enough to pull the ears off a bull. How about I tell you more on the way into town?"

"Anything you say, mister. I'll take whatever you're selling."

"Just be sure to spread the good word once we're in Bar-brady," Whiteoak said with a friendly nod. "And, please, feel free to call me Professor."

CHAPTER TWO

Both carts were pulled into town at the same time, but only one of them caught much attention. While Byron's disappeared into the closest livery, Professor Whiteoak's wagon drew curious glances from everyone who wandered past the lot where he parked it. The professor himself walked into a place called the Dove Tail Saloon where he chose a spot at the bar ideal for peeking out the window at the chattering locals studying his wagon.

"You gonna stand there admiring the view or are you gonna order a drink?"

Whiteoak turned toward the sound of that voice and found a tall, muscular fellow glaring back at him from the other side of a bar. Removing his hat to place it upon the beer-stained surface, Whiteoak declared, "I'll have a bottle of your finest whiskey, my good man!"

Nodding, the barkeep reached for a small shelf behind the bar where the dustiest and most decorative bottles were kept. Before touching the cork, he asked, "You got enough money for this?"

"How much is it?"

"Twenty dollars."

"How much for a glass?"

"Three."

"Well then," Whiteoak said while grasping his lapels with

19

both hands, "better make that a bottle of your second-finest whiskey."

The barkeep let out a huffing grunt, put the first bottle away and grabbed one from a more crowded and larger shelf beneath a painting of an equally large woman. After filling a glass and setting it next to the bottle in front of Whiteoak, he said, "That'll be five dollars for the bottle."

"Why, I've been to plenty of places that serve a fine brand of whiskey for half that price."

"You want horse piss? I got plenty of it under the bar."

Whiteoak picked up the glass, doffed it to the barkeep and swallowed its contents in one gulp. After setting the glass down again, he dug out some money from one of his pockets and placed it next to the bottle. "Very nice, sir. If I may be so bold, perhaps you'd like to attend my demonstration this evening? I have some wares that could greatly improve your spirits. And, by spirits, I mean your whiskey."

"I know what you mean," the barkeep replied. "That means you're the one who drove that garish wagon into town?"

"You were already told about my arrival?"

"Nobody can steer a thing like that down Main Street without everyone taking notice," the barkeep said with no small amount of distaste in his voice.

"Well, one man's garish is another man's flair." Noticing the confused tilt of the barkeep's eyebrow, Whiteoak added, "Yes. That's my wagon."

"So what's wrong with my whiskey?"

"Nothing at all." Leaning forward to rest one elbow upon the bar, the professor dropped his tone to a conspiratorial whisper. "One of my concoctions could filter, purify, and otherwise enhance the liquor kept beneath your bar well enough for it to be moved to more . . . shall we say . . . revered real estate." With those last words, Whiteoak pointed toward the uppermost shelf of dusty bottles.

The barkeep glanced over his shoulder. When he looked Whiteoak up and down, he seemed to regard the sharply dressed professor as something other than a minor annoyance. "You could do that?"

"Oh, yes. In fact, the process is so complete that rearranging your wares wouldn't even be considered a misrepresentation by the finest connoisseur. If you would come to my—"

Suddenly, another voice trampled over Whiteoak's pitch. "So you're the one who just got into town?" it said.

The barkeep jabbed a finger past Whiteoak toward a pale man with thick blond hair sprouting from his face and snapped, "Wait your turn, Swede. I'm talkin'!"

Whiteoak positioned himself so one elbow remained propped against the bar, one boot was crossed over the other and both other men were in his line of sight. Although there were other folks in the saloon, none seemed prepared to do more than watch the impending spectacle.

"It's quite all right," Whiteoak said. "I don't mind the occasional good-natured interruption. To answer this man's question, I most certainly did just arrive. If you're curious as to my reason for being here, all you'll have to do to get the answer is attend my demonstration at half an hour past sundown on this very night." When he said that last part, Whiteoak raised his voice so the time of his show could be heard by everyone in the saloon.

Swede was no kid, but his light hair and facial features gave him the appearance of someone younger than his twenty-odd years. Stepping up to within a few paces of Whiteoak, he dangled his left arm to his side while placing his right palm upon the grip of a holstered pistol. "I don't give a damn about no medicine show. I know why you're really here."

His eyebrows perking up ever so slightly, Whiteoak said, "You do? And why might that be?"

"You're one of those men the sheriff was told about. He's ready for you. We all are."

"You have the wrong idea, young man," Whiteoak chuckled.

"The hell I do."

When the barkeep's hand slapped down on top of the bar, it rattled every glass on it. "I already told you that's enough, Swede! I don't want any trouble in my place!"

"He's the one that brought trouble," Swede countered. "And if we let him be, he'll only bring more of it. Ain't you heard about the men that're supposed to be scouting this town?"

"That's nothing but a rumor."

"Rumor or not, maybe the sheriff would like to know about a fancy-dressed gunman posing as a huckster in a funny wagon."

Whiteoak stiffened and his expression lost the good humor that had been there since he'd walked in. "Huckster?" he said. "That's an unsavory term without the benefit of having seen my wares."

"I already seen enough," Swede said as he squared himself up with the professor. "What the hell does a salesman need with such a fancy shooting iron?"

Nodding, Whiteoak eased back the left section of his waistcoat to fully reveal the silver-handled Smith & Wesson .38 hanging beneath his arm. "I encountered a bit of trouble on the way into town and thought it might be wise to take precautions. I believe there's a young man at the stable who'll speak on my behalf in that regard."

"You know what a gun like that says about a man?" Swede asked.

"That he can afford a set of silver grips to match his stylish cufflinks?"

The barkeep as well as most everyone else in the room snickered at that. Swede, on the other hand, wasn't feeling so jovial. "That's the kind of weapon a gunfighter carries," he said. "We don't wanna see any gunfighters around here."

"And, by gunfighter, you're referring to someone who might shoot another in cold blood?"

"That's right."

"From where I stand, that doesn't appear to be me," Whiteoak pointed out.

The barkeep brought a shotgun to his shoulder and said, "Enough's enough, Swede. Get the hell out of here before you wind up in a pine box."

The light-haired man muttered a few unkind words in Whiteoak's direction as he stomped through the saloon's front door.

"Sorry about that, Professor," the barkeep said while replacing the shotgun into its spot behind the bar.

Dusting off the front of his waistcoat as if he'd taken a roll through a dusty field, Whiteoak said, "Quite all right, although I don't know if I should show my face in an establishment where I'm not welcome."

"Aw, don't get yer knickers in a twist. I'd still like to hear about that device or whatever you was talking about that would improve my whiskey."

"I don't know," Whiteoak grumbled as he wrung his hands and nervously fidgeted with his waistcoat. "Confrontations play havoc on my nerves. Of course, a man's opinion of an establishment like this one would greatly improve if he had something to calm those jangling nerves."

"How'd another drink be?" the barkeep offered. "On the house."

The professor's demeanor brightened as if someone had thrown a switch inside his head. "That would be splendid! And in reference to that other matter, why don't I sample something from the top shelf? That way, I'll be able to prepare something by tonight's demonstration to perfectly suit your needs."

The barkeep pulled in a breath, furrowed his brow, and studied the professor carefully. Just when it seemed he would refuse the request out of principle, he exhaled and reached up for the dusty selection. When he retrieved one of the ornate bottles and poured a splash of whiskey into a fresh glass, he gazed down at it as though he was handing off his firstborn.

"Ahh," Whiteoak said while picking up the complimentary drink. "My spirits improve by the second."

CHAPTER THREE

It was a cool night. Cooler than normal, which did nothing whatsoever to keep folks away from the lot beside the town's most prominent livery. Whiteoak's brightly colored wagon may have looked boxy and unbalanced, but it unfolded into a silent calliope, swaying and entrancing every eye fortunate enough to be cast upon it.

An awning extended from the side facing the street and lanterns hung from three of the wagon's four corners. Their flickering orange glow illuminated multilingual testimonials scrawled along the bottom of the wagon's cover, framing an array of picture advertisements painted upon the wooden structure that detailed the exotic wonders to be found within.

When Professor Whiteoak began his presentation, less than half a dozen locals wanted to take their attention away from his wagon to hear what he had to say. By the time he wrapped up his second demonstration, he had more than triple the original number gathered around the small platform he used as a pedestal. His silver-handled .38 was nowhere to be seen. Dressed in a freshly starched shirt and trousers sporting creases that were sharp enough to split an apple, he spoke in a booming voice that he wielded better than any firearm.

"Now this may sting for a moment," Whiteoak said to an elderly woman who stood stretching her hand up to him. The few drops of light green liquid he spattered onto her wrist caused her to recoil, but he patted her withered forearm and reached for a second glass vial on a rack behind him. "Fear not, m'lady. This is a cure that works in two stages. While the formula was inspired by a scholar from the Far East, the technique is my very own."

"This is a Chinese potion?" the old lady asked.

"Not that far east," Whiteoak corrected with a quick wink. "New York City." The crowd chuckled and Whiteoak used the same dropper that had carried the green liquid to draw up some of the clear fluid from the second vial. Both tonics were mostly water mixed with coloring and a few ingredients used mainly for effect, but the exotic diagrams on their containers' labels inspired as much curiosity as confusion.

Once there was the right amount of fluid in the dropper, he held the glass tube above a bulbous wart sprouting from the woman's second knuckle. The wart had been the center of this particular demonstration and now the entire crowd leaned in as if that lump of discolored flesh was a diva preparing for an aria. The solution hissed the instant it touched her skin, sending up a wisp of smoke that startled the crowd almost as much as an appearance from the devil himself.

"No need to be alarmed," Whiteoak said while removing a handkerchief from his pocket so he could dab the old woman's hand. "Merely the first treatment. Tell me, madam, do you feel any ill effects?"

She looked down at her hand where the raisin-sized growth was still smoking like a freshly snuffed candle. "Stings a bit, I guess."

"That means it's working! Now tell me . . . do you see any differences in that unsightly blemish?"

She studied the wart for a few moments, shrugged and replied, "Looks a bit smaller."

Since Whiteoak had been the one to doctor the second solution with the precise amount of acid to hiss and smoke on contact, he wasn't surprised. The scholarly man from New York City to whom he'd referred was a watchmaker who'd used the acidic solution to clean the gears and other metal parts in his creations before they were handed off to their owners. The mixture did a fine job of burning away tarnish and a bit of rust, but also cleanly removed a few layers of skin. Not only was the wart on the old woman's hand smaller and a somewhat different shape, but it was smooth and shiny as well.

"What about headaches?" Whiteoak asked to divert attention from her hand. "Do you suffer from headaches?"

"Why, yes, I do!" she replied, freely admitting to sharing an ailment with most people on earth.

"Then, as a gift for allowing me to demonstrate my miracle wart remover, allow me to present you with a tonic that eases headaches as well as most other pains associated with the cruel harshness of life." With a flourish, Whiteoak produced a vial that was half the size of the one containing the acid. He handed it to the woman, who stared at it suspiciously.

"I suppose this is laudanum?" she asked.

"Hardly, ma'am. It's a concoction I devised during some time spent with an Apache medicine man. Try some for yourself and enjoy the comfort that follows."

She sniffed the clear liquid in the vial, took a sip and then smiled. The man who'd taught Whiteoak how to distill it wasn't any sort of healer but he was, indeed, Apache. According to him, the process made a very crude and very potent version of what Europeans called vodka.

"Oh, my," the woman said.

"Do you feel better?"

"Why, yes!"

Whiteoak smiled and raised his arms as if introducing the small Kansas town to a new vice worthy of accolades. The smile spread even further across the old woman's face as she walked away from the wagon with a wobbly spring in her step, causing the clapping and chatter among the crowd to gain momentum.

"Thank you very much," Whiteoak said. "The wart remover and headache elixir are, of course, for sale at the conclusion of my demonstration. But first, I have a question. Does anyone here drink water?"

Several audience members looked around, obviously expecting a ruse. Eventually, most of them raised their hands.

"Of course you drink water," Whiteoak beamed. "We all do! But do any of you know what kind of impurities are in that water? Do you happen to know how much havoc you are wreaking upon your bodies by ingesting contaminants that can sully your water from any number of sources?"

A few of the men at the edge of the crowd scoffed and turned away, prompting Whiteoak to stab a finger at one of them and say, "You, sir! Would you ever drink a cup of rust? Or you?" he added while singling out another one of the disbelievers. "Would you ever bring a pail of mud in for your family to enjoy with a freshly cooked supper?"

"Course I wouldn't," the first man replied.

"You see, folks? Of course he wouldn't. But if you take your water straight out of most wells or from many streams, you're likely drinking silt, rust, copper, or even disgusting waste left behind by fish that you don't even want to know about."

Although the first man gave Whiteoak a final dismissive wave before leaving the crowd, the second one lingered with his arms folded defiantly across his chest. "What the hell are we supposed to do about any of that?" he asked. "We gotta drink from wells or the damn river!"

Dropping his voice so folks would have to work to catch every word, Whiteoak said, "What are you supposed to do about that, indeed?" When he raised his voice back to a booming pitch, everyone in the crowd jumped. "I'm glad you asked because *this* is what you can do about it!"

Whiteoak lifted a sheet that had covered a counter which folded down from the side of the wagon directly behind him. Stacked on that counter were several rows of tall, shiny metal cups that looked like something a highly paid bartender might use. Picking up a cup with each hand, Whiteoak said, "I see there is a pump behind you, my good man."

Once one of the men at the back of the crowd responded, the professor locked eyes with him and said, "Yes, sir. I mean you. Would you be so kind as to bring me some of that water?"

As the man walked to the pump, Whiteoak cast his eyes around at the members of the enraptured crowd. "What you see here," he declared while holding up one of the metal cups, "is a miracle of modern science! I won't bore you good people with specifics, but know that smarter men than I have been working on this particular innovation for well over a dozen years. Men from this country's finest institutions of higher learning have toiled to make great advances, but only a few of those men with a great enough vision found a way to put those ideas to immediate, practical use."

Now that a good mix of curiosity and confusion had been injected into the crowd, Whiteoak lowered his voice to bring the audience close enough for him to embrace them. "The metal in these containers has been attuned to attract and dispel any and nearly all contaminants that may strike a bad note with your palettes. Once you taste how good water can be, it will be next to impossible to partake of any liquid that hasn't been put through this simple process. And once you feel the health advantages for yourselves, you'll wonder why on earth you'd ever want to."

By now, the local man had returned with a bucket of water from a nearby pump. Whiteoak brought the man, the bucket and one other member of the audience up close to his platform.

"I'd like you two and anyone else who would care to do so to taste that water, please," he said. After those two and a few others took a drink, they showed the professor some unimpressed shrugs.

"I'm sure you've all tasted that water several times," Whiteoak said as he filled one of his metal cups from the bucket and then transferred its contents to a second cup. "But you haven't tasted anything like this." He poured the water from one metal cup to another, back and forth, forth and back, making certain that the small dose of sugar hidden in the tube attached to the back of one cup remained hidden. Before the audience's minds could wander too far, the sugar had been emptied into the water and mixed in thoroughly. Filling the cup without the hidden tube, Whiteoak offered it to the man who'd been the first doubter to speak up and said, "Try that on for size."

After taking a sip, the man raised his eyebrows and gazed up at Whiteoak. "What the hell did you do to that?"

"You saw what I did, good sir. Now pass it along so others may try."

Before doing so, the man looked down at the water and sipped it again. His face twisting into a disbelieving mask, he said, "That really is better!"

Every other volunteer who sampled the drink had similar reactions. Eyes widened. Cynical sneers curved upward into pleased grins. Several folks even licked their lips after passing the cup along as if they were sad to see it go.

"That water has been purified by a scientific method produced by some of our world's greatest minds," Whiteoak declared, "harnessed by my own patented devices and techniques." Pointing to the barkeep from the Dove Tail Saloon who stood in the crowd, he added, "And it doesn't just work on water!"

Stepping forward, the barkeep held out a half-empty bottle of whiskey. "If that's so, I got something else for you to try it on."

"I thought you might," Whiteoak said with a grin. Taking the whiskey, he walked to the back of his platform and selected one of the smaller versions of his shiny tin cups. "I assure you, ladies and gentlemen, this man is not in my employ. He is surely known to many of you as a local businessman and he has brought his own whiskey to test my miracle purifier for himself."

Holding up a finger, the barkeep clarified, "My *cheapest* whiskey."

"Indeed." Whiteoak handed the whiskey bottle to the man in the audience who'd brought him the bucket of water. "Here you go, sir. A small reward for your assistance at tonight's demonstration."

The man sipped from the bottle and handed it back.

"How was it?" Whiteoak asked.

"I had better."

"And you *will* have better as soon as I remove the impurities that make all the difference between cheap whiskey and the most expensive of brands." With that, the professor held up the smaller cups for all to see before setting them down to fill one with a healthy dose of whiskey. It was only a matter of posture and prestidigitation for him to stand with his back to the audience long enough to grab another cup from behind the display which he'd previously filled with some expensive liquor from his personal stash. Whiteoak turned around, leaving the cup of cheap whiskey on the table where it was lost among all of the display models and sloshed the premium firewater back and forth between the two tin cups in his hands.

"And now," Whiteoak said while dividing the whiskey evenly between both cups, "all of you can taste the purified spirits that have been cleansed by my wondrous devices!"

The barkeep was the first to step forward for a drink. After downing some of the whiskey, he sighed, "I'll be damned. That's the same stuff I gave you?"

"Indubitably."

After that, the rest of the audience couldn't rush forward fast enough to get a sample of the purified whiskey. Even though he'd lost a good portion of his favorite liquor, the professor knew it was a worthy sacrifice.

"So," Whiteoak said as he hooked his thumbs behind his suspenders, "since my demonstration is now concluded, who would like to purchase some of these miracles for their very own?"

Nobody responded.

After clearing his throat, the professor dropped his showy vernacular and asked, "Anyone want to buy something?"

The few people who stepped forward from the crowd were the first trickles to seep through a crack in a dam. Before long, the rest flowed behind them.

Whiteoak was quick to pull down another hinged countertop from the side of his wagon to separate him from his customers. He tended his makeshift store, accepting the locals' money before handing them watered-down elixirs and empty tin cups in return. If someone needed assurance before parting with their money, Whiteoak motioned to the words painted upon the wagon behind him while saying them out loud as if he was reciting the gospel.

"Guaranteed results!" he proclaimed.

For every local that was appeased by that, there was another who vowed to come back for a refund if they weren't happy with their purchase. Whiteoak nodded and smiled while telling all of them, "I stand by my wares. If you have any troubles, I'm not hard to find."

It was a good night for everyone gathered beneath the stars in Barbrady that evening.

Customers were excited with the prospect of bringing a little magic into their homes, while Professor Whiteoak was secure in the knowledge that he would be far away from town before too many ill effects could be felt. He was so secure, in fact, that he gave a friendly wave to the lawman who'd been standing at the back of the crowd during the entire show.

The sheriff nodded and returned the professor's wave. Leaning over to a deputy, he said, "Make sure that man doesn't leave town."

CHAPTER FOUR

A modest dining room was illuminated by the light from three lanterns, four candlesticks and one stove glowing with embers from the fire that had cooked the meal now being served. None of that light, however, was enough to outshine Henry White-oak's self-satisfied smile. He sat at an oval table, coat hanging on a rack behind him and sleeves rolled up past his elbows, beaming down at the plate of greens in front of him.

"You must be hungry," said Byron Keag who sat across the table from the professor.

"I am most certainly looking forward to a hot meal," Whiteoak replied.

The woman who brought the rest of their supper to the table had shoulder-length, sandy-brown hair, rounded cheeks and a pleasant face. Full lips curved into a smile that provided yet another source of light within the small room. "That was some performance tonight, Doctor."

Beaming even more, Whiteoak raised his eyebrows and straightened the front of his shirt with a few quick tugs upon the starched cotton. "Well, now. I appreciate the sentiment my fine lady, but I am not a doctor in the strictest sense of the word. And you can call me Henry if you so desire. What about you, ma'am? Do you have a profession?"

"I'm a seamstress," she replied. "And you can call me Lyssa. I do regular work for some of the tailors in town and pick up little jobs whenever they come around. It's not as prestigious as being a doctor, but it's steady work."

"He's a professor, Lyssa," Byron said.

"Semantics," Whiteoak explained with a wave of his hand. "A mere formality."

Nodding, Lyssa picked up a knife and fork so she could begin slicing the ham she'd brought to the table. "Whatever your title, it was still an impressive show you put on."

"Why, thank you, ma'am. If I was still wearing my hat," Whiteoak said, "I would tip it in your direction."

She bowed her head slightly and dipped at the knees in a miniature curtsy. When she looked at Byron, the expression on her face stopped just short of an eye roll.

Holding out his plate to accept the first slice of ham, Whiteoak said, "I do appreciate the invitation to dinner."

"It's the least we could do," Lyssa said, "considering how you saved my brother's life."

"Well, now," Whiteoak replied with a voice that maintained its smooth tone although its warmth was pointed inward. "You are right about that. Not that I charge into danger for the hope of reward. You're right that it was indeed a perilous situation that I—"

"He saved my life," Byron cut in. "Thank you, Professor Whiteoak. I've thanked you before and I'll thank you again. Would you like me to thank you a third time?"

"Don't be rude!" Lyssa snapped.

Whiteoak held up one hand and scooted his chair away from the table. "It's quite all right. I do have a tendency to prattle on, especially when there's a good story to tell. It's unbecoming of a man to blow his own horn, so to speak."

"Where are you going?" Lyssa asked.

"I don't want to make things uncomfortable in your lovely home. I can have a late dinner at my hotel."

"Nonsense. You'll eat here. You can stay here too, if you like.

35

There's an extra room."

"Really?" Whiteoak asked.

"Really?" Byron chimed in.

Looking to both of them in turn, Lyssa nodded once and said, "Really. My brother is alive thanks to the brave actions of another man. Since that man is at my table, the right thing to do would be to make certain he doesn't leave with a grumbling belly."

Whiteoak shook his head, albeit unconvincingly. "I wouldn't presume to intrude. My hotel will do fine."

"All right, but you also wouldn't come to someone's home, make a grand promise and then fail to see it through."

His expression turning from shallow humility to genuine confusion, Whiteoak asked, "I don't recall making a promise."

Lyssa sat down at the table and gazed at the professor with wide, blue eyes. "Everything from the way you presented your facts to the posture you took while saying them made it seem as though you were going to regale us with the full story of what happened with those robbers who tried to kill the two of you outside of town."

"I already told you about that, Lyssa," Byron said.

Dismissing her brother with a backhanded wave, she said, "You told me the bare bones of what happened. I want to know it all and I imagine Mister Whiteoak could tell me. Sorry. I mean Professor."

"Now how could I refuse a request like that?" Whiteoak beamed.

As Whiteoak scooted closer to the table and began laying a vivid foundation for his story, he filled his plate with food from the various helpings that Lyssa had brought from her kitchen. While his face was alight with enthusiasm for the verbal web he was spinning, Whiteoak's audience was divided on their response.

Lyssa may have been tolerating Whiteoak at first, but she wound up nodding at every appropriate moment, gasping under her breath when he came to a description of danger and smiling merrily when the story's conflict was resolved. Byron, on the other hand, did a modest job of appearing to be interested in a tale that painted him in anything but a generous light. Even though he kept quiet for most of the meal, he couldn't help but come to his own defense as dessert was being served.

"I probably could have made it to town on my own," Byron insisted.

"Made it," Whiteoak said. "A bit lighter in the pockets and cargo, but made it nonetheless."

Seeing the smirk on his sister's face, Byron snipped, "What's so damn funny?"

"Nothing at all," she quickly replied. "Would anyone like some tea?"

"I'd like some coffee if you have any," Whiteoak said.

"And I know my brother would like tea with a spoonful of honey and cream."

"Aww," Whiteoak said as if he was cooing to a child or small puppy. "That's just precious."

Through a sour face, Byron explained, "Our mother was English. She used to serve us tea a very specific way."

"Of course, of course. You'll never hear me accuse someone of being a little mother's boy."

Knowing that's exactly what the professor was doing, Byron crossed his arms and waited for his snickering sibling to leave the room. "If I didn't owe you a debt, I'd knock you on your ass for trying to make me look like a fool in my own home."

"It's good-natured ribbing," Whiteoak said as he dug into his breast pocket for a tarnished cigarette case. "And you'd try to knock me on my ass. Your success in that venture is a matter of some debate."

Byron couldn't help but notice the gun hanging from the holster covered by the expensive coat on the nearby rack. Suddenly, he didn't want to have that particular debate with Whiteoak.

Dropping the edge from his tone, the professor asked, "How about joining me on the porch for a smoke? Your sister strikes me as someone who would insist on me stepping outside before I touch a match to one of these exquisitely rolled beauts."

"You'd be right about that."

Both men headed for the front door. Reacting either to the professor's regal posture and stride or because of an unshakable need to be a good host, Byron found himself holding the door for Whiteoak so the dandy could step outside ahead of him. The night had cooled considerably in the short amount of time that had passed since Whiteoak's presentation of his wares to the town.

Leaning against a post supporting the wooden awning over the front porch, Whiteoak struck a match and lifted the flickering little fire to the cigarette clamped between his teeth. "I'd also be right in saying that those robbers didn't just happen to find you on that road," he said.

"Even if they'd had their way, those men wouldn't have gotten away with much more than ten dollars in cash and personal effects."

"That's not what they were after. You mentioned something about them asking about some documents?"

"I . . . umm . . . may have mentioned the documents first. From then on, I can only assume they were taking a stab in the dark that I might be carrying something valuable," Byron said.

"Would they have been correct?"

"I do owe you a debt, Professor, and I have every intention of repaying it. That does not, however, entitle you to know every last bit of business in which I'm involved. So I would be much obliged if you'd let the matter drop."

Whiteoak's face was an unreadable mask as his lips tightened around the cigarette. He drew in a breath, causing the tip to glow bright enough to illuminate his chin and cast a sinister shadow across the bottom of his eyes. "You do owe a debt to me and it would be wise that you don't forget it."

Tensing slightly, Byron asked, "Are you threatening me?"

"Take from my words what you will. I want to make it impeccably clear that I do not take debts lightly, whether they be large or small."

Byron nodded slowly as he regained the bit of composure he'd allowed to slip away a few moments ago. "I agree. Every man should honor his debts."

The smile that appeared on Whiteoak's face was genuine, but not overly friendly. "I never doubted you were a man of honor."

"Never?" Byron chuckled uneasily. "You act as though we've known each other for more than part of a day."

"I'm an excellent judge of character," Whiteoak replied with a flourish of one hand. As he puffed on his cigarette, whatever harshness he'd exhibited before left him like the smoke drifting from his nostrils. "Scoundrels are easy to spot and men without honor are even easier."

"I would think they'd be one and the same."

"You might think, but that would be an incorrect assumption. Scoundrels can have honor and plenty of it. They just adhere to a different sort of honor than common folk."

Both men stood in the cool night air for a short while. The quiet that settled around them wasn't so much a calm stillness as it was the burning of a long fuse without the hissing sound.

When Whiteoak took another puff of his cigarette, the scorching of the rolling paper and tobacco drifted through the air like a blaze in the distance. The smoke he exhaled as a series of wobbly rings smelled vaguely of exotic spices. "Who gave you those papers, Byron?" he asked.

"That's not something I'm supposed to discuss."

"I might understand your loyalty if this person was merely a paying client. After all, you are a professional and must maintain your business relationships. But under the circumstances, it seems . . . peculiar."

"Does it?"

Whiteoak nodded.

Furrowing his brow, Byron asked. "Why?"

"I don't know. It might possibly have something to do with the armed men who tried to kill you earlier today."

"They were robbers."

"Exactly."

"Common thieves," Byron continued. "Outlaws who were out to steal whatever they could get their hands on."

"For common, money-hungry outlaws, they seemed awfully interested in those papers you were carrying." Whiteoak took a slow pull from his cigarette and sent a few more fragrant rings into the air. "Didn't they ask specifically for those documents more than once? I could always be mistaken, though. After all, I didn't arrive until you were already engaged with them in conversation so I'm just going off of what you mentioned when describing the incident."

"No," Byron said thoughtfully. "They did ask for them."

There wasn't much left of Whiteoak's cigarette, so he finished it off and flicked it to the ground. "You were probably right in what you said earlier. They must have thought those papers were somehow valuable. Deeds or such. That must be it."

Whiteoak's verbal manipulations were anything but subtle, which seemed to aggravate Byron further as they burrowed like ticks beneath his skin.

Raising one eyebrow, Whiteoak glanced sideways at Byron and asked, "Were those papers deeds?"

"Sure. They were deeds. Whatever will bring this conversation to an end, that's what they were."

Whiteoak held up his hands in mock surrender. "I apologize for being a pest. Would it be all right if I passed on dessert?"

"Of course."

"Please give my best to your sister." The professor whistled a merry tune as he stepped off the porch and strolled away from the house. Byron shook his head, silently promising himself not to be swayed by any amount of talk and to maintain his composure until Professor Whiteoak left town.

The sooner, the better.

CHAPTER FIVE

It was late when Whiteoak returned to Lyssa Keag's home. Midnight was long past and not only was most of the town asleep, but everything for miles in any direction seemed to be in a deep slumber as well. Folks back in the old times used to call it the Witching Hour and all it took was a short taste of that time between night and day to know why.

The sky was a rich, inky black that would be chilling to the skin if it was possible to stretch out a hand and touch it. Even when a wind blew, it did so with the quiet reverence of someone sneaking through a museum afraid to knock over any one of a number of precious glass sculptures. The only animals out and about at that time were predators or soon to be prey. While Henry Whiteoak moved through the cool shadows of the Barbrady streets, he did so with the cautious skill of someone who knew what it was to be both of those things.

Still wearing the black trousers and shiny boots that he'd sported earlier that day, the professor had traded in his tailored suit coat for a more weathered black jacket. Every so often when his arms would swing a particular way, the holster strapped around his shoulder could be seen. The silver-handled .38 wasn't wrapped in that finely tooled leather, however. In its place was an older model of the same caliber with a dull gray surface that wouldn't reflect any bit of stray light that might happen to fall on it.

Whiteoak moved stealthily toward the Keag house. His stride

was fast enough to suit his purpose but not anything that might be construed as suspicious. Or, at least, no more suspicious than a man stealthily approaching a darkened house in the dead of night. Some things couldn't be helped.

Once he got closer, Whiteoak dropped into a crouch. No longer concerned with appearances, he approached one of the windows on the side of the home and slid his hat farther back on his head so he could look through the glass without bumping his brim. His fingers found the sill and could have slipped even further inside as the window was open about an inch. Since the room inside was just as dark as outside, Whiteoak's eyes didn't need to adjust. Right away, he could tell he was looking in a bedroom. However, it wasn't the bedroom he'd been hoping to find.

Lyssa Keag lay on her bed, sheets a rumpled mess and her blankets cast aside either by restless legs or in response to a warm spell. Whatever the reason, the lack of covers left her partially exposed to night air trickling in through the window and the eyes of unexpected visitors outside. During supper, she'd been dressed in modest attire that was pretty in a plain sort of way. Now, she was still wrapped in cotton but modesty wasn't much of a factor. More of a slip than a nightgown, the thin cotton twisted around Lyssa's body was loose and baggy around her hips and legs but had been drawn tight around her upper body and shoulders. Whiteoak's eyes lingered on her full, rounded breasts, which were more generous than her earlier garb had led him to believe. Thanks to the coolness of the breeze, her erect nipples pressed against the fabric making it seem as if her naked body had been drenched in a thin layer of cream.

Whiteoak shook his head as if he'd been splashed with cold water. Fighting every instinct to stay, he moved along to the next window. It too looked into a bedroom, but this one was more sparsely decorated than the last. The walls were bare except for one picture which looked to be a painting of a grassy landscape. The bed was small and bore only a mess of disheveled sheets and a quilt.

"Damn," Whiteoak grunted under his breath. His eyes were fixed upon a trunk near the foot of the bed which he recognized as having been on the cart that had brought Byron Keag into town.

Byron's window was also slightly open. This time, Whiteoak didn't stop himself from slipping his fingers through the crack and easing the window up the rest of the way. He was about to climb inside when he noticed something else about the room. There were no boots on the floor, no coat hanging from the hook, no clothes piled anywhere in sight.

Byron wasn't at home. The house was too quiet, too dark and too still for anyone else to be inside. Since he'd spotted a few of the young man's things strewn throughout the bedroom when he'd peeked through the door during supper, he knew that those articles of clothing were missing.

Why would a man leave his bed at such a late hour?

Could Byron simply be out for a stroll or could he be visiting some other female in Barbrady with whom he could share such a beautiful night?

Whiteoak's muscles tensed in preparation for his climb through the window. His mind wasn't nearly as ready for the short journey. What he wanted wasn't in there. He knew that without having to see definitive proof. And even if it was, he figured he stood to learn more by finding Byron than looking for the object that had captured his interest in the first place.

He closed the window, turned his back to the building and took a few steps away. On the off chance that someone might happen by, he walked slowly toward the street that led to the more populated areas of town. Whiteoak's eyes roamed the walkways and streets, looking for the path that was most likely taken by the man he was after.

"Byron is a businessman," he muttered under his breath. It did Whiteoak some good to talk his process through, but he didn't dare let his voice drift above a whisper. "While there are devious businessmen, Byron isn't one of them. He rode straight into town with his papers. Instead of hiding, he went straight to the home of his own sister. So when he sneaks out now, where would a man with such a limited capacity for sneakiness go?"

As he sifted through his thoughts, Whiteoak kept walking into town. If there was more light available to him, he might have attempted to look for fresh tracks in the dirt. Since the sunrise was still several hours away, he followed the next hunch that struck him.

Whiteoak took a sharp turn at the first corner which pointed him toward the section of Barbrady occupied by its two banks, the assessor's office and several storefronts owned by other professionals including two lawyers and a dentist. Although Whiteoak wasn't certain how many other offices were located in that vicinity, he was fairly certain that he was looking at Barbrady's closest semblance to a business district.

Like every other portion of town, except for the row of saloons and cathouses a few streets over, that street was almost completely dark. The only bit of light to break up the shadowy monotone was in a window on the second floor of a building in the middle of the block. Whiteoak's eyes narrowed as he focused on that spot and quickened his steps so he could arrive there before the source of the light was snuffed out.

"Could be some overworked clerk who lost track of time," he mused to himself.

With his gaze still fixed upon the single lit window, Whiteoak nearly ran straight into another man who was hurrying down the street without taking enough care to watch where he was going.

"What in the . . . ?" Whiteoak snapped.

"Oh," the man blurted. "Sorry, I . . ."

Both of them finally looked at each other long enough to see the other's face. Even then, it took a moment for either man to form another word. As it was for most verbal contests, Whiteoak was first to be heard.

"What are you doing here, Byron?" the professor asked.

Even in darkness, the shocked confusion could still be seen on Byron Keag's face. "What am I doing here? What are *you* doing here?"

"I'm out for a late night constitutional," Whiteoak lied. Given the condition of his audience, he didn't need to worry about being convincing. "I had trouble sleeping."

"I was just . . . actually, I don't need to explain myself to you!"

Whiteoak managed to cock his eyebrows at an offended angle, but couldn't unleash the tirade he'd prepared before footsteps crunched against the dirt not too far away.

"We need to go," Byron said in a rush.

"Why?"

"I can explain later. We need to go. Right now."

Whiteoak strained to look into the shadows. After a second or two, he could discern enough in the darkness to pick out a small group of figures near the base of the building with the single lighted window. At first, there appeared to be two of them huddled in the shadows. Then, as Whiteoak kept his eyes fixed on target, he picked out three distinct shapes.

"Does it have anything to do with them?" the professor asked, although he already had a good idea of what the answer would be. While he'd intended to elicit more of a response by playing on the tension already pouring from Byron, he hadn't expected his words to strike such a raw nerve.

"We've got to get the hell out of here," Byron snapped. "Or we're both dead."

"Dead?"

"You heard me, now let's go!"

"Surely, you're overreacting. Who are those men and why would they want to . . ." As he turned away from the figures he'd spotted, Whiteoak discovered that Byron had already vacated the spot he'd so recently occupied. More than that, the younger fellow was racing in the other direction without so much as a backwards glance over one shoulder.

The professor moved awkwardly at first, launching himself into motion from a standing start. After a few quick steps, however, he took a more graceful stride that allowed him to catch up to Byron in a scant couple of seconds. Once he was close enough, he reached out to grab the other man's elbow and rein him in.

"What are you doing?" Byron hissed.

"I'm still waiting for answers," Whiteoak replied.

"Are you deaf? I already told you we need to get away from there!"

"But I still don't know why."

Pulling his arm free of the professor's grasp, Byron said, "There's no time for this!"

Whiteoak meant to press the matter, but was unable to utter a word before his audience had dwindled from one member to none. Turning toward the distant group of figures, he saw that all three of them had fanned out to walk straight toward him. Since it seemed they weren't angry at him yet, he figured he still had some room to maneuver where a possible negotiation was concerned.

The three figures were wide through the shoulders and walked with solid steps that ground the loose dirt and gravel beneath their heels. Whiteoak straightened his posture and lowered his head a bit to present himself in a manner that would match the men's demeanor.

Their hands hung down near their hips without moving, hovering above the guns kept at their sides. One of them, the man in the middle, drew his pistol and brought it up.

"Oh, hell," Whiteoak muttered.

The middle man fired a quick shot which hissed through the air several inches to Whiteoak's left.

Figuring his window for negotiations had been shut, the professor spun around and ran to catch up to Byron.

CHAPTER SIX

Whiteoak's hand slapped down onto Byron's shoulder and closed to form a solid grip. Using the younger man's clothing as a handle, the professor forced them both into an alley by pulling with a combination of strength and momentum.

"What are you doing?" Byron gasped.

"Taking you out of the line of fire, in case you hadn't noticed."

Before Byron could protest, another couple of shots blazed through the night to burn into the darkness behind him. "Thanks," he said with a nod.

"You can repay me by telling me who they are," Whiteoak replied.

"I couldn't tell. It's dark."

Another shot was fired. Even though the bullet took a chunk out of the building Whiteoak was using for cover, he didn't flinch as splinters spattered against the brim of his hat. "You know them."

Byron shook his head, unable to speak as the sound of heavy footsteps drew closer.

Maintaining his grip on the younger man, Whiteoak began to shove him back toward the opening of the alley. "Then perhaps," the professor said forcefully, "we should see if they know you?"

"Fine, fine!" Byron sputtered. "I may know them. Or at least one of them, but this is no time for discussion."

"Agreed. If you want my help now, I suggest you make time for me at your earliest convenience."

"Yes, yes! All right. Just please, help me!"

Wearing a victorious grin, Whiteoak pulled Byron away from the street less than a second before more shots were sent in their direction. The already damaged corner of the building was chipped further by hot lead as echoing gunfire mixed with the sound of Byron's frantic wheezing.

Whiteoak pressed his back against the building a scant couple of inches away from where the last few shots had found their mark. The footsteps drew closer but slowed before entering the alley.

Several paces away, Byron had stopped so he could stare at Whiteoak and silently motion an unspoken inquiry as to what on earth the professor was doing. Whiteoak's response was an equally urgent gesture shooing Byron away. The younger man didn't need to see anything more to convince him to flee and he turned tail to bolt in the opposite direction.

"They're headed down the alley," one of the armed men said from the street. "I just heard 'em."

As the first man rounded the corner, the initial thing to come into sight was a gun hand and the pistol it held. Whiteoak reached out to grab that hand above the wrist. Long, slender fingers locked around the gunman's wrist like a shackle and once they were cinched in tight, the professor pulled while leaning back.

The man attached to that wrist was a burly fellow with muscles layered over a thick frame. His steps were already propelling him forward with enough speed to make it next to impossible for him to stop before hitting the corner of the building that had already been damaged by gunfire. When his face smacked against the splintered wood, his hat was knocked off and his mouth curved into a pained sneer. For a moment, he and Whiteoak locked eyes. As he tensed in preparation to break free of the professor's grip, the big fellow was pulled forward yet again to smack into the wall even harder.

Forecasting the other man's next attack with learned efficiency, Whiteoak ducked low to avoid a calloused grasping hand. Before the big fellow could try again to get hold of him, Whiteoak drove his heel into the other man's shin. The pain from that was enough to loosen the big fellow's hold on his pistol, allowing Whiteoak to take it away from him before hurrying away.

The big man reeled back, off-balance for a few steps since he'd been unexpectedly released from the fingers that had ensnared his wrist. Veins stood out on his thick neck, tracing crooked lines all the way up to his sweaty bald scalp. Behind him, two others approached. They weren't as quick to round the corner, however.

"Skinny little prick's stronger than he looks," the big fellow snarled.

"How would you know, Cord?" replied a man of average height with dark blond hair slicked down against his head. "You barely took a moment to look at him."

"I've seen plenty," said the third man in the group. He was stout with thick dark hair and a face covered in coarse whiskers. His dark eyes were pointed toward the far end of the alley and his hands brought a Sharps rifle up to one shoulder so he could take aim. Before he could squeeze his trigger, the blond man pushed the barrel of the rifle toward the ground.

"You may have seen enough, but I haven't," the blond said. "I want to get a closer look at that second fella."

"He wasn't no lawman," Cord offered.

"Which means neither of you has to be gentle when you bring him to me. Just don't kill him." Seeing the expressions on the other men's faces, the blond added, "Not yet, anyways."

The blond man stood in the alley as the other two split off in opposite directions to circle around either side of the dark passage. There was barely enough light for him to make out the far end of the alley, but not enough to pick out much detail along the way. He walked slowly between the two buildings, listening for every sound that drifted through the air. His hands rested upon the pistols kept in the double-rig holster strapped around his waist, ready to draw either weapon. Several sets of footsteps could be heard, but only one of them grew louder as the other two faded away.

Midway down the length of the alley, he planted his feet and squared his shoulders to the far end. Although his palms pressed against the grips of his holstered pistols, the blond man still did not draw them. Instead, he watched with eyes that narrowed intently to pick out everything they could from the shadowy gloom in front of him.

For a few seconds, the sound of boots scraping against dirt was the blond man's only company.

Soon, the two men making those sounds appeared in the alley. One was eager to rush all the way back to the street while the other blocked his path.

"What are you doing?" Byron asked frantically as he bumped against the arm that had been extended to impede his movement.

"Open your eyes," Whiteoak snapped.

Once he took a moment to catch his breath and truly look at what lay in front of him, Byron was no longer so eager to keep running.

Chapter Seven

Placing the professor between him and the blond gunman, Byron asked, "What do we do now?"

"We deal with this problem."

"Or we could go back," Byron offered.

Scraping footsteps grew louder as the big man named Cord circled around behind Byron and Whiteoak. Looking back at the big fellow, Whiteoak said, "I would imagine the other one isn't far away but sure, you can try to make a run for it if you insist."

Byron kept his mouth locked shut and his feet rooted to his spot.

"You know what we're after," the blond man at the front of the alley called out. "Best give it to us before this gets messy."

"Either you are extremely unlucky," Whiteoak whispered to Byron, "or you are in possession of something extremely desirable."

"Or," the blond gunman said, "it's a little of both. Where are those papers?"

Whiteoak let out a labored sigh. "How did I know it was going to be about the damn papers?"

"What do you know about them?" Byron asked.

"Just that they are turning out to be one of the largest inconveniences in my life since . . . well . . . other large inconveniences."

Byron squinted at the man next to him. "That's one of the

few times you've seemed to be at a loss for words."

"I'm flustered."

"You're about to be dead!" Cord bellowed as he stepped up to stand behind them.

"I can tell you where the papers are," Whiteoak announced.

Slowly, the blond man stepped forward. "Go on."

"They're in that building Mister Keag here was just leaving not too long ago. Don't ask me how I know, but I'm certain of it."

"No," Byron said shakily. "They're not."

Before Whiteoak could voice his surprise, the blond man said, "Go on."

"I've still got them. I was supposed to deliver them here tomorrow, but wanted to be rid of them right now. I was getting anxious because of the robbery and all and thought I might be able to slip into the building and leave them there, but the place was locked up tight."

"Who were you supposed to deliver them to?" the blond man asked.

"I don't have any names, but . . ."

The blond man cut him off by slamming Byron against a wall and roughly searching his person. It didn't take long for him to find the bundle of documents. "We already know that much," the blond man replied.

Whiteoak's turn came next when he was spun around by Cord and doubled over by a meaty fist driven into his gut. Cord's other hand remained on Whiteoak's shoulder, which was used to pull him back as if the professor was a wet shirt being peeled off a washboard. Whiteoak caught his breath. As he tried to straighten up, he was thumped in the stomach one more time. Despite his dandy appearance, the professor wasn't a frail man. However, being punched so hard in exactly the same spot took its toll.

As Whiteoak dropped to his knees, Byron was too nervous to move. Even when he flicked his eyes from one gunman to another, he twitched in expectation of the consequences. "You've got what you wanted," he said. "Leave."

Breathing heavily, Cord reached behind him to pull a blackjack from where it had been tucked at the base of his spine. He slapped the blunt weapon onto the palm of the blond man's hand and snapped Whiteoak's chin to one side with a quick left cross.

A cruel smile slid onto the blond man's face as he tightened his grip on the blackjack. Without another moment of hesitation, he pounded the blunt piece of hardened leather against Byron's ribs. "Neither of you two get to order us to do a damn thing," he growled before hitting Byron again.

"Stop it!" Whiteoak said, even as blows rained down on him as well. But as much as Cord struck him, Whiteoak didn't buckle.

The blond man tattooed Byron with the blackjack, tenderizing him like a slab of beef.

"Enough," Whiteoak gasped through a bloody mouth. His right hand drifted toward the gun in his holster and was immediately slapped away by Cord.

"I was wondering when you were gonna go for that smoke wagon," the big man said. "Thought you had enough sense to let it be. Guess not."

The pistol was taken from Whiteoak and tossed aside. It had barely touched the ground before Cord went about making Whiteoak regret he'd even tried to arm himself. After weathering a series of solid punches to his ribs, Whiteoak saw the other man pull back his fist in preparation for a straight punch to his face. In the space of time between preparation and execution, Whiteoak snapped his knee straight forward to slam into the side of Cord's upper leg. The impact hit the nerve running through that portion of Cord's anatomy, sending a jolt of pain through his entire body. It wasn't enough to end the fight, but it bought Whiteoak a few precious seconds in which he could act.

Whiteoak slammed his knee into the same nerve again, causing Cord to bend to one side like a plant wilting from lack of water. Whiteoak shifted his focus up a bit and pounded his knuckles three times in quick succession under Cord's left arm. With each punch that landed, Cord staggered back another step.

Although the big man obviously felt the blows, he simply used them as fuel for his fire. "Gonna tear your head off," he growled while lunging forward.

Whiteoak waited for the last moment before doing a quick sidestep to clear a path for the rampaging Cord. Before the big man could get past him, Whiteoak grabbed Cord's collar and leaned back with all of his weight to steer the other man straight into a wall. Cord hit with a resounding thump, twisted around as if he was going to charge again and then slid to a seated position on the ground.

Only now did the blond man seem to notice that his partner had been tripped up. Saliva trickled from his mouth, sweat rolled down his face and blood dripped from the weapon in his hand. He looked at Whiteoak with wide, expectant eyes as the professor stooped down to retrieve his .38.

"What're you gonna do with that, huh?" the blond man sneered.

Whiteoak thumbed back the pistol's hammer and immediately shifted his aim upward to the set of rickety stairs leading to the second floor of the building to the blond man's right. A third member of the blond man's group stood mostly obscured by shadows, watching events in the alley over the top of his Sharps rifle.

Both men pulled their triggers, filling the night with a single thunderclap that brought the scent of burnt gunpowder to the air. Although it was impossible to say which of them had been the distraction to the other, neither man hit their target. The one on higher ground took a moment to take aim before firing a second time while Whiteoak used one hand to fan back the hammer of his pistol and his other to squeeze off several shots in a row. The bullets flew wild, but the rifleman wasn't about to stand still for Whiteoak to steady his aim.

"All right!" the blond man said. "We'll go." Looking up to the top of the stairs, he jabbed a finger at the rifleman and added, "I said that's enough, Shawn. We made our point. No need to bring the whole damn town into this conversation."

Having found a new position so a good portion of his body was behind a handrail attached to the staircase, the rifleman grudgingly lowered his Sharps.

"How about you, fancy pants?" the blond man asked while staring at Whiteoak. "You wanna keep this up or should we part ways like gentlemen?"

"I'm always the gentleman," Whiteoak said between measured breaths.

"Good." The blond man offered a hand to Byron.

The offer was refused as Byron showed his attacker a bloody, defiant glare.

Chuckling under his breath, the blond man tossed the blackjack through the air to be caught by Cord who was climbing back to his feet.

"I'm glad we could resolve this without any further bloodshed," Whiteoak said.

The blond man was on his way out of the alley and the rifleman above had already disappeared from sight after presumably ducking into the door at the top of the stairs. Both Cord and the blond man turned away from the alley and walked casually away.

When Whiteoak made the offer to help him up, Byron accepted it. "You should have shot them," Byron grunted.

Whiteoak sighed and holstered his pistol. "I tried."

"You could have tried again while that maniac was busy making threats."

"Out of bullets, I'm afraid. I doubt he would have been so kind as to allow me to reload."

The two of them walked a few steps, neither one willing to fully let their guard down. Even though the other three men were nowhere to be found, Byron and Whiteoak kept looking as if one or all of them might spring from a dark corner like a beast from a nightmare.

"Is that truly all you know about those documents?" Whiteoak asked.

"I . . . I was paid to bring a package into town," was Byron's meek reply. "I'm just a courier. I've been working as a courier for some time. Like I already told that animal, I'm just the middleman. I accepted a courier job from a party who wished to remain anonymous and I was supposed to put that package into the hands of another anonymous party."

"And that didn't seem shady to you?"

Reluctantly, Byron said, "It did, but it paid well."

Since he'd taken plenty of worse jobs for similar reasons, Whiteoak didn't feel the need to climb onto a high horse at that moment. He simply nodded and kept walking.

"Thank you," Byron said eventually.

"For what?" Whiteoak chuckled.

"You scared them off."

"I fired blindly and got lucky."

"Good enough."

"Yes," Whiteoak replied. "But for how long?"

CHAPTER EIGHT

Byron winced in pain, started to swat at the source of his discomfort, thought better of it, and sucked in another labored breath.

"Sit still, will you?" Lyssa said as she tended to him with a wet cloth.

"I'm all right."

"You're a bloody mess is what you are!"

"Allow him to collect himself," Whiteoak said as he tossed the cigarette he'd been smoking and stepped into the house through the front door.

"You can keep out of this," she snipped. "My brother has been a courier for years and never had the kind of problems he's had since you arrived."

"It's not his fault, Lyssa," Byron said.

Whiteoak walked across the room and into the kitchen where he busied himself by setting a teakettle on top of the stove. "Indeed," he shouted into the next room. "In fact, I . . ."

"You saved his life," Lyssa said. "So you keep mentioning."

"It is true, you know," Byron said in a harsh whisper. "If he hadn't been there . . ."

"If he hadn't been there, perhaps none of this trouble would have happened," she snapped. "Did you ever think of that?"

Byron may not have been swayed by her argument, but he wasn't about to refute it.

Having silenced both of the men in her house, Lyssa dabbed

at the largest bloody welt on her brother's chin. "Why were you out so late?" she asked.

"I was nervous," Byron told her. "With everything that happened, I just wanted to get those papers away from here as quickly as possible. I thought that would divert any other problems away from here. At least I was right on that count."

Lyssa wrung out the rag she'd been using into a basin on the table before dipping it into a smaller basin of clean water beside it. "If this is what it's like when you're right," she said while cleaning some dried blood from his forehead, "then I think I prefer it when you're wrong."

"It seems I was wrong to accept this job in the first place."

"Did you know what kind of men you'd be dealing with?"

"I rarely do," Byron said. "Some of my duties are somewhat important, but a courier is never anything more than a tool."

"Then why do you do it? You're better than that."

"It pays well and it's easy, honest work. I'm hired through the company I've been working with for six and a half years. I got the assignment, a bundle was left on my desk and there was an envelope with instructions. Those instructions may have been a little more peculiar than normal, but . . ."

"Peculiar?" Lyssa said. "That's what you're calling it?"

"Well . . . more peculiar."

The way she scowled at him left no room for misinterpretation.

Byron averted his eyes before lowering his head like a scolded child. "I see what you mean."

"Of course you do," she hissed. "Because you're not stupid. Or, at least, I thought you weren't stupid. Maybe I should reconsider that now that I know you've been taking jobs that could very well get you killed."

Dropping his timid demeanor, Byron looked his sister in the

eyes and said, "I am not stupid. I knew exactly what I was getting into."

"Then perhaps you're just crooked."

"What?"

Busying herself by cleaning up the table and to keep her hands busy, Lyssa wiped at every little bit of water that had dripped onto the polished surface. "Arrangements like this obviously aren't on the square and if you weren't stupid then you would've known that."

"Well, that's . . ."

"And if you knew that and went through with the job anyway," she continued, "then you must have been at peace with taking part in such a thing."

"I don't know about . . ."

"And if you were at peace with something like that," she angrily concluded while picking up one of the basins and turning her back to him, "then you must be crooked yourself."

Byron didn't say anything, but he winced and gulped silently for air. Only when his sister was out of the room did he exhale and slump deeper into his chair.

Storming into the kitchen, Lyssa walked right past Whiteoak. Considering how small the room was and how much of its limited space was taken up by the stove and cupboard that was a fairly impressive feat. There was a small table wedged into a corner near the cupboard. That is where she placed the basin before snatching another rag hanging from a hook nearby.

"You're still here?" she snapped in the professor's general direction.

Whiteoak shifted on his feet. "There, uh, really wasn't anywhere for me to go without interrupting your conversation with your brother."

"Right. Because you are always the proper gentleman," she said in words dripping with so much sarcasm that her basin could have been put to good use in catching the runoff.

"Well, that is the case insomuch as I . . ."

"You look like an outlaw."

Furrowing his brow slightly, Whiteoak straightened the lapel of his rumpled jacket as though he was still wearing the finery in which he'd presented his tonics. "I beg your pardon?" he huffed.

"You heard me."

"Yeah? Well you interrupt people quite a lot."

Lyssa pivoted on the balls of her feet with the basin in her hands and put it into the cupboard. She then stomped past him into the next room so she could retrieve the smaller one. The only sound that came from the other room was Lyssa's angry footsteps. Just to be certain Byron was still in the vicinity, Whiteoak took a cautious peek. Sure enough, Byron sat at the table watching her. He wasn't about to move and he sure as hell wasn't about to open his mouth.

"I do not interrupt people," she snapped once she was back in the kitchen.

Against his better judgment, Whiteoak replied, "I'd beg to differ."

"And how would you know?"

"Because you barely let your brother or myself force two sentences from our mouths before you cut in."

"Seems to me like you've been doing plenty of talking your-self."

"Well," Whiteoak said with a tired grin, "I talk more than most."

"That's a fact." After tossing the remaining water out a small window near the cupboard, Lyssa used her rag to wipe out the basin. "And the only way you'd know so much about how I talk to my brother is if you'd been eavesdropping on us."

"To be perfectly fair, it would have been difficult to *not* hear your conversation since it was spoken in such loud . . ."

"So now I'm loud too?"

Whiteoak stepped forward to gently take the wet rag from her so he could place the cool cloth against his own swollen face. "I'll take back what I said about you being loud, but not the part about you interrupting."

For the first time since they'd returned that night, Lyssa seemed to relax. "I suppose that's fair."

"It would also be fair to give your brother some credit for wanting to shield you from danger. That's all he was doing, after all, where tonight's escapades were concerned."

"Tonight's escapades," she sighed, "and whatever trouble is to follow."

"What's going to follow?" Whiteoak asked.

"From what you told me, it seems obvious that this isn't over. Those men are still here and they still want whatever they came for."

"Sure, but this is surely the law's problem now."

"Oh, you know that for certain, do you?"

"Of course!" Whiteoak said with supreme confidence. "Not only was there trouble at an upstanding business here in town, but there were gunshots fired in the middle of the night. The law is more than likely sniffing around that alley as we speak."

"And morning," Lyssa sighed, "isn't far away. I'm so tired."

Wincing as he wiped some blood off his cheek, Whiteoak said, "I know how you feel."

When she looked at him this time, there was a hint of genuine compassion in her eyes. "I really do appreciate everything you've done, Henry," she said while reaching out to touch his cheek.

"That's nice." After Lyssa yanked her hand back, Whiteoak added, "I meant you calling me by my first name. It's not so formal. Also," he admitted, "a touch from such a soft hand was nice as well."

"It . . . slipped."

"Which one? The name or the touch?"

"Both," she replied in a voice that reflected some of her previous sternness.

Stepping closer to her, Whiteoak whispered, "A slip, perhaps, but not an accident."

"What's the difference?" she asked with a defiance that was only slightly convincing.

"One is something you didn't mean and the other is something beneath the surface that you merely didn't want to show. At least," he added while placing the side of his finger against the smooth skin beneath her chin, "not yet."

Her eyes were blue and unblinking as she looked at him. Although she lifted her head a bit, she didn't pull away. "It's late. We should both be getting to bed."

Whiteoak raised an eyebrow and smirked.

"That's not what I meant," she was quick to say. "Well, I did mean we should get to bed, just not . . . or should I say . . ."

"Just not together?" he offered.

"Yes."

"Not now or . . . not yet?"

"What a foolish question," she stammered as her eyes flicked toward the next room which was empty since her brother had snuck out some time ago. "We've only recently met and . . ."

"You're flustered," Whiteoak pointed out. "Or are your habits so deeply engrained that you're interrupting yourself now?"

She smiled, which brought more warmth to the room than the largest fire that could have been stoked in the belly of that stove.

Smiling also, Whiteoak slid the side of his finger along her neck before taking a subtle turn toward her shoulder. "We have only recently met," he said. "But there's something other than time that causes people to smile this way when they look at each other."

Lyssa started to turn away, but all it took was a gentle nudge from Whiteoak's finger against her chin to turn her back to face him again. "I'm still upset," she said. "With both of you."

"Of course. Perfectly understandable."

"And I won't tolerate anyone dragging my brother into danger."

"I didn't drag him into a thing," he assured her.

"And as far as you and I are concerned, I don't mind so long as . . ."

This time, he was the one to interrupt her as Whiteoak leaned in to place his lips upon hers. For a moment, her body shifted against him and her mouth pressed against his. A little moan came from the back of Lyssa's throat, which quickly turned into something of a growl.

"Well now," Whiteoak said with a smirk, which lasted right up to the point where she slapped it off his face and stormed away.

Placing his hand upon his cheek, Whiteoak mused, "That could have gone better."

CHAPTER NINE

The sheriff arrived bright and early the following morning. He and one deputy approached the Keag house and didn't need to bother knocking on the door to announce their arrival because Whiteoak was stretched out on the swing hanging on the house's front porch, wrapped in a thick wool blanket. He was just starting to stir when his makeshift bed was sent into motion by a kick from the lawman's boot.

Steadying himself by gripping the edges of the swing with both hands, Whiteoak tried to sit up and swing his legs down. It wouldn't have been such a difficult task if the swing wasn't pitching back and forth amid a shrieking chorus of rusty creaks.

"It's Professor Whiteoak, right?" the lawman asked.

"Yes, Sheriff Willis. It most certainly is."

"I don't recall properly introducing myself to you. Have we met before?"

"No," Whiteoak said as he finally managed to sit upright without falling from the swing. "I like to ask around about a town's law before I set up shop."

"Helps for when folks start to complain about all the snake oil you been peddlin', I suppose," the deputy said.

There was no mistaking the venom in Whiteoak's stare when he looked to the younger man and said, "It helps for when ignorant people assume my wares aren't genuine and decide to harass me for no good reason."

The deputy was twenty years old with light brown hair and

eyes that were too clear to pull off the imposing stance he was trying to use with the professor. The only feature that separated him from any young man who'd just learned to shave was the absence of the smallest finger on his left hand. Apart from that, he seemed to have avoided any harsh contact with the cruel world around him. Still doing his best to appear threatening, he asked, "Did you call me ignorant?"

"Why, no," Whiteoak replied in a droll monotone. "I wouldn't dare take such a risk with a bad man like yourself."

The deputy appeared to have something more to say, but was prevented from further posturing by the sheriff. The older lawman looked to be somewhere in his early forties with the grizzled lines in his face and streaks of gray in his hair that marked him as someone who'd been keeping the peace for some time. His build was solid, if not overly muscular. A somewhat rounded belly told Whiteoak the lawman had gotten used to town living a good while ago.

"All right, Avery," the sheriff said. "You've got this man sufficiently quaking in his boots."

The deputy had been perturbed before, but that fanned the flame even higher. As much as he wanted to laugh at the younger man's inability to defend himself to his superior, Whiteoak managed to keep a straight face.

As Avery moved back, Sheriff Willis stepped close enough to stare directly down at Whiteoak. Crossing his hands like a stone edifice, the sheriff said, "I take it you know why we're here?"

"I'm guessing it has something to do with the trouble last night?"

"That'd be a good guess. What was your part in it?"

"Why would I have any part in it?"

"I've spoken to some folks who were out and about when the fight took place. They say they saw you in the same area at that time."

Whiteoak patted down a stray piece of hair that was standing up after his night's sleep. "They could have mistaken me for some other handsome devil."

"You're very distinctive, Professor," the sheriff said. "Especially after all the attention you've been drawing after your medicine show."

"It just so happens that I was out for some night air," the professor explained, "and I happened to find my friend Byron Keag in a bit of trouble."

"Out for some air, huh?" the sheriff mused.

"That's right."

"In the middle of the night."

"Or very, very early morning," Whiteoak pointed out. "All depends on your perspective."

"Then what happened?"

"I found Mister Keag and then three unsavory characters found us."

"Who were they?" the deputy asked, eager to get back into the conversation as a participant instead of a distraction. Judging by the fact that neither of the other men deemed it worthy to give him so much as a quick glance, there was still some work to be done in that area.

"I didn't get all of their names," Whiteoak said. "I was too busy defending myself."

"Yeah," Sheriff Willis said as he gave Whiteoak's swollen, bruised face a gentle slap. "Looks like you did a real good job with that."

The professor didn't flinch at the casual smack. His eyes narrowed and his voice took a definite edge when he said, "The task may have been easier if the town's law was defending its citizens instead of . . . well . . . whatever it was you may have been doing while outlaws roamed your streets."

"What did these outlaws look like?" Willis asked.

Whiteoak gave a quick description of the three men who'd attacked him the night before.

Nodding as he listened, Willis then said, "You mentioned you got some names."

"Right. The big one was called Cord and I believe they called the one with the rifle Shawn."

"What about the third?"

"He had scars," Whiteoak said as he stretched his back. "On his face and neck."

"What kind of scars?"

"Deep gouges. Like claw marks, only they weren't."

"What were they, then?" the deputy asked.

Finally looking at the younger man as if he was something other than a buzzing gnat, Whiteoak said, "Bullet wounds. Near misses, by the looks of them."

Rather than keep up his angry scowl, the deputy turned to the senior lawman.

Willis gnawed on the inside of his cheek, sorting things in his mind as he asked, "You sure about that?"

"I may not be a doctor of medicine, but I've seen plenty of bullet wounds. They are quite distinctive, you know."

"Yeah. I do. Tell me something. You ever hear of a man by the name of Jesse Nash?"

"Sounds vaguely familiar. Some sort of bandit, I believe?"

Willis nodded. "Bank robber. One of the worst. He's got his sights set on something here in Barbrady."

"Could it be the bank here in town?" Whiteoak asked.

The deputy stepped forward with his hands balled into fists. "Don't act like you don't know! You were there and you got away without a scratch! You must've heard or seen something useful."

Motioning to his battered face, Whiteoak scoffed, "If you call this without any scratches then I'd hate to imagine what you'd consider scratched!"

In a much calmer tone than his deputy, the sheriff explained, "Most men who lock horns with Nash have scratches that look more like holes in their chest and head. Taking a beating from him and his men is getting off pretty light by comparison."

"Well, I can grant you that."

Turning to the younger man next to him, Sheriff Willis said, "Why don't you go back and see if them businessmen have anything more to say about that safe?"

"I can help here," the deputy said.

"You can help more over there. Just do what I say, Avery."

Reluctantly, the deputy complied. He made sure to shoot Whiteoak one last glare before walking away.

"What safe?" the professor asked.

The sheriff shrugged his shoulders. "Looks like you had a rough night," he said, dodging the question without much attempt at being subtle. "And I ain't talking about your ill-fated little walk."

Tracing the lawman's glance to the porch swing with the rumpled blanket on it, Whiteoak said, "Oh yes. That."

"Care to explain?"

"You are mighty curious this morning."

"Part of my job," Willis said.

Since the lawman obviously wasn't going anywhere yet, Whiteoak said, "Under the circumstances, I thought it best that I stay close to these good people in case they required additional protection. The lady of the house and I had a disagreement, however, and she felt it was better for me to sleep outside. Being a good guest, I complied."

"You stepped out of line and got booted out, huh? What did you do? Try to get your hands up her skirts?"

"Certainly not!" Whiteoak said. "And I resent the implication. Lyssa Keag is a fine woman!"

"She is," the sheriff said. "And if you'd answered that any other way, I would have given you a few more bruises to add to your collection."

"I can appreciate that."

"Then you should also be able to appreciate the position I'm in. You see, men like yourself aren't exactly reputable."

"Men like myself?" Whiteoak asked, feigning offended ignorance.

"Con men. Hucksters. Men who roll into towns filled with big words and promises, selling bottles of sugar water and three different flavors of laudanum. You come into Barbrady, put on your big show, and that very night some valuable papers belonging to Mister Halstead get stolen."

Sensing a good opportunity to fish for information, Whiteoak said, "From what I could see of those papers, they weren't all that impressive."

"Frankly, I don't care what's scribbled on 'em. They're gone and since that's all that was taken, I'd say that makes them valuable. Seeing as how Nash or those other two aren't around right now, I'm forced to pay a visit to this town's next disreputable citizen."

"Which would be me," Whiteoak said distastefully.

"Which would be you."

"Surely you don't think I'm some bandit sitting on a load of freshly stolen valuables. I spent last night getting beat to a pulp and then sleeping on a porch swing, for god's sake."

"And that," Willis said, "is why we're talking on this here porch instead of a jail cell."

"I already told you what I could, Sheriff. Isn't that enough for now?"

"I want to search your wagon."

"What for?"

"To make certain what I'm looking for ain't there. Look, this here visit is a courtesy. I could be turning your wagon upside down this moment and be within my rights."

"And you could also take whatever you like and claim it's what you were searching for."

The sheriff's face took a hard edge. "You accusing me of bein' some kind of thief?"

Whiteoak stood toe-to-toe with the lawman, staring right back at him without flinching at the growing embers burning within Willis's eyes. "Let's face it, Sheriff. Traveling medicine men like myself aren't the only ones with reputations that have been dragged through the mud."

"If you're calling me crooked, you'd best have some damn good proof."

"Merely acting out of experience," Whiteoak replied. "Isn't that the same excuse used by you and your deputy when you stroll up here and treat me like a criminal while the real perpetrators are still roaming free?"

The next few moments were long and taut as a bowstring. Finally, Willis took a step back. "You made your point. Don't push it."

The front door to the house swung open and Lyssa looked outside. The sheriff barely had enough time to tip his hat to her before she stepped aside and allowed Byron to move past her and walk onto the porch. "My sister thinks I should invite you in for breakfast, Sheriff Willis."

"That's mighty kind," Willis replied.

"I'm not feeling so charitable," Byron continued. "Especially since we didn't even get the first bit of help from you when me and Professor Whiteoak's lives were being threatened."

"A man can't be everywhere at once," Willis said. "Besides, you never told us you were there. We simply checked in on some gunshots that were fired. The offices of Mister Halstead were robbed at about the same time. I suppose you don't know anything about that either?"

Whiteoak shrugged. "I'm new to town. I don't know any Mister Halstead."

"Did I hear right when I thought you said the professor may be the guilty party?" Byron asked.

"Gotta be thorough. A quick check of his wagon will let us know if he's guilty or not."

"I can tell you he didn't take a thing," Byron said. Beside him, Whiteoak stood like he was posing for an inauguration painting.

The sheriff nodded. "Well then, seeing as how you're so willing to stand beside the good professor here, why don't I start my search with this house?"

Chapter Ten

The lawmen were thorough, but did their best not to make a mess. Even so, there was still a good amount of straightening up to do once they'd gone. It was several hours after Sheriff Willis's departure that the lawman returned. He was alone.

It was Lyssa who answered the door this time and she wasn't any happier than the last time she'd seen him. "What is it, Sheriff?" she asked. "Did you think of one more place in my home that you wanted to stick your nose?"

"No, ma'am. I just thought you might come down to my office when you get a chance."

"Why?"

"Nothing official, I swear. More like a request."

Exasperated by the whole affair, she said, "Just leave. I'll stop by when I can."

"Honestly, it's nothing to do with any suspicions I might have regarding that robbery at Halstead's office."

"So I'm not one of your suspects?"

"No, ma'am."

Shaking her head, she said, "I've lived here for years. We see each other every Sunday at church and suddenly you want to call me ma'am?"

"Feeling a might guilty, I suppose," Willis admitted. "You've got to know, Lyssa, that I didn't think I'd find anything to link you to those outlaws."

"Then why did you turn my house upside down?"

Although he and his deputy were as careful as possible when looking through the Keag home, Willis wasn't about to plead his case by questioning her choice of words. "You know how serious we take robbers in this town. We're a small community and if we don't protect ourselves, there's a whole mess of wicked men who'll be happy to ride in and take what we've got."

"Sounds like an awful lot of trouble to guard a courier's pouch," she scoffed. "Whatever is happening around here, my brother would never take part in it," Lyssa insisted.

Willis held up his hands as if to staunch the flow of pleas to come. "Not your brother, but the men that hired him. There also might be something suspicious about that professor fella that came to town. Seems mighty strange that he latched onto ol' Byron so quickly."

"So far, that part of it seems like a coincidence."

"Well I don't care much for coincidences. Frankly, I'm surprised you'd put up with the likes of that dandy."

"He seems . . . earnest."

"Earnest is one thing," Willis pointed out. "Honest is another."

"Believe me. I know."

Sensing he was no longer in her bad graces, the lawman let out a breath. "Well, since he's won you over like he has, it's no wonder he asked to see you."

"So," Lyssa said as she walked to the back of the sheriff's office, "what happened this time?"

Henry Whiteoak tried to play the part of a hapless fawn, but the fact that he was locked in a cell at the back of that office made the task especially difficult. He leaned against the bars, held on with both hands and showed her a crooked smile. "Would you believe I was a victim of circumstance?"

"No."

"How about an unfortunate recipient of a bad run of luck?"

Standing directly in front of the closet-sized cage built into the back corner of the office, Lyssa crossed her arms and cocked her head to one side while frowning disapprovingly. "How's that different than the first answer you gave?"

"Creative wording?"

"I don't have time for this," she grumbled while turning to walk away.

Whiteoak lowered his head which caused his brow to bump against the bars. "I might have said a few things to the sheriff that I shouldn't have," he admitted.

Having already turned her back to the cell, Lyssa stopped. "Go on."

"He was searching my wagon and found a few things."

"I'm listening."

"He found some guns and a small supply of dynamite."

Lyssa spun around to look at him. Dropping her voice to a harsh whisper, she asked, "What on earth would you be doing with those sorts of things?"

"I have many varied interests and travel to many varied places."

"Please, Henry. Don't talk to me like I'm another one of your customers. Speak plainly."

"I'm being perfectly honest with you, Lyssa. My entire life is in that wagon. It's my place of business as well as my home. I do travel quite often and sometimes find the need to defend myself. I stash weapons so I can better deal with robbers who may get the drop on me."

"And the dynamite?"

"I forgot that was in there."

She scowled at him even harder until Whiteoak buckled.

"Maybe I knew it was there," he said, "but I didn't think they'd find it. The only reason I have it at all is because I occasionally deal with miners and they need explosives. Selling to them provides a good amount of income. I didn't tell the sheriff about it because I feared he might confiscate it. In my defense, I was correct on that last part."

"He sure as hell was," Sheriff Willis announced from behind his desk on the other side of the room.

Turning to face the lawman, Lyssa asked, "Is having dynamite against the law?"

"Nope," Willis replied while turning over the newspaper that had been waiting for him on his desk.

"Is it against the law to carry weapons to use to defend yourself when riding alone?" she asked.

"Nope."

"Then putting this man in a jail cell seems to be unfounded, wouldn't you say?"

After taking a moment to peruse the newspaper in front of him, Willis said, "Why don't you ask him about what he told me when I asked him to unlock the other compartments in his wagon? The hidden compartments."

"I did unlock them, Sheriff," Whiteoak said.

"Sure. But what did you tell me when I asked the first time?"

"I told you there was no legal precedent for you to put me through such a degrading experience."

"And when I asked the next few times?"

"I . . . forget."

"He told me to go to hell, Miss Keag," the lawman said. "And he told my deputy to do some things to himself before joining me there."

Turning to look at the cage, Lyssa asked. "Is that true?"

"Well, not in those exact words," Whiteoak replied.

"And," Willis continued, "when I informed the good professor that I was acting within my responsibilities as sheriff, he decided to try and stand between me and my task."

"For God's sake, Henry," Lyssa sighed.

"Oh, I'm not through," Willis said. "My deputy stepped in to lend a hand and the two of them got into a shoving match."

"Which that young man started," Whiteoak was quick to say.

"Punches were thrown."

"I believe he threw the first one," Whiteoak chimed in. "That thug in a badge even tried to draw his gun on me!"

"He told you to settle down before things got worse," the sheriff said. "We both did. Why don't you tell this nice lady what you did when my deputy's hand touched the gun which, by the way, he never drew?"

Whiteoak sighed, held on to the bars and once again tapped his forehead against the rounded iron. "I relieved him of his weapon."

"He plucked the gun from its holster and tossed it like a hot potato," Willis said. "Damndest thing I ever saw. Damn quick too. The least any man should expect after a display like that is to spend some time in a cell to cool his heels."

"On that, I agree," Lyssa said in an icy tone.

"Nobody was hurt," Whiteoak explained. "I wasn't being particularly violent. I was just defending myself and standing up for my rights as a citizen of this great country."

"You were being an asshole," Willis snapped back as he slammed the newspaper down onto his desk.

"I wasn't the only one!"

"Avery is cooling his heels also, but not in a cell."

"A travesty of justice if there ever was one."

Standing up, the sheriff asked, "You really want to keep spouting off?"

Whiteoak choked back the words he obviously wanted to say and instead replied, "No, sir."

"That's better. Now if you behave yourself for a little while longer and prove you can be trusted, I'll open that door. If you'll excuse me, I've got rounds to make. Miss Keag, a word?"

Lyssa walked over to the sheriff while shaking her head. "I sincerely apologize about this," she said softly. "While he is difficult to be around, the professor has been a genuine help to my brother and I do think he has the best intentions."

The door came open with a squeak as the sheriff pulled it with one hand while using his other to place his hat upon his head. "I know he ain't a bad man," the lawman said in a faint grumble of a voice. "But he's a menace to this town."

"Isn't that a bit harsh?" Lyssa asked in a voice that matched the lawman's.

"Fine, then. He's a pain in my ass and I imagine several others' as well."

Lyssa couldn't deny that. She couldn't even keep herself from nodding her agreement. "If that's all it took to be locked away," she said, "then I doubt there'd be many free men left in this world."

"You got that right," Willis said good-naturedly. His smile barely got a chance to become attached to his face before it was wiped away by the crack of a few gunshots in the distance.

"What's that?" Lyssa asked as she tried to get a look past him and out the door.

Unshaken by the noise, the sheriff let out a tired sigh. "Never fails. Whenever I barely get any sleep, the drunks come out of the woodwork and decide to get rowdy. Now's about the time when the saloons are clearing out the all-nighters. I'll go and see how many of them need an escort out of town."

"And what about him?" she asked while nodding back toward the cell.

"He can sit and stew for a while longer." After a stern look from Lyssa, the lawman sighed and marched to the back of the office while snatching a ring of keys from his desk. He unlocked the cell and was on his way back to the front door before the hinges had a chance to squeal. "Any more trouble from you, Whiteoak," he announced without looking back, "any more smart-ass comments to me or my deputy and you'll be back in there."

"Yes, sir!" Whiteoak said happily while strutting outside the cell.

"And you won't be getting out after another couple hours, neither!" the sheriff warned before slamming the door shut.

"Once again, fine lady, I am in your debt," Whiteoak said to Lyssa.

She shook her head and was surprised when he placed his hands upon her cheeks to give her another kiss. It was a gentle meeting of their lips that lasted for about a second. When it was over, the professor retreated and crossed the office to a locked cabinet.

"What are you doing?" she asked while placing her fingertips upon her lips.

Whiteoak tested the cabinet, found it to be locked and went over to retrieve the keys from the lawman's desk. "My property is in here and I'm reclaiming it."

"No, I meant before." Her voice was breezy and slightly dazed. As much as she tried to sound upset by the surprise show of affection, Lyssa couldn't muster the necessary ire. And before she could think of anything else to say about the kiss, she was distracted by more gunshots. "What was that?" she asked while snapping her eyes to the closest window.

"Whatever it was, it's more than some drunks firing at the clouds."

"How do you know?"

"Call it a hunch."

Stepping behind him as Whiteoak gazed out a window, Lyssa raised up her tiptoes so she could get a better look. "I don't see anything."

"I do."

"What is it? Tell me!"

Pointing to a small cluster of people across the street, he asked, "See that?"

"Yes. They're a few people I know walking down the street."

"They're moving quickly and look like they're in a rush to find someplace safe. You should do the same." As soon as those people ducked into the closest doorway, he added, "See? That means there's trouble and it seems the trouble is in the vicinity of the bank."

Chapter Eleven

Having just emerged from the sheriff's office, Whiteoak slipped on his shoulder holster and checked the .38. Without looking at the woman trailing behind him, he said, "I thought I told you to stay put."

"Even if you did, I don't take orders from you."

"Then follow the example of your fellow townspeople and find some shelter."

"They're not trying to find shelter."

"Then go with one of them to keep them company," he snapped. "Frankly, I don't care where you go, just get away from here!"

As soon as those words were out of his mouth, Whiteoak knew they would have the opposite effect than what he'd intended. His hastily formed theory proved correct when Lyssa planted her feet on the boardwalk and her hands upon her hips. "Don't talk to me like that," she said through gritted teeth.

The next series of shots came from the part of town that Whiteoak had deemed the business district. It was in the general vicinity of the office that had been robbed after Byron's visit, but it was also the location of the ripest apple in town for any robber to pluck. Whiteoak hurried in that direction.

"Where do you think you're going?" she hollered while dashing to catch up to him.

"I think the bank is being robbed," he said.

"Nobody would be stupid enough to try that!"

"Nobody ever accused outlaws of being overly intelligent. They do tend to be fairly decent shots, so it might be best for you to find somewhere else to be right now. Somewhere safe."

"I agree," she said, much to Whiteoak's surprise. Lyssa took him by the hand and dragged him a few steps toward one of the buildings where other locals had ducked in for shelter. "Let's both get off the street. It's about to get bad out here."

"I realize that," he said while pulling his hand free. "That's what I've been trying to tell you. Why do you insist on making this so difficult?"

"Fine. You want to get shot? Go right ahead. See if I care."

As she stormed toward it, the door was opened for her by a wrinkled old man who stared past her at the flustered professor. After a few whispered words between him and Lyssa, the old man shut the door and worked the latches that would lock it.

Whiteoak moved down the street. "Good," he grumbled under his breath. "Her heart's in the right place, but her brain simply isn't. That's the problem with headstrong women. Especially the pretty ones. They get so used to leading men by the nose that they start thinking they know what's good for everyone all around."

Having made it to the corner, he was able to see a portrait of chaos drawn in the near distance with smears of gun smoke drifting through the air churned by the movement of desperate men. At the far end of the street, the bank's shattered windows and flung-open doors made it look like an egg that had been cracked by the men scattered in front of it. There were six men in all, only three of which Whiteoak recognized.

The blond gunman with the scars on his face who'd led the attack in the alley was there. Whiteoak assumed he was Jesse Nash. Although Nash had the reins the last time he and the professor had crossed paths, he wasn't in control of anything anymore.

The second face to strike a chord with Whiteoak sat atop Cord's thickly muscled neck. Like most big men, Cord was accustomed to being at the top of the pecking order or at least somewhere in that general vicinity. Normally, that would give him an air of confidence. In this situation, however, it didn't serve him so well. He stood with his feet shoulder-width apart, gripping a pair of saddlebags that had been thrown over a shoulder with one hand and hefting the weight of a .45 pistol in the other.

Two of the remaining men wore bandannas covering most of their faces. One had it pulled up over his nose to create a mask and the other was simply disheveled in general and the slip of material was skewed across his chin. That one was Shawn, the man who'd brought the Sharps rifle to the fight in the alley during Whiteoak's late-night stroll. The fifth man stood perched on the edge of the boardwalk in front of the bank carrying a shotgun. His face was etched into a defiant visage that looked around for a target.

"Lay down your guns and put your hands up!" Sheriff Willis called out.

Until then, Whiteoak hadn't been able to see the lawman. Tracing the voice back to its source, he picked out Willis and his deputy. The former stood with his back pressed against the corner of a building directly across from the bank while the latter lay on the dusty ground mostly concealed in shadow behind a water trough.

Nash stood in the doorway of the bank. Leaning to one side, he grabbed hold of a petrified woman dressed in a simple gray dress with her hair tied in a bun. Obviously several years older than Nash, the woman seemed to age a few more years as Nash cinched an arm around her scrawny neck from behind.

"You men toss *your* guns!" Nash demanded as he held a pistol to his hostage's temple. "Or this one here will get blown to hell."

"You already got caught in a robbery," Willis said. "Don't add murder to it."

"If this bitch dies it'll be your fault!"

"If she dies, you'll hang for it," the sheriff replied. "You got my word on that."

"And you already got my word that I'll kill her," Nash said. "Don't make me repeat myself."

Whiteoak took a few steps down the street after turning the corner, but was stopped by tension that hung so thick in the air it formed a solid wall in front of him.

The street had become quiet.

Although both lawmen froze intently in their spots, the outlaws shifted anxiously on their feet. Whiteoak noticed Cord's eyes darting upward and to the sides, prompting him to take a look in that same direction.

There were several buildings neighboring the bank, either next to the square building or across from it. Most of those structures were at least two floors high and a few were three. Plenty of windows had a view of Barbrady's financial institution, several of which were slowly being opened. From his angle, Whiteoak couldn't see much more than a few flapping curtains being tugged by the wind or the occasional wrinkled face gazing out for a look at what was about to happen.

"One last chance, Nash," Willis proclaimed.

The outlaw answered quickly and loudly. His pistol erupted in his hand, its report muffled by the skull of the woman he'd grabbed from inside the bank. Before the pulpy mess of blood had a chance to slide down the door frame, Nash dropped the dead husk he'd been using as leverage and disappeared inside the bank. When he returned, he was holding another hostage.

"You wanna keep bargaining?" Nash asked. "There's plenty

more in here, although this is the last lady."

"Fine," the sheriff said. "Let that woman go and come on out of there."

At first, Whiteoak couldn't tell the person Nash had grabbed was a woman. Once Nash took a step outside, it was easy enough to see that Willis was right. The outlaw dragged a dark-haired woman along with him, wrapping an arm around her neck and pressing his pistol against her head. She winced at the touch of the warm, wet barrel and tears began streaming down her cheeks.

"Let my boys go too," Nash shouted.

"You let the woman walk away and I'll think about it."

Sensing weakness in the lawman, Nash added, "Bring the bank president in here so he can open this safe! I'm taking some of this here money as well. I don't do any job for free."

"Let her go."

"Or what?" Nash asked. "You ain't got the stomach for all the blood me and my gang's prepared to spill!"

There was more silence, but it was short-lived. After a second or two, Willis stooped down to set his pistol on the ground near his right boot. He stood up again, stretching his arms halfway to the sky in a lazy surrender. "This what you want?" he asked.

A filthy grin spread across the lower portion of Nash's face like fungus overtaking a tree stump. He leaned his head out from behind the woman he'd grabbed so he could use both eyes to drink in the sight before him. The woman was slender and had short black hair with streaks of gray. Too frightened to move, it was all she could do to stay on her feet.

"Your deputy too," Nash said.

"You heard him," Willis told the younger lawman. "Put the gun down."

Although he wasn't happy about it, Avery left his gun on the ground while rising to his feet.

The other four outlaws had been content to let Nash do all the talking. Now that it was time to put that bank behind them, they all seemed more than eager to be on their way. Several horses were tied to a rail near the bank and it was there that the outlaws started to converge.

"Leave the woman," Willis said.

"She's our ticket out of this shit hole," Nash replied. "I'll cut her loose when we're away from here."

"You'll do it now."

Nash pulled her close while backing toward a gray mare tied to the rail. "Nah. I'll do as I please. And maybe," he added while pulling her close to take a long sniff of her hair, "I'll do it more than once."

Whiteoak's hand tightened around the grip of his pistol. Even though he was well outside of the .38's range, he wanted nothing more than to put an end to Nash's threats.

All of the gunmen were gathered around their horses by this time and a few were climbing into the saddles. Some, either from nerves or overconfidence, were laughing loud enough to be heard from where Whiteoak was standing. The professor looked over to Sheriff Willis, glaring at the lawman while silently urging him to do something, anything at all, to put an end to this nightmare.

Nash had his back to his horse and stood so the woman was between him and Willis. Keeping a hand locked around the woman's neck, he lifted one foot into a stirrup. It was an awkward motion, but one that had surely been practiced many times over the years with countless other poor souls he'd taken hostage.

Whiteoak looked back and forth frenetically between the outlaws and the sheriff. "If he's not going to do something," the professor grumbled to himself, "then by God . . ."

"Take him," Willis said in a voice that cut through the air like a sickle through dry wheat.

Nash had just started climbing into his saddle, which took him farther away from his hostage than he'd been since grabbing the poor woman. The space between them was only a few inches, which was enough for a well-placed shot. That shot came from one of the upper windows overlooking the bank, announced by the solitary crack of a rifle.

Whiteoak twitched at the sound, crouching a bit.

Snapping his head back, Nash toppled to the ground in a jumble of arms and legs. He hit the dirt with a loud crunch and when he scrambled to his feet again, the woman hostage was already bolting.

Cord and one of the others were still on their feet and the two remaining outlaws had mounted their horses. Cord lunged for the woman and grabbed a handful of her sleeve as she hurried past him.

Before the outlaws could get their second wind, Sheriff Willis dropped to one knee and retrieved his pistol with a sweep of his hand. As his fingers wrapped around the familiar grip of his shooting iron, the lawman shouted, "Take them all!"

Nash's men found themselves staring up at dozens of gun barrels pointing down from the windows overlooking the street.

CHAPTER TWELVE

Nash looked up at the windows around him with a broad grin on his face. He was clearly amused by the show of force in much the same way a prizefighter might think it adorable if his seven-year-old son balled up a little fist and popped him in the rigid muscles of his stomach. Blood poured from the fresh wound in his cheek. Another scar to add to his collection of mementoes from near misses throughout an eventful career.

Each shot made a sound that smashed through Whiteoak's ears like a boulder through the shimmering layer of ice on a newly frozen lake. His nerves were jangled by the eruption of gunfire; a feeling that was clearly shared by all the outlaws who, like the professor, didn't think the locals had it in them to pull a trigger. All of them were wrong.

It didn't take long for the initial surprise of that first shot to wear off. After that, survival instinct kicked in. Before they could take aim at the window that was the source of one shot, rifles from all of the surrounding windows spat a torrent of fire and lead down upon them.

"Jesus!" Shawn hollered. He was one of the men who was already in his saddle and he pulled his reins while firing up at the windows directly in his line of sight. His shots punched into the wall, drilling a random pattern accented by flying splinters and chipped boards.

"Take what you can and get the hell out of here!" Nash shouted. He kept his head down and his movements concise as he focused all of his efforts on mounting his horse.

Panic caused another of the robbers to point his shotgun at the opposite side of the street and pull both triggers. The thunderous roar instilled some degree of confidence in his belly, but did nothing to help him. Well beyond the effective range of the shotgun blast, the buildings received nothing more than a spattering of buckshot. In return, the people inside those buildings sent a stream of rifle rounds his way with more than enough power to reach their target. The shotgunner was cut down where he stood.

Shawn twisted as if he still meant to leave town at his own pace. Every second or two, his body twitched and flailed with the impact of one bullet after another. Only a fraction of those fired at him were hits, but that was enough to send him to the ground in a bloody heap. He let out a pained scream on impact that was swallowed up by the unrelenting gunshots coming from above to finish him off.

"Get out of here!" Nash cried out. "Move!"

The remaining outlaws stuck together. Cord was on foot and the masked man sat atop a white spotted horse that was aching to run. Until now, the sixth outlaw had been content to stand quietly near the bank as if he could blend in with the scenery. Gripping his reins in one hand, the outlaw on horseback tried to control his mount while reaching down to help the wallflower. Before the petrified outlaw could make it up behind the rider, he was hit twice by incoming bullets; once in the knee and another in his side. He let out a pained yelp but still somehow got on the horse's back.

Cord must have recognized that the gunfire was focused on the two men on horseback because he turned away from them and ran across the street. Seeing that the burly gunman was headed straight for Deputy Avery, Whiteoak forced himself to run toward the lead-filled tempest raging in the street.

"Look out!" Whiteoak shouted to the younger of the two lawmen.

But there was too much chaos filling the air, and the professor could barely hear his own voice. Avery had no chance of hearing the warning. Whiteoak straightened his gun arm and fired a shot in Cord's direction. His bullet didn't draw any blood and didn't even stand out enough from the others whipping by to catch Cord's attention. Rather than waste ammunition with another hurried pull of his trigger, Whiteoak steadied himself to take proper aim.

His body loosened a bit. He drew a breath, held it, and let it out while squeezing his trigger. The .38 bucked against Whiteoak's palm, sending a round directly into Cord's thick torso. The impact knocked the outlaw off his stride and stopped him long enough to be hit by one of the shooters looking down from a nearby window.

Ignoring the pain from his wounds, or perhaps too overwhelmed to feel it any longer, Cord bared his teeth in a feral snarl while shifting his aim to Whiteoak. The deputy only now realized how close the outlaw had gotten. Before he could fire a shot in his defense, the professor burned another hole into Cord's chest. This one, having been aimed with even more precision, bore a tunnel through Cord's heart and sapped the big man of all his remaining strength.

Cord dropped to his knees, shuddered with a wheeze and flopped dead onto his side in the dirt.

Once his target was down, Whiteoak's senses opened to everything happening around him. The sensations were almost enough to make him dizzy as screams, gunshots and shattering glass all mingled with the sound of hooves beating against the street. Whiteoak took particular notice of the latter since those hooves were drawing closer with alarming haste.

Leaning low over his horse's back, Jesse Nash tapped his

heels against the animal's sides to milk every last bit of speed from the horse's able body. Firing wildly into the windows on either side of him, Nash raced down the street and through the middle of town.

The masked outlaw had remained in his saddle with the wallflower behind him. He meant to follow Nash, but was forced to turn sharply as more rifle rounds hissed down at him. So many chunks of hot lead hit the street that they kicked up a small cloud of dust in the path of the masked outlaw's horse. He turned and decided to make a run for the opposite end of the street. Sheriff Willis stood in the middle of the confusion, sighted along the top of his pistol and sent a round directly into the wallflower's back.

At least one of the rifle shots hit the horse beneath the masked outlaw, causing the animal to rear up and churn its hooves in the air. The wallflower was thrown and landed heavily on the ground. An easy target for the shooters above, the fallen man was peppered with lead that slapped into his flesh and drilled bloody holes under his flailing body. By some miracle, the masked outlaw managed to jump from his saddle and roll clear so his spooked horse could gallop away.

Nash was out of sight, but there was more gunfire erupting from the direction he'd gone. Since most of those shots rippled through the air like a summer storm, Whiteoak assumed they came from more citizens in the upper windows.

"Give it up," the sheriff said as he marched forward to approach the only gunman left alive anywhere near the bank. The masked outlaw climbed to his feet and held his hands high above his head.

The shots from the nearby windows came to a halt. Most of the faces looking down at the street were covered in weathered skin with more wrinkles than a basket full of prunes. Their eyes were sharp, however, gazing down over rifles held in steady hands. Many of them had also been at the professor's medicine show, watching Whiteoak with almost as much scrutiny as they watched the outlaw now, waiting for a single misstep.

"You . . . you'll kill me," the outlaw whined.

"Not if you do as you're told," Willis assured him.

"You killed all the rest."

"Because they were stupid. They fired at us or put innocent lives in danger. You're standing there like a frightened kid holding a bag of money."

Flinching, the outlaw looked at his shoulder as if he'd forgotten he'd grabbed one of the saddlebags full of cash taken from the bank. Once he was reminded, he couldn't get rid of it fast enough.

Nodding slowly, Willis said, "Good. Now toss the pistol."

"If I do, will you call them off?" the outlaw asked while nodding up to the windows.

"If you do, they won't have any reason to shoot. Ain't that right?"

"Yes, sir, Sheriff," one of the wrinkled faces hollered down.

"There's been enough bloodshed for one day," the sheriff said, even though he hadn't caught so much as a scratch. "The robbery is over. There's no reason for you to make things any worse for yourself." When the outlaw glanced longingly down the street that Nash had chosen for his getaway, Willis added, "He's gone. Either dead or out of town. Whichever it is, he ain't coming back for you."

The outlaw let out a tired breath, lowered his gun arm and allowed the pistol to slip from his grasp.

"Good choice," the sheriff said. "Now, my deputy's coming over there to put some cuffs on you. Don't give him a fight because you know plenty well that I've got to bring you in."

The outlaw nodded.

Avery straightened up and brushed himself off before holstering his pistol so he could retrieve the cuffs dangling from a loop on his belt.

Above the street, many of the windows were closed. Whiteoak counted less than a third of the faces looking down now compared to before. Since the show was over, it seemed they weren't interested in watching the cleanup. The professor couldn't help but notice the outlaw studying the upper floors of those buildings also.

"All right, Sheriff," the outlaw sighed. "I'll come along without a fuss."

"That's what I like to hear."

Willis relaxed his posture as his deputy approached the outlaw. Avery looked down one more time to make sure he was holding the handcuffs correctly and the movement sparked one last bit of fight from the would-be prisoner. The outlaw turned and ran away from the lawmen when one more shot cracked through the air. Now that the rest of the town had become quiet once again, that single shot roared louder than the wash of thunder that had come before.

The bullet clipped the outlaw's thigh, knocking him into a wobbly dance that carried him several more steps before he lost his balance altogether. Dropping to one knee, he reached down to brace himself before falling onto his face.

"Sneaky bastard," Avery said as he approached the outlaw and kicked the supporting arm out from under him, sending him face-first to the dirt. With a loud curse, the outlaw was out of the fight and allowed himself to be unceremoniously cuffed by the deputy.

Whiteoak stood with his smoking .38 in hand. Noticing that he was under harsh scrutiny from the sheriff, he smirked, shrugged and loosened his grip on the weapon so it could dangle from his finger by the trigger guard. "I suppose you'll want to relieve me of this as well?"

"That's the way it normally works," Willis said as he stepped up to Whiteoak. "Especially when a man was killed."

"He doesn't look dead to me."

"Maybe not that one," Willis sighed as he watched his deputy perform his duty. "But there are a few others who seem plenty ready to fill a deep hole."

"You saying I killed those men?"

"I'm saying men died and you shot at one of them. And here I thought you were gonna be cooperative."

Handing over his pistol, Whiteoak said, "Of course I want to cooperate. I'm making certain I'm not being blamed for more than my part in this."

Willis took the fancy pistol from him and tucked it under his gun belt. "You were just in my jail for another shooting last night, Mister Whiteoak. And here you are with a smoking gun in your hand a short while later. Don't you think I got a right to be a little suspicious?"

"Am I going to be tossed into that cell again?"

"I appreciate your help, Professor. Seems I may have misjudged you. As for the jail cell, I suppose there's no reason for that. Not yet, anyway."

"Then be as suspicious as you like, my good man," Whiteoak beamed. "I find it's a habit that keeps a man healthy."

CHAPTER THIRTEEN

Once again, Henry Whiteoak found himself sitting at the dining table in the Keag house being tended to by Lyssa and a wet rag. This time, however, her efforts were gentler and even occasionally bordered on tender since all he'd acquired this time was a few bumps and bruises. Her words, on the other hand, were nothing of the sort.

"What in the hell is wrong with you?" she groused while dabbing at a dirty spot on Whiteoak's cheek.

Sitting in his normal spot, Byron said, "You didn't see what happened. I heard he played a part in stopping that robbery."

"Strictly speaking," Whiteoak offered, "the robbery had been concluded. What I helped stop was the escape."

"Either way, you're a damn fool," Lyssa told him.

Whiteoak leaned in to her and angled his head so she could apply the damp cloth to a spot on his forehead that was particularly achy. "Not a very nice way to speak to a hero."

"Nice?" she challenged while leaning back to get a good look at him. "Hero? I don't know which of those words offends me more."

"You have no good cause to be offended at all," the professor said.

Making sure to keep his voice down, Byron made his way to a small cabinet where the liquor was kept while muttering, "Oh, dear lord."

"First of all," she said while allowing her brother to slip out of the room, "I can be any way I choose inside my own home. Nice, rude or anything in between."

"Fair enough."

"And as far as the other title is concerned, I'd rank you as more of a nuisance than any sort of hero."

Whiteoak cocked his head to one side like a vaguely confused dog. His face went through a series of changes ranging from heartbreak and disbelief before settling on perturbed. "Perhaps you didn't see how I saved that deputy's life."

"I saw plenty. Perhaps Avery wouldn't have been in need of saving if you hadn't stepped in where you weren't needed."

"Things were going straight to hell already, which is something you would have noticed if you'd been there."

After taking her wet rag and throwing it at Whiteoak, Lyssa placed her hands on her hips and said, "Things were going according to plan. Everyone was doing what they were supposed to."

At that moment, some of the confusion drifted back onto Whiteoak's face. It didn't last long, however, before he brightened up and snapped his fingers. "Of course! The sheriff gave the signal and everyone took their places."

"And I thought you were supposed to be this big, smart professor."

"You'll excuse me if this sort of thing is somewhat out of my range of experience. A man can't be an expert in all things. Has the bank been robbed before?"

"There were a few who've tried."

"How many?"

"Enough for the sheriff and some of the others in town to organize a committee to . . . what's so funny?"

Covering his mouth to hide a grin, Whiteoak quickly attempted to disguise his subtle laughter by turning it into a cough. "Oh, nothing. Something caught in my throat."

"You were laughing."

He lowered his hand and shrugged apologetically. "Not laughing at you, in so much as at the words themselves. Why is it that when women form a committee it's to organize a picnic or a quilting circle? When men form a committee, it's usually to shoot something."

"This committee was formed to help protect the town and its bank from dangerous outlaws."

"And," Whiteoak added with a gently raised finger, "to shoot said outlaws."

"I don't have to explain anything to you."

Seeing that she meant to leave the room, Whiteoak got to his feet and moved forward to take hold of her arm in a gentle yet firm grip. "You're right."

Although she'd tried to squirm free of him the moment the professor took hold of her, Lyssa eased up when she heard those words. Picking up on how difficult it was for him to say them, she looked him in the eyes and asked, "What was that?"

Whiteoak let out a haggard breath. "Today has been very trying. I started off in jail. I was in a gun battle."

"Say what you said one more time."

"You're right," Whiteoak repeated. This time, however, it was as though he was forcing the words through an iron mask clamped to his jaw.

Lyssa raised herself to his level by standing on her tiptoes so she could give him a quick kiss. "You should learn to humble yourself more often," she said while giving his cheek a quick pat. "It suits you."

Remaining steadfast so as not to give her the pleasure of seeing him flinch when she patted his bruised face, Whiteoak replied, "No. It doesn't. Tell me more about this committee."

"It's more of a plan of action, really. When there are outlaws spotted in town or if there are suspicious men lurking about, a group of folks who live here are put on notice."

"So Nash was seen in town before he attacked your brother and I?" Whiteoak asked.

"I don't believe so."

"Would you know if he was?"

"There isn't a lot of excitement in Barbrady," she said. "Something like that would keep this town mighty busy."

"I suppose one of Nash's men could have been spotted."

"Not that I know of."

Again, Whiteoak snapped his fingers. "The shooting involving me and your brother last night! That's what put everyone on their guard!"

"No," she said timidly. "That wasn't it."

Timidity suited Lyssa almost as well as a harness fit a duck, which made Whiteoak immediately suspicious. "What was it, then?"

Eventually, she told him, "You. You're the suspicious character that put the committee on their guard."

"And what might happen if I draw more of their ire?"

"It's likely they'll just keep an eye on you," she told him.

"What's the worst that could happen?" Whiteoak asked, gingerly testing the waters.

Her face became grave. "You've seen the worst," Lyssa replied. "The worst is shooting down from the windows, filling the streets with lead and blood. I hate it when it comes to that, but sometimes such things are necessary."

"Ah."

"I hope you're not offended," Lyssa assured him, even though the grin on her face said otherwise. "It's just that the folks around here are suspicious of a lot. They need to be."

"Really? And why is that?"

She recoiled slightly. "This town was founded by elderly folks and elderly folks like to settle here. They say they like the quiet, but they never stop gossiping and spreading rumors, which makes them all twitchy. I tried to tell you everything was under control once the sheriff arrived at the bank," she said. "And even after that I tried to get you to come with me where you'd be out of harm's way."

"I did manage to take care of myself. And, despite being unaware of the entire situation, I also managed to hold my own as well as pick up some of the slack. If this committee had such a good plan worked out, that deputy didn't seem to be fully aware of it."

"Avery is new around here. He tends to get rattled."

"So you've seen him under fire before?" Whiteoak inquired.

"There was one other time when some rough men came through town looking to stir up some trouble. We were forming our committee, and some of the men thought it would be a good test."

"We?"

Lyssa shrugged her shoulders. "I may have come up with part of the committee's formation."

"So it was a trial run," Whiteoak said.

"Exactly."

"A trial with a dubious amount of bullets."

She narrowed her eyes as if that would make her displeasure burn Whiteoak's skin even more. Strangely enough, it worked. "A town has a right to defend itself."

"Indeed it does."

"You don't approve?"

"Does it matter?"

When Lyssa relaxed, her entire body became softer and she drifted a bit closer to the professor's side. "Sheriff Willis isn't always here. He has to ride to neighboring towns a lot. Also, with the bank . . ."

"What?" Whiteoak asked as she allowed her words to drift off into silence. "What about the bank?"

"It's a juicy target for men like those robbers today. Without something like you saw today, it would be in the sights of every rough gang of men that rode through Kansas. Even more people would be shot." Suddenly, Lyssa's face went pale and she placed a hand to her mouth.

Recognizing that she'd become unsteady upon her feet, Whiteoak took hold of her before she fell. The instant his hands were on her, she wilted like a flower in a vase that had gone bone dry. He guided her to a chair, sat her down and picked up the rag. "What is it, Lyssa?"

"Missy Stanson," she said.

"Who?"

"The woman who works . . . worked . . . at the bank. The one that was shot. She's gone, isn't she? I heard she was shot." Her mouth kept moving slightly, but no words could make it past her trembling lips.

Tears threatened to assault her eyes and before they could fall, Whiteoak sat beside her and took Lyssa's hand. "You heard right. She's gone. I'm sorry."

"But maybe it wasn't so bad. Maybe the doctor can tend to her."

Now Whiteoak had to distract himself as the gruesome memory of that previously unnamed woman's death played through his mind. When she was just another terrified face in a chaotic drama, it had been difficult enough. But now that she had a name, friends, and people that would miss her, that woman's passing took its proper spot among a cruel world's many tragedies.

"She's gone," Whiteoak said again, simply because he didn't know what else to tell her.

Lyssa nodded and leaned over to rest her head on Whiteoak's

shoulder. When he gently stroked her soft, fragrant hair, she closed her eyes and let out a vaguely contented breath.

CHAPTER FOURTEEN

The stink of burnt gunpowder and panic still clung to Whiteoak like the stained fabric of an old, filthy shirt. It crawled up into his nose, reminding him of the events of the last several hours as he walked down First Street in something of a daze. It wasn't the first time he'd been shot at and it wasn't the first time he'd seen others cut down by gunfire, which did nothing to soften the blow delivered by a morning such as the one he'd endured.

After excusing himself from Lyssa's frail company so she could collect herself in private, Whiteoak thought some fresh air would clear his jumbled thoughts. The dusty wind swirling through town did carry the scent of distant prairies and wildflowers, but wasn't quite enough to do the job. Once he'd turned a corner and made it to the end of Wilcoe Avenue, he spotted the very thing that he needed.

"Whiskey," Whiteoak said as he stepped into the Dove Tail Saloon.

The barkeep smiled, placed a glass in front of the professor, and filled it. He watched Whiteoak down the firewater with so much beaming pride that one might have thought he'd fermented the liquor himself.

"Another," Whiteoak said after setting the glass down. It was refilled and he was proven correct in thinking that, while fresh air was nice, fresh air and whiskey was a whole lot nicer.

"Can you tell?" the barkeep asked.

"Pardon?"

"That whiskey. It's been sloshed around inside those cups you sold me."

"Oh, yes," Whiteoak said as he went through a practiced set of motions that made it appear as though he was examining the drink in his hand. After swirling the liquid in his glass, holding it up to the light and sniffing it, he nodded and drank what remained. "Very nice, indeed."

"So far, nobody's complained that I started charging more for my cheaper brands. Whatever them cups do, they work great."

"I'm glad you're satisfied."

The barkeep placed both hands on the warped wooden surface in front of him and studied his customer. "You don't look so good."

"I was present at the trouble earlier today."

"Oh, the bank robbery?"

"That's it."

"I heard about what happened to poor Miss Stanson," the barkeep replied. "Crying shame. She was a good gal."

"Does that sort of thing happen a lot?"

"Not for a while. Not after what happened to the Garza brothers."

Now that the whiskey was working its way through him, Whiteoak felt somewhat better. The sugary residue smeared within the cups he'd sold to the barkeep tonic left a familiar taste in the back of his throat, but didn't do anything to take away the liquor's natural bite. "The Garza brothers were here?"

"You know them?"

Silently cursing the effect of the hard morning combined with that of the whiskey, Whiteoak quickly said, "Garza is a fairly common name. Why don't you tell me about the ones you were referring to?"

The barkeep was all too happy to tell his story and saw

straight past any discomfort that might have shown on Whiteoak's face. "They took a run at the bank and were gunned down like dogs. Didn't even make it off Trader Avenue, if I recall."

"They were gunmen of some repute?" Whiteoak asked, despite already knowing the answer all too well.

"They thought they were, anyway. Now they're nothing but fertilizer in some field outside of town. Ain't even a marker to show where they were planted. Serves 'em right if you ask me."

"Doesn't that whole course of action strike you as somehow . . . I don't know . . . barbaric?"

It was unclear which of those words had confused the barkeep, but the haze behind his eyes made it clear that he'd been lost somewhere along the way. "Having the law around is one thing," the professor restated. "Don't you think slaughtering innocent men in the street is going too far?"

"*Innocent?* Ha!"

"Fine, then. Slaughtering any man in the street seems quite savage to me."

"No more savage than stringing them up and making a day of it," the barkeep pointed out. "Bring the young 'uns. Pack a lunch!"

Whiteoak had to smile at that. "A friend of mine met his wife at a hanging in Abilene."

"And I suppose that's perfectly civilized to your delicate sensibilities?" the barkeep asked in an English accent that was thicker than the paint over a pair of bullet holes in the wall near the front door.

"Hanging a man is within the letter of the law," Whiteoak said. "And it happens after a trial."

"Usually. And have you ever been to many trials?"

"Yes. Plenty of them." At such events, the professor was more than a bystander, but he decided not to expound on that particular aspect.

"And can you tell me that some of those men wouldn't rather get shot down outside before going through all the headache of them men in suits talking gibberish in front of another idiot with a hammer in his hand?"

After taking a moment to form a logical retort, Whiteoak admitted, "It sounds silly when you put it that way."

"Sounds silly because it is. This way, if a bunch of armed men get caught in a bad spot, they get what's comin' to them. *Adios, hermano.* You want another?"

Following the barkeep's line of sight to the empty glass in his hand, Whiteoak shook his head. "No, this is my limit. At least for this time of day."

"Needed to steady the ol' nerves, huh?"

"Precisely. I am suitably settled."

"And since you got them words out without a hitch, I know you ain't drunk."

"You're a man of good humor," Whiteoak said. He then furrowed his brow and turned to look at the barkeep directly. "I never caught your name."

"It's Robert."

"Pleased to meet you, Robert. Since it seems I'll be staying for a while, is there a chance I can start an account at this fine establishment of yours?"

"After all them tonics you sold, you need a line of credit?" Robert asked. "Don't take me for a fool. You must've made more at that show than I make in a week."

"Not as much as you might think, but I see your point." Whiteoak dug into his pocket and fished out a small bundle of cash. He made sure it was plainly visible to the barkeep and peeled off a few bills. "This should cover my drinks," he said while handing over what he knew to be more than double the necessary amount. "And you can keep the remainder if you do me a favor."

Having already taken the cash and squirreled it away beneath the bar, Robert asked, "What's your favor, Professor?"

"I'd like to know a few things about your sheriff. Also, tell me about this committee I've heard about. The one that organized Barbrady's unique methods for guarding its bank."

Robert started his tale at the beginning when he arrived in Barbrady and went through several years of his experiences without pausing long enough to take a full breath. Although Whiteoak was partially listening to the barkeep, much of his attention was diverted elsewhere. Mostly, he observed the other people inside the Dove Tail and those who walked past its large front windows.

Whiteoak's eyes darted from one spot to another, taking his gaze outside to the street and back again to various points within the saloon. All the while, his ears soaked up every word Robert was saying. Most of it wasn't anything that couldn't have been pieced together on his own or with a few short conversations with the locals, but it did him some good to hear it all from one of the most reliable sources in town. Bartenders were never to be taken fully at their word, however. Whiteoak had learned that lesson well enough over the years. Even so, enough of what Robert told him rang true when compared to what Whiteoak had seen earlier that day.

According to the barkeep, Sheriff Willis had been in town for a few years and did a good job of mopping up drunks and escorting rowdy transients out of town. There wasn't much violence in Barbrady to speak of and what few scuffles there were had ended with the participants in a cell for a few days.

On the few occasions when there was real trouble, extra steps had to be taken. That's where the committee came in. According to Robert, nearly every man in town old enough to sprout whiskers from his chin was a member of the committee. The group had been called into action only a few times, each resulting in something similar to what the professor had witnessed for himself. In one instance, the men looking up at all those rifles pointing at them from the windows had taken the sheriff's offer and surrendered. Other times had turned into a bloodbath.

"Very effective," Whiteoak said.

Having reached the end of his story, Robert glanced over to Whiteoak as though he'd almost forgotten he had an audience. "Huh? Oh. Yeah. I suppose you could say that. Them boys didn't bother anyone again after that day, let me tell ya."

Whiteoak wasn't certain who, exactly, Robert had been talking about but it didn't matter. Setting his glass down, he said, "It looks like you've got more customers to tend."

Robert glanced over to the tables that had filled up since he'd started gabbing with the professor. "Not much of a surprise considering the excitement. Speaking of that, I hear you might have some interesting tales to tell since you were at the bank and all."

"You're interested in my stories? I thought you already had plenty of your own."

"More is always good," he said with a wink. "Gives me some good stuff for the regulars. You know how folks come in to a watering hole like this and expect to hear colorful chatter from the man behind the bar."

"Yes, I do know about colorful chatter," Whiteoak replied. The smile he showed to Robert was tired, but genuine. "I'll be back later. You have my word that I'll be much more talkative then."

Holding his fingers like a thin pistol and aiming them at Whiteoak, the barkeep said, "I'll hold you to that." After pulling his invisible trigger, he set his sights on the next man at his bar and dug into a fresh conversation.

Whiteoak left the Dove Tail and strode outside, tipping his hat to all the familiar faces he spotted along the way. Not surprisingly, there were more than a few unfamiliar faces who recognized him right away. The professor tipped his hat to them as if they were old friends and moved along.

He hadn't been in town for long, but was already piecing more of Barbrady together like a map in his mind being sketched and colored bit by bit. No matter how sharp Whiteoak's eye might have been, he would need to get a closer look if he wanted to get a clearer picture of what had gone on. For that, he needed to return to the Bank of Barbrady.

"Perhaps I should have another drink first," he muttered as the scent of burnt gunpowder became stronger in the air.

Instead, the professor steeled his resolve and soldiered on.

Chapter Fifteen

Now that the shooting had stopped, the street outside the bank was mostly quiet. Folks still went about their business, walking to and from the various businesses nearby. They even entered and exited the bank itself as though nothing out of the ordinary had happened. That, along with the whiskey he'd drunk, helped settle Whiteoak's jangled nerves as he approached the bank's front door.

"Hello, Professor Whiteoak," said a young man who stood behind the second teller's cage in a row of four. "What can I do for you?"

The teller wasn't really a young man in the strictest sense of the word. He may have been a year or two shy of Whiteoak's thirty-four, but he was a spring chicken compared to the rest of the wrinkled faces he'd seen that day. Tipping his hat, Whiteoak stepped up to the counter and said, "Looks like it's business as usual, and on such an *un*usual day."

"Not exactly, but we can't exactly close on the third Tuesday of the month."

"Ah, yes. Lots of banking to be done, I suppose."

There was a subtle shift in the teller's features. While nothing more than a little twitch to the inexperienced eye, a seasoned poker player would pick up on a hint of nervousness.

"What can I do for you, Professor?"

Leaning one elbow on the counter, Whiteoak said, "I'm surprised you remember me."

"That was an impressive show you put on."

"Did you purchase any of my tonics?"

"Oh, I meant what happened earlier today. You charged right in to lend the sheriff a hand. Very impressive."

"Yes. I wish I could have been there for the poor woman who wasn't so lucky."

"I wish that too," the teller said as he shuffled some papers in front of him just a bit too hard. His knuckles whitened and tense lines showed around his eyes. Any man who would have missed that was either blind or dead. "But business moves along."

"And why is that?" Whiteoak asked.

"We do what we're told. I'm sure you've worked for bosses before."

"While I run my own affairs now, I know all too well what it's like to be on someone else's payroll. They crack the whip and we jump. Am I right?"

"Very true."

No, Whiteoak thought. The teller wasn't merely upset with having to carry on like this was a normal day. There was something more. Something else was eating away at him. Every one of Whiteoak's senses told him as much.

"The owner of this bank must have some important matters today," Whiteoak pressed.

"He always does."

"Perhaps I could have a word with him? Maybe a voice from a concerned outsider could open your employer's eyes to the callousness of his policies."

A smile tugged at the corners of the teller's mouth, only to be quickly suppressed. "You might have better luck with that than any of us."

"And I imagine the owner of this institution was already bent out of shape after what was stolen."

"Only one of those robbers got away and he didn't take much with him. Just some of the loose cash from a few of the drawers."

"Not that," Whiteoak said. "I mean what was stolen before. You know, from those offices not too far from here."

"I don't know about that," the teller said, even though Whiteoak could tell the true story was quite different.

"The only reason I ask is because I'd like to know how safe a place like this is before I open an account."

"I can assure you it's perfectly safe," the teller said. "As you saw for yourself after today of all days, the Bank of Barbrady can weather any storm. In fact, I believe you're acquainted with the Keag family."

"I am."

"Byron Keag made a deposit before the robbery occurred and his money is secure in our safe."

Raising his eyebrows, Whiteoak said, "That is impressive. Even so, I'd like to get a look at that safe."

"Why?"

"My funds are considerable," Whiteoak replied. "And I need to be absolutely certain my money will be secure. And, after today of all days, you must see why a man in my position would like to have some assurances before committing to the Bank of Barbrady."

Glancing over his shoulder, the teller said, "It's still a mess back there."

"And it's a mess in here," Whiteoak said while gesturing to the fresh bullet holes in the wall to his right. "But business must go on." Sensing that he was falling out of the teller's good graces, Whiteoak added, "After putting my neck on the line and witnessing the demise of that poor soul today, I want to speak to the owners of this bank about a few things. I'd like to do so, not only as a concerned and upstanding businessman, but as a

nigh-deputized member of this town's law and an account holder as well."

"You were deputized?"

"Not yet," Whiteoak pointed out. "Nigh. I am nigh-deputized."

"What's that mean?"

Normally, it was a safe bet that people wouldn't admit to being lost by a fancy turn of phrase. Losing that bet, on the other hand, put Whiteoak at risk of looking foolish as well as ignorant. "It means, almost," the professor said, fairly certain he was correct. "Anyway, I have considerable funds and don't think my request is out of line, even considering the circumstances."

There was just enough ire in the professor's tone to push through the awkward moment he'd created. The teller nodded and quickly shut the drawers beneath his section of the counter. "Of course. Although, I can't guarantee much more than a glimpse."

"That should be more than sufficient."

Whiteoak was led around the counter to a narrow door that nearly came off its hinges when it was opened. A quick inspection was all Whiteoak needed to verify the door had recently been busted open. On the other side of the cracked frame was another, much sturdier, door.

"There," the teller said while motioning to the tall, cast-iron door of a large safe. "As you see, our safe is still quite formidable."

"Yes, formidable indeed," Whiteoak said. "Let's get a look at the inside."

"The inside?"

"Yes. Inside the vault. Let's have a look." When all he got was confused silence, Whiteoak asked, "Isn't that a fairly common request?"

"Not really, no."

Another customer entered the bank and loudly cleared his throat to catch the teller's attention. Whiteoak tapped his foot and stared at the man in front of him as though they were the only folks in town.

"I'm not asking for a peek into every nook and cranny," the professor assured him. "Just for reassurances that this isn't some ruse to gain the confidence of large depositors like me."

"A ruse?"

"You know. A trick."

"Yes," the teller snapped. "I know what a ruse is. After everything you've seen and all that's happened, you think I would want to deceive you by showing some sort of trick vault?"

"Stranger things have happened," Whiteoak said with a shrug he knew wouldn't be well received.

The teller reacted even better than Whiteoak had hoped. All of the anger, fear and frustration that came along with being put through an ordeal like the one that had transpired earlier that day built to a head and promptly exploded. For a second, the professor felt a little bad about how easy it had been to push the other man over that edge.

"You think this is a trick?" the teller growled. "You think we have nothing more important to do than build stage dressing to impress the likes of you? One of us was killed today and you think it was all to protect some sort of lie to make this bank look good?"

Whiteoak ignored the disdain in the teller's voice as well as the aggression in his movements so he could focus all his attention on that safe. According to every instinct at his disposal, he wouldn't have very long.

The heavy iron door would most certainly require some bit of effort to open. The hinges looked sturdy and the manufacturer was difficult to determine from where he was standing.

"Looks like there's some wear and tear," Whiteoak said.

"We were just robbed," the teller huffed.

"What's going on here?" asked a man in a voice that sounded almost as well polished as the cedar trim in the lobby.

The teller straightened up quicker than a cabin boy in the presence of his captain while Whiteoak turned as though he'd barely heard the stern voice. It would have taken a deaf man, on the other hand, to miss the sound of dress shoes knocking against the floorboards. "I'm here as a potential depositor," the professor said while turning on the balls of his feet. "My name's—"

"I know who you are," the other man said, ignoring the friendly hand Whiteoak offered. He was in his late sixties with the tough, weathered skin of someone who'd spent every one of those days under an unforgiving sun. His thick white hair was combed back into a mane and the spectacles he wore were attached to the bridge of a sharp, angular nose. "Everyone knows who you are, Professor Whiteoak."

"I'm honored."

"Why are you here?"

Retracting his hand, Whiteoak asked, "Does a customer need a reason to be in your bank?"

"To be this close to the safe on such a trying day, yes."

"Mister Bailey," the teller said nervously, "I was showing him that our safe is still intact."

"Of course it is," Bailey said, staring so intently at Whiteoak that he nearly fogged the lenses of his spectacles. "The men who thought otherwise are dead and buried."

"All of them?" asked the professor.

Somehow, Bailey poured even more consternation into his gaze when he said, "Enough of them. You happened to be in the vicinity and somehow fought back the urge to turn tail and run. That's not exactly the heroic story I'm sure you've been telling anyone who'll listen."

"Then you must not have been wearing your eyeglasses, sir," Whiteoak said tersely. "All I wanted was to open an account."

"Where's your money?"

"I'd rather bury it in a hole than put it in this place," the professor replied.

With a sneer, Bailey said, "Then get out of my sight and find yourself a shovel."

For a few seconds, both men eyed each other. They sized up one another like two boxers circling a ring after already having traded several testing blows. In the middle of that, the teller squeaked, "This really is my fault, sir. I shouldn't have brought him here."

"Nonsense," Bailey said. "We have nothing to hide from our customers. Once Mister Whiteoak decides to be a customer, he'll be more than welcome to see where his assets will be kept. Until then, he surely realizes this is not the time to come in here and harass our tellers."

"You're right, of course," Whiteoak said. "Forgive me. It seems we're all a bit wound up. I'll come back with my funds and discuss opening that account."

"And it will be our pleasure to help you with that."

Some lies were smooth, floating through the air like a slip of paper. Mister Bailey's was a blunt instrument wrapped in spiteful disrespect.

Chapter Sixteen

The frosty reception he'd gotten from the manager at Barbrady's financial institution stuck with Professor Whiteoak for about three minutes. That was the amount of time it took him to walk down Trader Avenue all the way to Second Street where he'd spotted a nice barber shop. Whatever hostility he carried with him during that short journey would be washed away by warm water and fragrant lather. A few swipes from a straight edge in the hands of an old man who weighed less than the smock he wore would put the professor right back into his cordial frame of mind.

"Tell me something, Salvatore," Whiteoak said while stretching out in the barber's chair. "Why is everyone in this town so old?"

"We've all lived long lives, I suppose," the fossil of a man replied. "Isn't that how it works?"

"I suppose so, in general, but why do so many old folks live here? Did Barbrady drop off the map as far as new settlers are concerned? Is there some kind of ill effect from the sun in this particular region of Kansas?"

"This is just a quiet town where important men come to enjoy their twilight years."

"Important, you say?" Whiteoak asked. "How important?"

"Well, let's see," Salvatore mused while snipping at Whiteoak's sideburns. "I can think of at least three cattle barons, one timber baron . . ."

"Never heard of a timber baron."

"If there's money to be made in something, there's a man out there who makes enough to become a baron."

"What about medicine?"

Salvatore shrugged. "I suppose so."

Whiteoak's gaze drifted to the large mirror taking up most of the wall directly in front of him. "Baron Whiteoak. Now that has a ring to it."

Like any good barber or someone working for gratuities, Salvatore nodded sincerely and said, "That, it does."

"So, all these important gentlemen just decided to come out to the middle of Kansas. Why not someplace near the ocean or close to some mountains?" Whiteoak asked.

"I've lived here all my life. Seems like a perfectly good spot to me. Better than Saint Louis, anyhow."

"I've been to Saint Louis and there are some fine eateries out there."

"If you say so."

"So all these rich fellows come together," Whiteoak said, veering sharply back to the previous topic, "and they all put their money in the bank."

"Where else would they put it?"

The professor fell silent as he thought about everything he'd heard and seen throughout the day. He liked taking time to contemplate while in a barber's chair because he could say anything at all and most barbers would roll with the verbal punches. Or he could not say a word at all and be left in peace. Whiteoak got the same results talking to his horse and always the option of talking to nobody at all, but that would be crazy.

"So," Whiteoak said, "these upstanding businessmen decided to live the quiet life out here. Makes sense I suppose. Like-minded people frequently make good neighbors. Many a town has sprung up that way."

"Upstanding?" the barber snorted. "I guess."

And there was the nibble for which Whiteoak had been hoping. "You don't agree?" he asked.

Whiteoak could see Salvatore shrug in the mirror as he muttered, "Who am I to say? I suppose they're friendly enough."

"Some of the most despicable men I've met have been friendly," Whiteoak pointed out. "Even the devil wore a smile when he offered his fruit to Eve."

"Got a point there. Eh, I don't know much. Just what I hear around this shop and most of that's got to be rumor."

"Are you finished with my haircut?"

"Yes."

"What about a shave?"

"I could start on one if you'd like," Salvatore said hopefully.

"Shave away, my good man. And since we have time, regale me with these salacious rumors you've heard."

Between the additional fees he'd be collecting for the shave and the chance to gossip with a willing customer, the barber's face lit up in the mirror like a flash of reflected sunlight. "The main fellows around here are the group of men who put Barbrady together. We call 'em the Founding Four."

"As in the Founding Fathers? Very prestigious."

"Between them, they're responsible for plenty of jobs all over the country and a few others as well. There's Jeremy Christian who made his fortune digging whatever he could out of the ground or scrape off a rock. Copper, gold, silver, guano, whatever could be put on the open market, he delivered. Then there's Michael Davis. He runs more lumber mills than I can count between here and Oregon. Also, there's Adam Bailey."

"Mister Bailey and I have met."

"Sounds to me like you ain't too happy about that."

"Granted, it has been a rough day for him with the bank being robbed and all. Even so . . ."

"He was a prick?"

"I was searching for a more diplomatic turn of phrase," Whiteoak chuckled, "but yes. That about covers it."

"It's best that you let him be however he wants to be."

"Why? Does he get worse?"

"When it comes to Mister Bailey," Salvatore said warily, "it could always be worse."

"What else have you heard about him?"

Suddenly, the barber didn't seem so eager to gossip. In fact, his hands went through the motions of scraping the lather from Whiteoak's chin with such haste that the professor was hesitant to move for fear of getting his throat slit. Proving to be a true master of his craft, Salvatore finished the shave without so much as a nick in his customer's flesh.

Once it was safe to sit up, Whiteoak swung his legs down from the chair and took a towel to wipe away the stray flacks of soap that remained. "You only mentioned three of the Founding Four," he said.

"Oh. The last one's George Halstead. Not to be confused with his boy, George Junior. They made their money building carriages and selling horses to pull 'em."

"You don't seem to hold these men in very high regard."

"I shouldn't speak out of turn."

Whiteoak watched the barber for a hint as to what had caused his sudden change in spirit. Before long, he couldn't help but notice the older man's eyes drifting toward the front window of his shop. When Whiteoak took a look out there for himself, he picked out two men standing across the street staring into Salvatore's shop.

"Who are they?" Whiteoak asked.

Without looking through the window himself, the barber replied, "Couldn't say."

"They seem fairly interested in your shop. Perhaps they need their hair cut?"

"If they do, they'll come in."

Judging by the tone of Salvatore's voice and the faint tremor beneath it, the barber wanted anything but for that to happen.

Whiteoak stood up, put his back to the window and positioned himself so he blocked the older man from being seen by anyone outside. "I've already crossed paths with Bailey and it was far from pleasant," Whiteoak said. "Come to think of it, much of what's happened to me since arriving in this town has been unpleasant."

"Then perhaps you should leave."

"No man can let himself be pushed around by unpleasantness, whether it be from impolite people or harsh circumstances."

"Professor, you seem like a good sort. I even bought some of your vitamin tonic and I haven't felt better."

That was a common accolade given to that tonic, which wasn't surprising considering the amount of barley, hops and poppy oil that was mixed into it.

"Speaking ill about the Four ain't a good idea," Salvatore continued. "They've got eyes and ears all over this town."

"Do they run Barbrady?"

"No more than any other men with influence. They have interests here and protect them with everything they got. Trust me, they have a lot."

"You're talking about their committee?" Whiteoak asked.

"Not really. Hell, I'm a member of that committee and proud of it. We don't do much more than protect our homes and town from getting busted up by the occasional bunch of rampaging animals."

"But what would bring those animals to Barbrady? This isn't the only bank in Kansas and it's not even close to being one of the largest."

Salvatore was growing more anxious with each passing second. Even Whiteoak could feel the hairs on the back of his neck standing up the longer he stood with his back to that window. Unfortunately, that was the only way he figured he might keep the barber talking.

"There are two men outside," Whiteoak said in a hurry. "You've seen them too."

"Yeah."

"They can't tell what you're saying to me right now, so tell me who are they?"

"The squat fella is Yance and the skinnier one's Eastman. I don't know which of the Four they work for, but it's one of them for certain. Maybe more than one."

"What do they do to earn their money?"

"If you don't go soon, you'll find that out for yourself," Salvatore said while nervously looking past Whiteoak and through the window. "They're headed this way."

"Then perhaps they want a trim."

"Perhaps," Salvatore said. "Or perhaps not. If it's the latter, I'd rather the lot of you not be inside my shop amongst so many breakables."

Whiteoak could see the sense in that reasoning. "You're sure they're coming this way?"

"Yes," the barber replied less than a second before the shop's front door was pulled open.

Whiteoak turned on his heels and smiled at the new arrivals. "I was just leaving," he said to the two men standing in the doorway. With all the ease of a man casually about to stroll out the door after getting a haircut, Whiteoak reached for the jacket he'd hung on a rack and draped it over his arm. That way, the two pistols hanging from the holster strapped around his shoulders could still be seen.

If the men in the doorway were at all concerned with the

silver-plated weapons, they gave no indication. Instead, one of them stepped forward so the other could also have a clear view into the shop.

"Excuse me," Whiteoak said cordially while placing his wide-brimmed hat on top of his head.

The man closest to him was Yance. Several inches shorter than Whiteoak, he still outweighed him by at least thirty pounds. The professor tested that bulk by attempting to bump him aside as he passed. Since most of that bulk was muscle, he bounced off of Yance instead of pushing him from his spot.

"Excuse me again," Whiteoak said while slipping into his coat. Once he stepped around the stout barricade and reached the door, he was face-to-face with Eastman. "Would you mind?"

"Why don't you help Fancy Britches out?" Yance said in a scratchy snarl of a voice.

Eastman had high cheekbones and a pug nose that most likely earned him some attention from the ladies. That was about all of the younger man's face that Whiteoak could see before he was picked up by the coat and collar like a cat being lifted by the scruff of its neck. Both of the other men laughed as the professor was tossed outside where he landed on his feet and used one hand to straighten his lapel.

"That's the nice thing about simpletons," the professor said loudly. "Doesn't take much to amuse them."

Yance emerged from the shop and stood at the edge of the boardwalk. "What did you call me?"

Stepping up to within a foot of the squat man, Whiteoak matched Yance's severe tone when he said, "You heard what I said. Or are you so simple that you don't understand my words? Shall I try to use shorter ones?"

"You got a smart mouth, Fancy Britches."

"And you've got an ugly face. I'd say that still puts me ahead of the game." Whiteoak looked over both men and scoffed distastefully. "If you're done acting like dumb animals, I'll be on my way." Adding insult to more insult, the professor turned his back on them and calmly walked away.

"Son of a bitch," Yance growled.

When he heard a calloused hand slap against leather, Whiteoak stopped and extended the arm that had been covered by the coat draped over it. "Looking for this?" he asked while displaying the pistol he'd lifted from Yance's holster when he'd bumped into him inside the barbershop.

Not only did Yance slap at his empty holster a few more times, but he also had to look down to make absolutely certain his weapon was gone. Much to his displeasure, he was just as weaponless now as when he'd checked the first time.

"You're the leader between the two of you, am I right?" Whiteoak asked.

The silence between the other men was more than enough to tell the professor that he was correct.

"And," Whiteoak continued, "as such, I would imagine you're the better shot. Now you, Eastman. Care to try your luck outdrawing a man who was fast enough to take your boss's weapon away without him realizing it was gone? Come to think of it, who's to say I didn't take your pistol as well?"

As if on cue, Eastman looked down to check his hip. That gave Whiteoak plenty of time to pluck one of the silver-plated .38s from his shoulder holster. When Eastman looked up again, he got a good look at the smiling professor.

"How's that for a Fancy Britches?" Whiteoak chided.

Too stunned to act, Eastman and Yance could only glare menacingly at the professor.

"Who sent you boys?"

"Boys?" Yance said through clenched teeth.

"Sorry. Upstanding men of this fine community. Scholars. Gentlemen. Whatever you prefer. Who sent you?"

"We're not telling you shit."

"Then why did you come to bother me?" Whiteoak asked. "Clearly it wasn't for a haircut even though you both need one."

Although surprised at first, Yance had regained his composure enough to approach Whiteoak without showing much concern for the guns in his hands. When the professor thumbed back both hammers, the metallic click served as a very good reminder.

"You're to pack up your things," Yance said, "and drive that god-awful wagon out of town."

"Is that it?" Whiteoak asked. "All this trouble just to try and shoo me away? I'm almost disappointed."

"You're nothing but a thief who sells dressed-up liquor in little bottles. You've been in the right place at the right time too many damn times." Stretching out one hand, Yance asked, "Now are you gonna return my property?"

"Why would I do that? So you can take a shot at me?"

"That's what I thought, thief. Come on," the squat gunman said to Eastman. "This son of a bitch thinks nobody's smart enough to figure out the part he played in robbing our bank."

"Wait a second," Whiteoak snapped. "You think I had something to do with that robbery?"

Yance's eyes narrowed as he studied the professor. "I know a scallywag when I see one."

"And I know killers when I see them," Whiteoak countered. "You were here to do more than try to frighten me off."

"Maybe we was," Yance replied. "If you're so sure about that, you'd best put bullets in both of us right now. Otherwise, we'll just come around some other time and get the job done. What do you say, Fancy Britches?"

"Here," Whiteoak said as he tossed Yance's pistol to him. "You shouldn't force another man's hand when you don't have

125

the slightest notion of what kind of hell that man is willing to unleash."

While Eastman looked at Whiteoak with the same amount of ill intent as before, there was something different in Yance's eyes. It was a small measure of trepidation mixed with the slightest hint of respect.

"I guess we'll see what kind of hell that is," Yance said. "From both of us."

"Yes," Whiteoak replied. "We certainly will."

Chapter Seventeen

The rest of the day passed and the only thing to bother Professor Whiteoak was making preparations for that night's medicine show. Although he would vehemently deny that they were shows in the strictest sense of the word, that's exactly what they were. Calling them demonstrations or expositions made them sound more official and upstanding, but showmanship was a large part of his craft and everyone knew it.

The longer he stayed in a particular town, the better acquainted the professor became with the quirks and eccentricities of its residents. He also needed to consider the climate, local concerns and some bit of history to put together the approach he would take as well as a batch of tonics that would best appeal to his audience. All of those things went into play as Whiteoak strutted in front of his wagon while touting the virtues of his newest concoction.

"And this, my good friends," he said to the audience gathered around him that evening, "is guaranteed to cure those sleepless nights, bestowing upon you the most refreshing couple of hours you've ever experienced."

"And give us some sweet dreams, I imagine," groused one old man who'd taken it upon himself to complain about the amount of laudanum he'd gotten in one of his pain relievers. Laudanum wasn't any kind of secret ingredient, but it was usually not something folks complained about.

"Actually, this is for sleep," Whiteoak said. "If you're looking for intoxication, might I recommend the Dove Tail Saloon on Wilcoe Avenue."

"I know where the Dove Tail is," the old man grumbled as the man beside him gave him a nudge with his elbow.

The size of the audience may have dwindled slightly with each one of Whiteoak's shows, but the people who came were a profitable mixture of those loyal to his products and fresh faces passing through town. The professor spoke to each one of them in turn, locking eyes with every single person in front of his wagon at least once. That was all he needed to pick out sources for the night's income.

There was a ripple of laughter after the grumpy old-timer was needled back into silence. Whiteoak picked up another bottle and launched into a pitch that was as convincing as it was colorful. During his flamboyant presentation, Whiteoak's attention was diverted slightly by two faces in the crowd. They weren't customers and they weren't even there to shout criticisms. Yance and Eastman stood silently on the periphery of the group with arms crossed and eyes narrowed into predatory slits.

"But my eyes are strained by the sun!" Byron said from the same general direction as the two gunmen. Using a simple technique to goose a sagging crowd along, he played the part of a customer so Whiteoak could further his pitch. "How could that possibly help me?"

Shaken by the appearance of Yance and Eastman, Whiteoak had to look down at the bottle in his hand and read part of the label to formulate a response. "Of course you might believe that," he said, "but these drops have been specially blended to relieve strain from the sun as well as from reading or even a stray kick from a mule."

Byron scowled in a convincingly skeptical fashion while shaking his head as if he'd heard the most ridiculous thing imaginable. Having just arrived at the demonstration, he hadn't had time to notice the foul temper of the two gunmen beside him. "That's plain crazy."

"A man in Leadville, Colorado, was kicked by his mule and was told he'd go blind," Whiteoak proclaimed, picking up steam in his speech. "Only a few weeks of applying these drops to his eyes reduced swelling, relieved pain and saved the precious gift of his sight."

From there, Whiteoak and Byron went through the banter they'd practiced an hour beforehand. Although the professor's performance was polished and charming, his heart wasn't fully invested. Even so, the presentation went over well and managed to draw some more spectators who were interested in the new product. Samples were given, a few volunteers were allowed to sample the drops and several bottles were sold. While he was packaging up a small box of wares for an old woman who'd been in his audience since the first night, Whiteoak allowed a somewhat genuine smile to drift onto his face.

"I simply cannot thank you enough for what you did to your celery tonic," said an old woman with one of the kindest faces Whiteoak had ever seen. She had the solid build of a farmer and a nose that more closely resembled a small potato set beneath wide, friendly eyes. "Once you added that extra ingredient, my hands have never felt better." Whenever she spoke, she was as earnest as could be. If he could find a way to bottle that for himself, Whiteoak knew he could really do some damage as a salesman.

"My pleasure, Sophia. In fact, why don't you take this extra bottle? My compliments."

"Oh, I couldn't."

"Don't be silly," Whiteoak insisted while placing the bottle in with the rest of her order. "I couldn't sell it anyway since I brewed it especially for you."

"Really? What is it for?"

"Headaches." With a wink, he added, "The kind that you get from long days and hearing too much guff from your husband."

She pulled out the stopper, sniffed the bottle and chuckled. "This isn't medicine."

"Good for whatever ails you, as my grandpa used to say. And if it was good enough for him, who lived well into his nineties I might add, then it's good enough for you. Enjoy."

"You are too kind," she said while reaching up to pat his cheek. "Next time I see you, I will bring you some of my potato kugel. I promise, you will like it."

"Can't wait."

Whiteoak couldn't stop smiling after Sophia walked away. He then turned his attention to the display he'd constructed in front of his wagon and started taking it down.

Once the crowd had completely dispersed, Byron worked his way over. "I think that went well," he said in a hushed voice.

Making certain to speak in a normal tone, Whiteoak replied, "I'd say so."

"Some of them did seem to be a little leery of me, though. I think they know we're on friendly terms."

"Of course they do. One of the biggest mistakes a man can make in this business is assuming your audience is stupid."

"Then perhaps we should do something differently?" Byron offered hopefully. "Maybe I shouldn't try helping you during your shows?"

"Why would you think that?"

"Because we're not fooling anyone."

Now that his samples had been packed up, Whiteoak folded the display counter back up into the side of his wagon and latched it in place. "The point tonight wasn't to fool them. It's to make them listen and, once they're listening, to make sure they hear what they need to hear."

"So you're saying you never set out to fool anyone?"

"That's not what I said. That just wasn't the point tonight."

Byron followed Whiteoak around to the back of the wagon and helped load some boxes into the wagon where they could be stored with the rest of the professor's supplies. "So you do set out to fool people sometimes?"

"Of course, but only at first. That first show and maybe the second. Those are the only ones where you have any chance to lay groundwork. After that, it's too late. They either already have you pegged as a charlatan or have written you off completely. If either of those things happen, it's time to pack up and move along to the next town."

"Speaking of moving along, why haven't you done that yet?"

"You mean from Barbrady?"

"Yes!" Byron replied with some amount of urgency. "Lord knows there's plenty of good reasons for you to want to put this town behind you."

"And why did you put it behind you?" Whiteoak asked, sidestepping his own response with the nimbleness of a ballet dancer.

Byron's eyes took on a faraway quality. "I'm still here, aren't I?"

"As a visitor. And yet your sister lives here by herself. While the two of you don't always seem to be in agreement, there is affection between you. A familiarity that comes from proximity."

Scowling at the professor's words, it took a few moments before Byron said, "We're close. Is that what you mean?"

"Yes."

"We're brother and sister. And sure we were in the same proximity as well. We were raised together like most other brothers and sisters."

"I was raised among plenty of family," Whiteoak said. "When the time came for us to part ways, we were all the happier for it.

131

You and Lyssa are on better terms than that. You lived here in Barbrady for some time?"

"No," Byron replied plainly. "But we did live in Wichita together for some years. We left town when . . ."

Whiteoak gave the other man a few moments to gather his thoughts, but prodded him a bit when it seemed Byron was retreating into a shell. "Yes?"

Looking up again, Byron's eyes flashed with anger for a split second. "We left because she made it intolerable to live there. I was tired of indulging her every little whim and so I set out to pursue my own fortune."

"Now that," Whiteoak sighed, "sounds more like the family I'm accustomed to."

"One more time, she insists on staying somewhere that's more trouble than it's worth." As he spoke those words, Byron seemed to be thinking out loud instead of conversing with anyone else. "I mean, what the hell is keeping her in this dusty town full of even dustier old men?"

Whiteoak cocked an eyebrow and nudged him with an elbow. "Perhaps she's cleaned the dust off of one old man and made him shine?"

"Good Lord," Byron gagged.

"Or maybe she doesn't like being told where she should be and how long to stay there."

Still green from the prospect of his sister being a woman in every aspect of the word, Byron pulled in a breath and nodded. "That's always been true. You figured it out after such a short time, so what's that say about me?"

"Actually, it's what it says about me," Whiteoak said through a beaming smile. "I've known plenty of women and I have studied them quite well."

The greenness came back to Byron's face.

"So," Whiteoak continued, "why were you run out of Wichita?"

"Lyssa wanted to be a lawman."

"Is that so?"

"She wouldn't let up about it, no matter how many times she was told how ridiculous it was. And yes, before you spout off about women and their character, I do realize that's the sort of thing that would steel her resolve. Even so, it didn't change the minds of all the men she tried to put in their place while showing them up at their job."

"She showed them up, eh?"

"Every now and then," Byron said with a glimmer of pride. "She'd take a run at doing the job and wind up doing it just well enough to turn some unkind attention her way."

"And the lawmen who'd been put in their place ran you out of town?"

"Not per se, but they did make it a trial to live there."

Now it was the professor who took on a disgusted pallor. "I am quite familiar with how difficult lawmen can make someone's life."

Byron chuckled to himself. Then, he started laughing until his shoulder shook and his head drooped as though the muscles in his neck had finally relaxed.

"What is it?" Whiteoak asked as some of the other man's laughter rubbed off on him as well.

"I was thinking. About . . . about you and my sister."

"Really?"

Byron's face was reddening now and he reached out to grab Whiteoak's shoulder for support. "The way you look at her. The way sometimes she looks at you."

"I don't know if that's funny in as much as it might be amusing in a whimsical sort of way."

That only made Byron laugh harder. "You keep talking and

talking. Just like she said."

"What did she say?"

Byron shook his head, either as a refusal to betray his sister's trust or an inability to catch enough breath to do so. "The very thought of her . . . and you . . ."

"I know," Whiteoak said with a wistful grin.

"She wants to be a peacekeeper. And you . . . she calls you a swindler who won't give her a moment's peace with all your blathering."

"All right," the professor snapped. "Enough. I get it."

"You're so loud! And you must have a price on your head in at least . . ."

Byron couldn't stop laughing long enough to finish his sentence. And that was just as well since he no longer had anyone else with him to listen.

CHAPTER EIGHTEEN

The next couple of nights were quiet. Of course, compared to the nights that had come before, a hurricane might have seemed quiet. Some men thrived in a good storm and Professor Henry Whiteoak was certainly one of those. His shows continued, selling wares to customers who rarely missed a performance. Even the most skeptical townsfolk occasionally found a reason to be within proximity of the garishly painted wagon to hear the bombastic claims of its owner.

When Whiteoak wasn't selling his products, he was busy inventing new ones. During the day, smoke curled up from the narrow pipe used to ventilate the wagon's interior. Every now and then, the professor himself would emerge from the cramped quarters like a miner hunched over from working in tunnels that were barely fit for a rat. On one such occasion, one of the grayer citizens was passing by to watch Whiteoak step from the wagon.

"You a magician too, Professor?" the old fellow asked.

Straightening his back and craning his neck, Whiteoak asked, "Pardon me?"

"I've seen a man in Prescott who had a cabinet that him and a few girls all stuffed into like they was stepping into a sitting parlor. They stepped right back out again and took a bow without nary a feather on either girl's dress being rumpled."

"I've had a lady or two in here over the years," Whiteoak replied. "But it was a different sort of magic that happened if you catch my meaning."

Both men had a good laugh and the old-timer shuffled along, leaving Whiteoak to catch a few moments of fresh air before getting back to work. The smoke that curled from the ventilation pipe was normally dark gray. Every so often, however, it shifted to a lighter hue while taking on a sweeter odor. When the scent became too sweet, Whiteoak hurried out of his confined workspace. His face was sweaty and he gulped in the clean air like a man who'd been pulled from a lake a few seconds shy of drowning.

The next time the sun dipped low on the horizon and Whiteoak took a quick breather, some folks were waiting outside of his wagon for him. One of them, a squat silver-haired woman who owned a bakery, watched the professor gasp and wipe his brow without the slightest bit of concern. "Will there be a show tonight?" she asked.

"No, Mrs. Cassaday," Whiteoak said between coughs into one closed hand. He tapped a sign hanging from the rear corner of his wagon. "Next presentation is tomorrow half an hour after sundown."

The old woman squinted through a pair of round spectacles, pushed them higher up onto the bridge of her nose and then squinted some more. "Is that what the sign says?"

"Most certainly. Perhaps you couldn't read it due to a condition that produces fogginess behind the eyes?"

Although Mrs. Cassaday's eyes weren't particularly foggy, they were most definitely wider than they'd been a moment ago. "What's this now?" she asked.

"It's a rare condition, indeed." Looking around at the few others who still lingered nearby after hearing that there was to be no show, Whiteoak added, "It's a condition that can take hold and rob us of one of our very senses! The best one, some might say!"

The other locals grumbled to themselves, gave the professor a polite nod and moved along. All except for the silver-haired woman. "What's this condition called?" she asked.

As far as Whiteoak could tell, the condition was called needing new spectacles. He had a drawer full of them in his wagon and could probably find a pair that suited her better than the ones she currently wore. To her, however, he said, "Optimicum Fataltis."

Any string of Latin-sounding phrases with a derivative of "fatal" tossed in was usually taken quite seriously to Whiteoak's most valuable customers and Mrs. Cassaday was one of the best customers he'd found in all of Barbrady.

"Oh, dear!" she said.

"Indeed. I'll mix you up something very special and have it ready for the show tomorrow. It will require a new apparatus for delivery into those beautiful eyes of yours, which I'll toss in for free."

Mrs. Cassaday smiled and fanned herself with her wrinkled hand. "Oh, my. How very generous of you."

"Such is the benefit of being in a town like this one long enough to become acquainted with the good people within." If he'd been wearing his hat, Whiteoak would have tipped it. Instead, he tapped his fingers to his temple in a friendly salute.

Once inside the wagon again, Whiteoak allowed the well-practiced and very convincing smile to melt away from his face. The interior of the brightly painted box on wheels was a chaotic assault upon the eyes as well as the nose. Every inch of space was carefully used, with some drawers removed from specially made cabinets to form a small space in which a miniature burner could heat a vial of chemicals within a protective layer of tin. Shuffling down the narrow aisle to the back of the wagon, Whiteoak extended both arms to reach for a powder from one shelf and a pestle from another.

"I'll need more if this is going to work," he muttered to himself as the powder was poured into a stone bowl and the pestle was used to make it even finer. "And perhaps a little stronger. There's always the chance that they won't drink as much as they need right away. The fossils living in this town may be rich, but they still act like every other coot I've ever met. They find something they like and sock it away, divvy it out and try to make it last forever."

Once the powder was turned into white ash, he took the vial from the heater stand and let out a pained hiss as the tips of his fingers sizzled against the glass. When he added the liquid to the powder he'd ground, smoke rolled upward like the spindly arms of an insect. Whiteoak leaned down as much as he could and sniffed the smoke. Almost immediately, he shook his head and staggered drunkenly for the door.

Without stepping all the way outside, he leaned through the opening and filled his grateful lungs with air. "No, Mrs. Cassiday," he said in response to the old woman's shouted inquiry. "I'm fine! Just slaving away to serve my customers."

The woman shouted something back at him, which Whiteoak could barely hear.

"I know it's not midnight," he replied to what he hoped was the general intent of whatever she'd said. "But I must make certain I've prepared all the . . ." Dropping his voice to a breathy whisper, he said, "Aaand you're walking away. Give me that little wave you always do because if I don't wait for it, you'll only come back."

She stopped, looked over her shoulder and waggled her hand at him.

Whiteoak smiled wide enough for it to be seen from a distance and waved back. "That's it, Mrs. Cassaday. See you tomorrow."

There was still a lot of work to be done, but not all of it

could be completed at once. Whiteoak mixed and cooked and mixed some more until the wagon and his lungs were filled with almost enough smoke to send signals across the prairie. Thanks to a tolerance built up over years of perfecting his craft, the professor was able to soldier on without falling over. When his body reached its limit, he stowed everything back in its place and locked the wagon up for the night.

Leaving behind a few mixtures that were stewing and some compounds that were drying, Whiteoak headed across town. Not all of his efforts were left behind, however. Placing his hands into the pockets of his suit coat, he found a small piece of folded paper and used a fingertip to make sure it was still sealed.

"Should be enough for at least two trials," he said to himself.

CHAPTER NINETEEN

It was late, but not too late for poker. If there was one constant throughout every one of the states and territories of a wild, incredible land, it was that it was never too late for poker.

Whiteoak sat at a table nestled in the middle of the Dove Tail Saloon. To his immediate right was Byron, three beers in his stomach and a dwindling stack of chips in front of him. A thick fellow by the name of Sammy Owens sat to Whiteoak's left. He had black hair, a thick beard and a paunch that came from eating too much of his aunt's cooking. Dell North sat directly across from the professor, fiddling with his cards, nervously touching his money and dabbing at the sweat on his brow. Alan Weir sat between Dell and Byron, a quiet man with salt-and-pepper whiskers sprouting from a mostly friendly face.

"Who do you think that is?" Byron asked.

Whiteoak propped a single chip onto its edge with one finger while using the thumb on that same hand to set the chip to spinning. "Who are you talking about?"

"That man at the back of the room with his back to a wall. He looks like a gunfighter."

"What makes you say that?"

"Because he's got his back to a wall and . . . well . . . he's wearing a gun."

Whiteoak let out a sigh and shook his head.

"What?" Byron said defensively. "I've never seen him around here before and he's been glaring in this direction as if he's set to kill everyone at this table. You don't think he might be a gun-man?"

"On the contrary. I think he is absolutely a gunman."

"Then why the sigh?"

"Because he might as well be wearing a sign around his neck as he sits there trying to look like a bad man." Giving his chip another spin, Whiteoak added, "It's no wonder that so many men like him wind up dead so early in their careers."

"Wanna know why I'm sighing?" Owens asked.

Whiteoak looked over to the dark-haired fellow and asked, "Why's that, Sam?"

"Because there'll be snow falling outside by the time Dell makes his damn bet."

Dell, a large man whose clothes were so poorly tailored that he looked like he'd stuffed a lumpy mattress under his shirt, bobbled his head and continued to rearrange his chips. "Laugh all you want, mister. I'm about to take down one hell of a pot and I need to figure how much I can fleece you gentlemen for."

"Is that a fact?" Alan grunted. "You're gonna do all of that fleecing with two pair?"

Dell snapped his head toward Alan, causing multiple fatty chins around his neck to wiggle. "What makes you think you know what I'm holding?"

"You drew one card, missed your full boat, and now you're trying to figure how to make the best of it," Alan replied.

"Maybe I got my full house and am trying to figure out how much to bet."

Alan raised his eyebrows as if entertaining the notion of play-ing along with the larger man's serious tone. A second later, he took a drink from the whiskey glass in front of him. "Yeah," he chuckled. "Maybe you did."

His charade deflated, Dell tossed in a modest raise and checked his cards for the fifteenth time.

"Call," Alan said immediately.

Byron was already out of the hand, so he looked over to Whiteoak who was last to act.

The professor looked at Dell for less than a second, shifted his glance to Alan and shrugged. "Raise," he said while tossing in twenty dollars.

"I call," Owens replied, which was what he said to pretty much every raise anyone made.

Dell was next and when his pudgy hand remained on his chips for more than a trio of heartbeats, Alan told him, "You take another forever to make your play and I'll toss your fat ass through that wall."

Doing his best to maintain some semblance of dignity, Dell looked at his cards one more time before shaking his head. "I know when I'm beat," he said before tossing his cards onto the stack of dead wood.

"You don't know shit," Alan muttered. "I'm out. What've you got, Dandy Dan?"

"I'm guessing that would be me," Whiteoak chided as he straightened the lapel of his pearl-gray waistcoat. He placed his cards face up in front of him and then reached into his breast pocket for a silver cigarette case.

All of the men looked at the cards, but not all of them were pleased with the sight. "Tens and jacks?" Alan said before leaning forward to spread the cards even further apart. "You only had two pair?"

"That's the hand I was dealt," Whiteoak replied.

"And you didn't think I could beat that shit?"

"Of course you could."

Knowing he'd been read like a book was one thing. Bringing that knowledge into the open was another. Recognizing that he would only make himself look worse, Alan kept his mouth shut and shifted his focus to the one man at the table that might help ease his flaring temper.

Sammy Owens looked at Whiteoak and gnawed on the same piece of beef fat that had been wedged between his teeth all night. "Eh, you got me," he said while tossing his cards without showing them.

"He got you?" Alan snarled. "*You* can't even beat two damn pair?"

Owens shrugged, his eyes already drifting to one of the girls working the saloon.

"What the hell is goin' on here?" Alan sighed while settling back into his seat. "If I'd known I was playing with a bunch of idiots, I'd change my strategy."

Whiteoak glanced over to his right. Even though Byron hadn't shared the professor's company for very long, he could practically hear the professor making a barbed comment about Alan's supposed upcoming strategy. Thankfully, the words weren't spoken out loud and the game continued without bloodshed. Before the next hand could be dealt, however, Whiteoak pushed back from the table and stood up.

"Where the hell you going?" Alan snapped.

"Not far, I assure you," Whiteoak said. "After that last hand, I thought I'd buy a round of drinks for the table. Would anyone care for something else?"

"I'll take a steak," Alan said.

"Naturally." The smile Whiteoak wore was as bright as the polished watch chain crossing his midsection. It lasted all the way until he reached the bar and waved for Robert's attention.

Stepping up beside him, Byron said, "You ruffled some feathers, I think."

"Did I?"

"Wasn't that your intention?"

"My intention was to win." When the barkeep stepped over to him, Whiteoak said, "I'll take a round of beers for my table.

Also," he added grudgingly, "one steak."

"I don't got any food left. None fit to eat anyway," the barman said.

"What do you have in the way of meat?"

"Just some scraps that're mostly fat and gristle," Robert told him.

Putting on his warm smile, Whiteoak turned to cast a wave at his table. Alan was watching him closely and responded with a curt, upward nod. "That will do fine," Whiteoak said to the barkeep. "Just throw it over a flame and serve it to the fellow over there with the mean look on his face."

"If you say so."

When he looked over at Byron, Whiteoak was greeted by a grin that he might expect if there had been genuine steaks in front of them. "What's got you so happy?" he asked.

Byron nodded sagely. "You were testing them, weren't you?"

"Testing them how?"

"To see if they'd get their feathers ruffled. That's why you made such a strange play on that last hand."

"What was strange about it?" Whiteoak asked. "Seemed rather straightforward to me. Dell wasn't going to make the call and Alan was convinced that anyone with functioning eyes and ears would know he had two pair beat. He was so full of himself on that account that any raise would have frightened him off."

"And what about Owens?"

"He's a wild one," Whiteoak said. "But there's one thing of which I'm absolutely certain."

"Which is?"

"He's playing with found money."

That put a perplexed expression onto Byron's face. "How do you know that?" he asked.

"He tosses it around like it doesn't mean a thing."

"So does any other gambler," Byron pointed out. "Or at least the ones who are any good at it."

"Gamblers aren't there to lose. Even the professional sporting men enjoy their victories and flinch when they lose. They may not show it like some drunken cowboy who lost his earnings, but it shows. You need to know how to look for it. That man back there was killing time and didn't much care if he lost or not. That means he's either filthy rich or playing with someone else's bankroll. I'm putting my bet on the latter."

"That's an impressive talent you've got."

Whiteoak perked up a bit. "Really? Which one?"

"Reading people."

"That's a skill and one that was very hard to earn."

"Teach me," Byron said.

Scowling at him, the professor replied, "I said it's hard to *earn,* not learn."

"So it can't be taught?"

"Experience, my good man," Whiteoak said. "I can tell you some of the basics, but it takes experience to figure out the rest. After all, people react to me differently than they would to you."

"All right, so teach me the basics."

Impatience cracked Whiteoak's exterior like mold splitting an old log. "What do you think I've been doing?" At that moment, the beers he'd ordered were lined up in front of him. When Robert was done with that, he turned to check on the slab of leftover meat that was already beginning to smoke on a stovetop in the next room.

"Here," Whiteoak said while taking hold of two mugs and sliding them closer to Byron. "Take these over to the table. Serve Alan and Sammy first."

"Fine."

Refusing to let go of the mugs even after Byron took hold of them, Whiteoak said, "This is important. Serve those two first."

"Why?"

"Because they're the ones with the most to prove. If you walk over and show preference to anyone else, especially if it's one of those two and not the other, the man without a drink in front of him will feel slighted and that's trouble."

"All this fuss over beer?"

"It's not just beer," Whiteoak said. "It's the point. Also, it's one of the basics of what I do. Would you like to learn the basics or not?"

"I want to be a good businessman. That's all."

"Would your business involve selling anything?"

"Of course," Byron replied.

"Selling to people?"

Byron didn't dignify that with a response other than a frown and cocking his head.

"Whether you're selling tonics, lumber or land, it doesn't matter," Whiteoak explained. "You read people and make little adjustments when dealing with them. Want another bit of advice for dealing with someone?"

"Sure."

Finally, Whiteoak let go of the beer mugs. "When it comes to simple requests, just do what you're told. It makes things that much smoother."

"Fine, I'll serve the drinks. Any other simple requests?"

"Next time it's only you and me in a hand, I'd appreciate it if you lost to me."

"Seriously?"

"Yes. Lose profusely."

"Why?" Byron asked eagerly.

"I need the extra money."

It took a moment, but Byron eventually grumbled to himself and walked away. Whiteoak watched him just long enough to make certain the beers were delivered correctly. Once both mugs were set in front of Owens and Alan respectively, he set his sights on the gunman who kept his back against a wall.

CHAPTER TWENTY

Whiteoak threw the gunman off his game in the quickest and easiest way possible. Where the armed man was obviously comfortable watching from afar and glaring with intimidating eyes, he wasn't as ready to have one of the men in his sights walk directly up to him and sit down as if he'd been invited to supper.

Quick to reclaim his posture, the gunman asked, "Can I do somethin' for you?"

"You can start by telling me your name. I'm Henry Whiteoak, by the way. Professor Henry Whiteoak."

"I know who you are."

"Then how about you return the favor?"

The gunman said nothing. Instead, he shifted his weight so the holster around his waist was more visible.

Narrowing his eyes, Whiteoak tapped his chin and squinted across the table as though he was gazing into a crystal ball. "You're Chuck Monroe."

The gunman was surprised, but did a fairly good job of masking it. "How the hell do you know my name? Have we met before?"

"I saw you in Topeka about a month or so before I came here. You were splitting logs at one of Michael Davis's lumber camps, I believe." Snapping his fingers, Whiteoak corrected himself. "And stealing from the till. Or, that was the accusation that was made."

"Them charges didn't come to anything," Monroe said.

"Not from lack of trying. The law in those parts was keen to get their hands on you. Apparently you've been known to take part in some very unsavory pastimes."

"You know a lot, don't you?"

Whiteoak nodded. "One thing I don't know is why you're sitting here watching my card game. If you wanted a seat at that table, all you had to do was ask."

"You think you know so damn much," Monroe snarled, "then you should know why I'm sitting here."

"Having a drink?"

Monroe picked up the glass that had been sitting in front of him and lifted it slightly as if to toast the man sitting across the table.

"Perhaps," Whiteoak continued, "you're here to try and spring that bank robber from jail?"

"Any robber that winds up in jail ain't worth savin'."

"An excellent point. But not all of those men were captured. Judging by the look in your eyes, I'd say you know that all too well."

"There ain't no look in my eyes," Monroe pointed out.

"Precisely."

"This right here is why nobody likes you double-talking sidewinders. You flap yer gums and say a fat load of nothin' along the way."

"You're here for Nash, aren't you?"

"Nash who?"

Whiteoak nodded. "That's got to be it. Otherwise, you'd be involved in some sort of business, playing cards, keeping company with one of the many feminine distractions around here. Instead, you're sitting there watching me."

Monroe chuckled in a most genuine way, leading Whiteoak to a singular conclusion.

"Or," the professor mused, "you weren't watching me at all."

"Anyone ever tell you you're a smart fellow?"

"Why, yes!"

Standing up, Monroe glared down at the professor like an angry storm picking the next spot to send a dose of lightning. "They'd be wrong."

When Monroe started walking around the table to the saloon's front door, he found his way was quickly blocked by the well-dressed professor. Anger flashed in the gunman's eyes in response to the challenge, making it seem much likelier that he would carve a path through Whiteoak than step around him.

"You're still working for Davis," Whiteoak deduced. "That's why you're here."

"What's it to you?"

"I'm not sure yet, but I'm starting to put a few things together."

Monroe stepped close enough for the scent of his last few drinks to fill the air between them.

"Whatever the job is, it must pay well," Whiteoak said.

"Some men I'd kill for free," Monroe told him plainly. "I'm lookin' at one right now."

"What did I do to deserve that kind of hostility?"

"I don't like the look of you and I've sent men off of this earth for less."

"I can be a valuable asset. I've cultivated a good amount of respect from folks around here."

"Then run for mayor. Until then, you'd best step aside before I decide to move you myself."

Whiteoak held his ground for as long as he dared. It may have only been two seconds, but it was a long couple of seconds by anyone's measure. Even though he cleared a path for Monroe, the gunman was very deliberate in his effort to knock the professor aside even further as he passed. Whiteoak's narrow frame nearly toppled over, which gave Monroe no small amount of amusement.

"Keep your distance, medicine man," Monroe said through his leering smile. "You don't want me to set my sights on you. Understand?"

"Most certainly, yes. I do."

"Good." Monroe turned his back to him and strutted away like a dog that had finished kicking dirt onto the most recent shit it had taken.

Whiteoak looked over to the table where Byron sat with the others. The next hand had already been dealt and Alan Weir was grinning down at his cards. Dell looked nervous as always and Sammy Owens let out a loud belch before slamming down his empty beer mug. The professor checked his watch and nodded to himself on his way over to them.

"I'm turning in," he said while collecting his chips.

"Sit your ass down," Alan said. "Give us a chance to win some of our money back."

"You'll have plenty of opportunities for that," Whiteoak assured them. "For now, I must bid you all farewell so that I may retire for the evening."

"Whatever you say," Owens said with a backhanded wave. His arm came up and clipped the top of his beer mug without knocking it over. Whiteoak checked his watch again and walked away.

Byron watched him go, but didn't say anything due to the strength of his cards. The look in his eyes let Whiteoak know that he would definitely have to answer for his quick exit sooner rather than later.

Once outside the saloon, Whiteoak ducked into an alley and took a zigzagging path toward Barbrady's business district. Cutting across First Street, he peeked at the main walkway whenever he could safely lean out of the shadows. The first time he did so, Whiteoak saw nothing and could only hear the distant knocking of boots against the boardwalk.

He was closer to Trader Avenue when he took another look. There was slightly less light along those streets since most of the buildings were locked up for the night. The sputtering flames of a few untended streetlights barely provided enough illumination for someone to avoid falling off the edge of the boardwalk. The knocking steps Whiteoak was following were steady and strong, leading him toward Second Street.

In the distance, he saw a man strolling alongside the deserted street. The silhouette was vaguely familiar, but Whiteoak wasn't going to place any bets as to who it might be. He waited for the man to walk past one of the few streetlights on Trader Avenue. It was Chuck Monroe, all right.

Even better, there were more figures walking toward Monroe from the direction of Second Street. By the looks of it, the group meant to meet up at the intersection of Second and Trader Avenue.

Dashing down the next alley, Whiteoak raced behind a few smaller stores so he could wind his way back again. When he reached the mouth of that alley, he couldn't hear the footsteps anymore. The professor stuck his head out and looked back in the direction from which he'd come. Nobody was there. As he turned to look in the other direction, he heard the scrape of a matchstick against a wall. The flaring of that little flame was less than five paces away from him, causing Whiteoak's heart to skip a beat.

He wanted to pull his head back into the shadows, but that movement would most likely give away his position. There was always the chance that he'd already been spotted, which meant he should find some cover as quickly as possible. When he heard the crunch of feet against the hard dirt behind him, Whiteoak held his breath. There was still a slim chance that he had yet to be spotted.

"What the hell are you doing?" someone hissed behind him.

Some chances were slimmer than others.

CHAPTER TWENTY-ONE

Weighing his options in less than a second, Whiteoak knew he had to make his move quickly before he was put down for good. He turned on the balls of his feet, dropping into a crouch while reaching for the pistol at his side. Whiteoak didn't have his stance situated well enough to take a shot by the time he faced the man who'd gotten behind him. Fortunately, that man was too petrified to do him any harm. Byron's empty hands shot up and his eyes grew wide as saucers.

"What are you doing?" Whiteoak hissed.

"I asked first."

Angrily holstering the .38, Whiteoak grabbed Byron by the front of his shirt and pressed him against a wall. He kept him in place while leaning out to carefully check the street once more. Monroe had already lit his cigarette and was walking toward the corner in the distance.

"I don't think they saw us," Whiteoak whispered. "Or heard us. No thanks to you."

"Who is that? The gunman that was watching us at the Dove Tail?"

"One and the same. Why aren't you at the game?"

"It's over," Byron said. "Owens downed that beer faster than he did the others he'd been swilling all night long and all that liquor caught up to him in a rough way. Wound up tripping over his own feet on his way to the outhouse."

"What about Weir?"

"He was losing."

"That's not what I meant."

Both men stopped talking when the sounds of other voices drifted through the air. A conversation was taking place some distance away and when Whiteoak hurried down the alley to cut behind the next couple of buildings, he dragged Byron along with him.

"What's going on here?" Byron asked while struggling to keep up.

"You keep insisting on tagging along with me wherever I go," the professor replied as he carefully stretched his body forward to be that much closer to the meeting taking place nearby. "That's what's going on."

They approached the end of the next alley, bringing them even closer to the other men who were conversing nearby. The shadowy figures were huddled in front of a darkened building with an assayer on the first floor and a dentist's office on the second.

"It's—" Byron was silenced by a hand that clamped over the lower portion of his face. It took two tries, but he swatted that hand away. "This is exactly what bothers me," he said in a harsh whisper. "Being watched by a gunman is bad enough, but following that same gunman in the middle of the night is even worse!"

"Will you keep quiet before you get us both killed?"

"If you're so worried about getting killed," Byron asked in an admittedly quieter voice, "then what are you doing out here in a dark alley?"

Abandoning the possibility of getting the other man to leave without additional fuss, Whiteoak nodded toward the corner in the distance and asked, "See those men?"

"Yes."

"One of them is Chuck Monroe, the gunman from the Dove

Tail. He did some work for Michael Davis some time ago. Isn't that one of this town's Founding Four?"

"He is, but that other fellow isn't Davis."

Whiteoak squinted into the darkness splayed in front of him. "Which other fellow?"

"The one in the dark suit with the diamond cufflinks."

"How can you possibly see the cufflinks from this distance?"

"First of all," Byron said, "they're the only things catching any light apart from the shooting irons on their hips. And second, that is George Halstead. He always wears diamond cufflinks."

"George Halstead? Are you sure?"

"I've done business with both Halsteads, Junior and Senior. That's Senior, as sure as I'm standing here."

Whiteoak spun around and charged down the alley. For as quickly as he moved, he made surprisingly little noise. It took some amount of effort for Byron to catch up without creating footsteps that echoed all the way down Second Street.

"Where are you going now?" Byron asked after he'd managed to close some of the distance between himself and the professor.

Without breaking stride, Whiteoak replied, "To get a closer look."

"Don't you trust me?"

"I need to be certain."

"Of what?"

When he didn't get an answer to his question, Byron added some steam into his steps and caught up to Whiteoak. Grabbing the professor by his starched collar, he slowed him down with a hearty pull. Whiteoak came to an abrupt halt and yanked free of Byron's grasp.

"Do you know how expensive this shirt is?" Whiteoak snapped.

Ignoring the professor's love of his accoutrements, Byron asked, "What do you need to be so certain about?"

"I suspected Monroe was a bounty hunter when he was working for Davis and now it seems even more probable that that's the case. It also makes it that much more vital that I find out who the hell he's meeting with."

"Why?"

"Because something is going on here and I aim to find out what it is."

"What does it matter to you? It's only a matter of time before you pack up your medicine show and drive that wagon to another town. Just make sure it's a town with fewer greedy old men than this place and you'll be fine."

"There are more greedy old men out there than you might know," Whiteoak pointed out. "And unless you haven't noticed, I'm in this too deep to pick up and leave."

"Something put a bee in your bonnet within the last few minutes. Tell me what it is or so help me, I'll rain all kinds of hell on you."

Although he wasn't overly concerned by the threat, Whiteoak sighed and cast one more glance at the corner. There was still a bit more alley to traverse before he could get a good look at the men having the conversation, but he could still hear their voices. By the sound of them, they were still too wrapped up in their own business to take notice of anyone else's. Knowing that good fortune wouldn't last, Whiteoak positioned himself so he could watch Byron and the end of the alley at the same time.

"There's something going on . . . ," Whiteoak started to say.

"So you've already told me."

"Whatever it is could start something that might affect this whole state."

Byron's face twisted into an expression of pure disbelief. "What?"

157

"Monroe has done some very nasty work for Michael Davis. George Halstead, Senior, is talking to him at this moment. Unless my skill at arithmetic is severely lacking, that's half of this town's Founding Four linked to a known killer. As you've already told me, those four men are responsible for a great deal of business in this state, hell, this entire region of the country."

"I'm sure this isn't the first deal those men have struck with violent men in the dead of night."

"Maybe not," Whiteoak said, "but it's the first one I've been able to witness."

"And what the hell does that matter?"

Stricken by the other man's tone, Whiteoak looked at him exclusively for a few moments. He suddenly realized he'd taken his eyes away from the street corner and quickly checked to make sure nothing there had changed. "What's gotten into you?" the professor hissed.

"I don't believe a word you're saying."

"Can't we get into this some other time? Like when there isn't an armed killer nearby?"

"And when will that be, exactly?" Byron asked. "From what I've seen, there could be armed killers around you at any given moment."

"Nobody's been forcing you to follow me."

"You've already been seen with me and my sister on plenty of occasions. In case you haven't noticed, this is a very small town and word spreads quickly through it."

"And?"

"And if anyone might ask about you, like some killers from out of town for example, odds are pretty damn good my sister and I would be mentioned right along with you."

The men at the corner were still talking. While their gestures were becoming more intense, their voices had dropped so low that they would've been tough to hear even for someone much closer than the alley Whiteoak had chosen. Although his eyes were still on the group of huddled men, Whiteoak's thoughts circled around the points Byron had made.

"You're right," the professor admitted. "I apologize."

"I don't want your apology. I want real answers to my questions. And if you mention some nonsense about danger to the state of Kansas or the world at large, I swear I'll knock your head off your shoulders."

Whiteoak grinned. "Money."

"Huh?"

"You want to know what this is about? Money," the professor said. "That's all it's ever about."

"You'd get killed for money?"

"I have no intention whatsoever of getting killed. Those men are connected to a large amount of money and they're up to something. If we find out what that is . . ."

"We? I'm not going to lock horns with a killer and at least one of the town's Founding Four."

Whiteoak took hold of Byron by the shoulders and shoved him into the relative safety of the alley. "You want me to be level with you? How about you do the same for me?"

"I don't want a part of something like this."

"Then you could've stepped back and let me go about my business. Better yet, you could have kicked me out of your home or told the law to come after me. Your sister's got connections to the sheriff, right?"

"Yes," Byron said insistently before removing Whiteoak's hands from where they gripped his shoulders. "And if she got wind of what you're up to, she might do something about it."

"Now you're the one feeding me a line of nonsense," Whiteoak said as he took a quick glance at the corner where the other men were still talking. "You just don't want her to mess this up."

"I still barely know what there is to mess up!"

"But you wanted to keep pestering me until you found out. I think you wanted to be a part of it because you knew it would lead to more profit than you could get ferrying papers and such from one town to another."

Now it was Byron who glanced at the trio of armed men. "Looks like they're about to disband. The arguing is settling down."

"You'd best get home. Make certain your sister is safe."

"Why wouldn't she be safe?"

"I don't know. All I'm doing is trying to think of every eventuality."

"What about you?" Byron asked. "Have you figured some way to rob them before they move away from that corner?"

"Not yet," Whiteoak replied, "but I'm working on it. And unless you want one or both of us to get shot, I'd suggest you decide what it is you're after. Either go back to your family and home where it's safe or throw in with me where it's profitable."

"Throw in with you?"

"Of course. Isn't that what you wanted?"

"All I wanted was to keep you from getting yourself killed. It's the least I could do after you saved my life."

As the three men in the distance said their farewells, they each walked in different directions. Whiteoak put his back against a wall and used one arm to push Byron back as well. "You're a businessman," he said in a whisper that was almost too quiet to be heard. "And you have a taste for adventure."

Byron let out a snort of a laugh. "That's a bit dramatic."

"Drama adds spice to life. The trick is knowing how much spice to add. Too much, and you become something you hadn't bargained on becoming."

"And what's that?"

"Dead, if we don't both keep our mouths shut. Now do you

want to help me or leave? Choose right now."

It only took a moment for Byron to make up his mind, although he let more time pass in the event that he had second thoughts. If he had them, those reservations were pushed out of his head when he got a closer look at one of the men who'd been talking on the corner. "Is that . . . ?"

"Yes," Whiteoak snapped. "It's Jesse Nash. I'll follow him and you follow Halstead."

Before Byron could say anything, Whiteoak's hand was clamped over his mouth. Not only did it snuff any sound he was about to make, but Byron was also pushed against the wall with a surprising amount of force.

Nash came to an abrupt halt.

Neither Whiteoak nor Byron dared to move as Nash approached the alley.

"Run," Whiteoak said.

Byron refused to make a sound and he was either unwilling or unable to move.

Giving Byron a mighty shove toward the far end of the alley, Whiteoak insisted, "Run!" and then turned to face the armed man who was now headed straight for them.

CHAPTER TWENTY-TWO

Nash's eyes set upon Whiteoak like a wolf that had just spotted its prey. The bank robber went for his pistol as Whiteoak lunged for him. Being more practiced with his gun, Nash was able to clear leather before Whiteoak landed his first punch. Even when he did land his punch, however, the professor wasn't able to do much damage.

"That all you got?" Nash sneered.

"No," Whiteoak replied. In the time it had taken for Nash to react to the ineffectual punch, Whiteoak had drawn his .38 from its holster. While it was a smooth motion that brought the gun to bear, he couldn't pull his trigger before his arm was knocked aside by a chopping blow from Nash. The .38 barked once, sending its round into the dirt.

Nash took aim from the hip and fired a shot that would have burned a hole through the professor's midsection if Whiteoak hadn't dived to one side beforehand. Although that first shot missed its target, Nash was quick to sight along the top of his barrel to fire again.

Whiteoak rolled to one side to avoid a fatal injury, but felt the bite of hot lead gouging through the flesh in his side. As soon as he could stop himself from rolling any further, Whiteoak pointed his .38 in Nash's general direction and unleashed two consecutive shots.

Both bullets hissed from Whiteoak's barrel toward Nash. The bank robber had been fired at plenty of times before and didn't panic on this occasion. By the time he'd taken his third shot, Whiteoak was climbing back to his feet and Nash had ducked out of the alley.

Gritty smoke burned the professor's eyes and scraped at the back of his throat when he took his next breath. He backed up until he felt the wall against his heel, knowing there were three bullets left in his cylinder.

"You through?" Nash asked. Judging by the sound of his voice, he was around the corner at the mouth of the alley.

Whiteoak kept his mouth shut, took more careful aim and blasted a hole through the edge of the building that Nash was using for cover. Wood splinters flew from the spot he'd hit and more smoke smeared the air.

"You're a real pain in the ass," Nash called out. "Nothin' we can't handle, though."

"We'll see about that," Whiteoak said, knowing all too well that Nash would use the sound of his voice as a guide for his next shots. Sure enough, the bank robber leaned around the corner firing several rounds into the alley without wasting a moment to get a clear look at his target. If Whiteoak hadn't anticipated the other man's skill and speed, he'd be dead where he stood. Instead, he dropped to a crouch and threw himself toward the other side of the alley.

Stabbing, burning pain lanced through the fresh wound in the side of Whiteoak's lower back. He could feel his shirt and suit coat growing wet with his blood. Due to the thick haze of gun smoke in the already inky shadows, Whiteoak was all but blind. The only saving grace was that Nash was in the same predicament.

"What're you after, huh?" Nash asked in another attempt to get a feel for where his next bullets should go.

Whiteoak wasn't about to make a sound. The first time he'd spoken had been to draw Nash into the alley, but now he had a limited amount of time to act before the smoke dissipated or Nash found him on his own. It had been a stroke of luck that the professor was wearing a darker suit in the first place and the dirty smudges that now sullied his clothing helped him blend in even more. Reaching out with one hand, he found a broken bottle on the ground near one foot. Whiteoak picked it up and tossed it across the alley so it cracked against the wall directly opposite of him.

Nash's first shot was quick as a thought, but he only wasted one bullet on the distraction before stepping closer to find what he was really after. Whiteoak charged straight at him with pistol in hand. His eyes burned with the smoke that still hung heavily in the air. When he fired at Nash, he did so while in a hurry and on the move, violating two of the biggest rules he'd been given when learning how to effectively use a pistol.

Without so much as flinching at the gunshot, Nash stepped to one side. His back leg came forward, driving his knee solidly into Whiteoak's gut. The impact doubled the professor over while forcing the air from his lungs. Lifting his .38 took a great amount of effort and before he could take proper aim, Whiteoak's wrist was encased in a vice-like grip.

"You're a real pain in the ass, you know that?" Nash snarled.

"So . . . I've been told."

"Where's the other fella?"

"I don't know . . ." Pain lanced from Whiteoak's wrist all the way up through his shoulder as Nash twisted his arm in the wrong direction. Whiteoak's finger nearly clenched around his trigger, but the thought of wasting his last bullet gave him some extra incentive to resist.

"Last chance, asshole," Nash said. "You working with the law or one of those rich men?"

"You mean, like one of the men you're working with?"

"To hell with this. You ain't got nothing I need."

Even if there were any live rounds in his pistol, Whiteoak couldn't move his gun hand well enough to fire a shot that would hit anything but the ground or a wall. His legs were too wobbly to kick and his vision was growing blurrier by the second. He couldn't think of many other options and he figured there were precious few seconds for him anyway.

The next sound he heard was a gunshot, but it didn't come from Nash. Although the bullet didn't hit the outlaw, it came close enough to make him let go of Whiteoak and run in the opposite direction. Whiteoak spun around to find the closest thing to an angel he'd ever seen.

"Lyssa?" the professor said. "Is that you?"

She stood holding a gun in her hand as well, smoke curling up from the barrel. Once she got a longer look at Whiteoak, she gasped, "You're hurt. There's blood on your clothes."

"I'll be fine."

"What are you doing?"

Whiteoak hefted his .38 in hand while fumbling to open its cylinder. "Reloading."

In a stern voice, Lyssa said, "Henry! It's over."

"No, it's not! He needs to be dealt with."

"He will," she said softly. "Just not now. Looks like it's been a rough night. Come with me and I'll clean you up. Again."

"But he'll come back."

"When he does, Sheriff Willis will deal with him. He's probably already on his way."

"Not fast enough," Whiteoak grumbled. His grip tightened on the .38's handle as well as the trigger. Seemingly without an ounce of fear, Lyssa stepped up to him and placed her hand on top of the gun so she could lower it.

"It's over," she repeated.

Reluctantly, Whiteoak eased the hammer back down and holstered the pistol.

CHAPTER TWENTY-THREE

Whiteoak sat on the edge of the same chair he'd occupied when eating dinner in the Keag's home. Instead of plates and glasses on the table, this time there were rags, a washbasin and a pitcher. And instead of using his hands to hold a knife and fork, he placed one on his knee while raising the other to give Lyssa an unimpeded view of the wound in his side.

"What were you doing out there?" Whiteoak grunted.

"You're welcome, by the way."

"Thank you. Now what the hell were you doing out there in the middle of the night?"

"Looking for my brother," Lyssa said. "His nerves have been a jangling mess since you got to town and I suggested he take a walk to calm them. When he didn't return right away, I thought he might have gone to a saloon. He's not much of a drinker, so I went after him before he got into trouble or passed out drunk in a gutter somewhere. When I heard the shots, I feared for the worst."

"Do you always carry a pistol when searching for your brother?" Whiteoak asked in a softer tone.

"When he insists on spending his time with the likes of you . . . yes."

"I suppose that's fair."

"I'm so glad you approve," she scoffed while wringing a small towel over the basin. "Now take your shirt off."

"I beg your pardon?"

"You're wounded and I told you I'd clean you up. Nothing more than that. Weren't you listening before?"

"I was," Whiteoak said as he peeled off his coat and unbuttoned his shirt. "But hope springs eternal. After all, we are all alone here."

Shaking her head, Lyssa removed Whiteoak's shirt to examine the bloody mess underneath. "Just be quiet before I change my mind and tend to you outside so you don't bleed on my floor."

"I think you're sweet on me. Maybe even a little bit?"

Without addressing that, she said, "Let's clean you up so I can see the wound better."

"Do you bring a lot of men to your home in the middle of the night?" he asked while holding his arm up high to give Lyssa an unimpeded view.

"Oh, sure. Usually just to give them a roll between my sheets."

"Oh, my."

"Just sit still."

Whiteoak followed that order for all of three seconds before saying, "This is a nice house. A little sparse, though. I'm surprised you allow me here at all, considering how distasteful you seem to find me."

"Would you rather I bang on a doctor's door in the middle of the night? Then again, from what I've seen so far, it seems that's the only time you're out and about. Just because I won't have you bleeding to death, don't get any funny ideas, Mister Whiteoak."

"That's Professor, if you please."

Lyssa announced the fact that she'd found the wound responsible for the bloodstains by pressing her finger against it.

"Damn!" Whiteoak yelped. "If that's how you treat every man who isn't your brother, it's no wonder you haven't found a husband."

"To be honest, I did have some other ideas for you once I got you alone, but I've changed my mind."

"Why?" Whiteoak asked.

"You talk too much and say the wrong things. It makes you much less desirable."

"I'm sure I can change your mind," Whiteoak purred.

"Maybe I should have left you in that alley," she grumbled.

"You wouldn't have done such a thing," Whiteoak said with utmost confidence.

"What's that supposed to mean?"

"I mean you don't let anything lie. You charge into distraction headfirst with gun drawn," Whiteoak replied.

"I heard the shots and so I went to see what might be behind them."

Stretching his arm up a bit more as Lyssa cleaned off his wound with a wet cloth, Whiteoak watched the young woman's face as he pointed out, "Most people would have run in the other direction."

"Maybe," she replied as she uncovered a gash in Whiteoak's flesh that looked as if it had been opened by an eagle's talon. "But I'm not most people. When we were kids, I was often the one stopping fights between other children while Byron ran for help."

"Also, more recently, you were taught by a lawman."

She stopped what she'd been doing for a moment and looked up to meet the professor's gaze and then returned to her task. "My brother told you about my aspirations, did he?"

"Yes."

"I wasn't taught in a formal sense, but I did learn a lot from observing. I wish Byron wouldn't say so much about me when I'm not around."

"Don't blame it all on him. I might have figured it out on my own from watching you in action."

"I was married to a lawman some years ago back in Topeka."

"Really? Byron didn't mention that part."

In a softer, sweeter tone, Lyssa said, "Because he didn't know."

Whiteoak started to turn so he could face her more directly, but was held in place by a portion of skin that felt as if it had been snagged on a fishhook. "What are you doing to me?" he screeched.

"Just a few quick stitches."

"Stitches?"

"You were shot," Lyssa replied. "You're lucky this is all you need."

"Are you qualified to sew stitches in a man?"

"I know how to sew well enough."

"I know how to sew!" Whiteoak bellowed. "That doesn't make me a doctor!"

The next time the needle punctured his skin, it was somehow more painful than the others. "If you can sew, then you can see to your own damn stitches."

Since he couldn't squirm anymore without tearing at his own skin, Whiteoak collected himself and tried to catch his breath. "How do you even know I need stitches?"

The professor wasn't currently interested in looking at her so she leaned over to fill his field of vision. "Are you honestly asking me that question?"

"Yes. You are not a physician."

"I have eyes and I see you're cut open badly enough to need stitches. Now stop being a baby and let me do what needs to be done."

Blinking quickly and lifting his chin slightly, Whiteoak asked, "Can I at least have something to drink? Possibly some whiskey to dull the pain?"

"You have the pain tolerance of a small child."

"I served in the army, I'll have you know."

"Were you ever wounded?"

Whiteoak's mouth hardened into a straight line. "I was."

"Let me guess," Lyssa said as she continued to sew his skin together. "You were knocked unconscious and woke up when the doctor's work was done."

"You are mostly correct and it is nothing to be ashamed of."

"No," she said with only a slight chuckle. "There isn't. I'm almost done here, but I imagine the skin's a bit raw. Do you still want that whiskey?"

"No," Whiteoak tersely replied. "I can barely feel the stitches anyway."

Lyssa kept working, tactfully ignoring the winces and suppressed grunts from her patient whenever she pierced his skin with the needle. As promised, she didn't have many more to do and she was soon tying off the last of them.

"How could Byron not know you were married?" Whiteoak asked.

Her voice was soft and a little sad when she replied, "There was a few years when he preferred to stay away from the rest of his family. I don't want to go into the ugly details, but let's just say I didn't blame him. We all lived separately for those years, during which I lived in Omaha and married a lawman."

"He mentioned Wichita."

"That's where I went after my husband died," she told him. "I was in a bad way, so I went to Wichita where things got worse. That's when Byron came back and decided to take care of me for a while. I didn't make things easy for him, or anyone else for that matter. In fact, I was a real nuisance to anyone and everyone."

"That's the sort of trouble Byron was talking about," Whiteoak said. "I imagine you were a real pistol. Still are, as a matter of fact."

Smiling, Lyssa said, "Speaking of trouble, I hope something

was accomplished after all that trouble you and my brother got into tonight."

"I learned a lot."

"Other than what my brother told you about me?"

"My lady, not everything that goes through my mind has to do with you."

"Oh," she said while giving the final stitch one last tug. "Excuse me."

Whiteoak clenched his teeth, unable to keep from grunting louder when he was surprised by the painful pull on the thread holding his flesh together. "That bank is going to be hit again."

"What do you mean?"

"I mean the bank is going to be robbed."

"It already was robbed."

"Whatever those outlaws were after," Whiteoak explained, "they didn't get it. Jesse Nash is still in town. And if he's still in Barbrady, that means he's still got work to do. Him sticking around for any other reason doesn't make sense."

"What if he intends on breaking his partner out of jail?"

"Men like him aren't so loyal," he told her.

Gently washing off the wound, Lyssa muttered, "You know from personal experience, I'm sure."

"Yes. From personal experience. A man who travels and trades as much as I do has to deal with all sorts of folks, reputable and otherwise. Also, if Nash intended on a jailbreak, I doubt he'd be meeting with the likes of George Halstead."

"Junior or Senior?"

"Is one of them a bank robber?" Whiteoak asked.

"Well . . . no."

"Then what's the difference?"

Lyssa put her needle and thread away so she could clean up the rest of the supplies she'd used to help Whiteoak. "I don't like the sound of that."

"As well you shouldn't."

She shook her head while letting out a tired sigh. "I didn't like it when Byron started acting as a courier in the first place. He said I was just fretting for no reason, but I always thought that anyone willing to pay so much just to deliver papers from one town to another had to be up to no good."

"Your instincts were correct this time."

"And I don't even know what all the fuss was about," she continued as if talking to herself. "There wasn't much of anything on those papers anyway."

"Wait. You know what's on those papers?" Whiteoak asked.

Lyssa nodded.

Leaning on the edge of the chair, Whiteoak said, "The papers that those men tried to take from him before Byron got to town?"

"Yes. I . . ." She glanced toward the door. Even though there was nobody standing there, she lowered her voice when she said, "I told Byron it couldn't be anything good in those bundles, but he said it was only papers." Lyssa stood up and wrapped her arms around herself as if the room had suddenly grown cold. Walking to a window she looked outside at nothing in particular and continued, "He insisted it was business as usual. Papers needed to be delivered."

Whiteoak, sensing he was drawing closer to something truly big, stood up and cautiously approached her. "Yes?" he prodded.

"Normal papers are mailed, I told him. Normal papers are taken by normal couriers on trains or stagecoaches. They're not tucked away and hidden so they can be delivered at a higher fee and nearly stolen by armed men who should be after money or something of real value. The whole arrangement seemed suspicious. I suppose it was mostly instinct."

"And so?"

"And so . . . I looked at them."

"At the papers, you mean?"

"That's right," she said. "When he got here that first night, I took a look at them to see what my brother had gotten himself into. I wanted to see what was so important that armed men would try to take it from him."

"And what did you find?" Whiteoak caught himself leering hungrily at her in anticipation of Lyssa's response. When she turned to look at him, he quickly pulled back a bit and relaxed his expression into something less wolfish.

"It wasn't much," she said. "He wore a money belt with some cash and one other piece of paper."

"What was on the paper?"

"I really shouldn't. After everything that's happened . . ."

"I've been shot at too, you know." Lifting his arm, Whiteoak winced in exaggerated agony while gesturing to the spot on his side bearing the freshly placed stitches. "I was wounded. More than once, actually. I'm in this. We all are. The only way to come out of this in one piece is for us to know what we're dealing with."

"That's if you intend on fighting."

"I believe the fight has been brought to me, instead," Whiteoak scoffed. "Me and your brother."

"We could all leave town and put whatever dirty business is being done here behind us."

"Is that what a peace officer would do?"

"Why would that matter to me?" Lyssa asked, even as a twitch in the corner of one eye told the professor that it mattered to her very much indeed.

"You're not the kind of woman who picks up and runs when there's trouble, just like I'm not the sort of man who would run from anything, either."

"Really? Aren't you the same man who lives with all of his

possessions in the back of a wagon?"

"That is my career," Whiteoak replied. "Facing adversity head-on is my way as I believe it's yours."

While his words may have been more than a little dramatic, their effect on Lyssa was undeniable. She turned away from the window and crossed her arms into a more severe posture as she faced the professor eye-to-eye.

"What would you do if there was a chance to face whatever is going on here?" she asked skeptically. "Almost get yourself killed again? Maybe even succeed at it? Or would you get my brother killed instead?"

"I never asked your brother to do anything. He's simply following his instincts, which are most likely telling him the same thing as yours and mine."

"Which is?"

"That when powerful men like this Mister Halstead and the other rich old men here in town lock horns, there's got to be lots of money involved."

"How could that benefit us?"

Whiteoak smirked. "All we need to do is figure out what they're doing and we might be able to turn it to our advantage."

"How?"

Whiteoak squared himself to her so he could take both of her hands in his. It was like closing a circle between them that shut out the lesser thinkers of the world. "It all depends on what they're doing. At the very least, we know Nash is involved with at least one other gunman and one of your town's founding fathers. Whatever was on that paper you saw could have something to do with it as well."

"I doubt it. There wasn't much. Just some numbers."

"There had to be more than one paper with some numbers," Whiteoak said.

"The rest was cash."

"Do you happen to know how much?"

"Twelve hundred dollars. It was all separated into neat little parcels of two hundred each, all six of them wrapped up in strands of twine." Seeing the questioning look on Whiteoak's face, she shrugged and added, "Byron is a sound sleeper. I had plenty of time to look at it all."

"And what about the numbers?"

"Three, four, seven, nine, twelve and sixteen."

Whiteoak blinked and shook his head quickly as though he'd been swatted on the end of the nose. "Were those the actual numbers?" he asked.

"Yes."

"You're certain?"

"Yes. Do they mean something to you?"

"No. I'm just surprised someone could remember something so . . . random."

"They're not random." Lyssa grabbed Whiteoak's hands and spoke with the speed of a fan that had caught a stiff breeze. "I mean, they can't be if they mean anything at all and they must mean something otherwise they wouldn't have been written down and sent here by a courier. Don't you think?"

"I agree wholeheartedly. You're certain those were the *exact* numbers?"

She nodded quickly. "I've always had a good head for figures. Besides, I read that scrap of paper so many times trying to figure out what it could mean that I see it in my sleep. Does that seem crazy?"

Professor Whiteoak showed her what he thought of that by taking hold of Lyssa's face in both hands and planting a kiss on her very surprised lips.

Chapter Twenty-Four

On the following night, Whiteoak was preparing for his demonstrations as always. The locals found some reason to be near his wagon so they could appear to wander by out of nothing but curiosity as always. Three things, however, were out of the ordinary.

Whiteoak's movements were stiffer than usual due to the tender skin around his stitches.

The tonic he mixed wasn't something that he'd made while in Barbrady.

Something else he'd managed to forge during his stay was some degree of respect from the sheriff since the lawman knocked once before pulling open the door to the wagon and saying, "Come on out of there."

"I'm busy," Whiteoak replied.

"Now."

"I already told you—" was all the professor managed to say before being dragged outside.

"What on earth do you think you're doing?" Whiteoak fumed. "My next show will be starting soon!"

Once he had the professor outside, Sheriff Willis stood with his hands propped on his hips and glared at him like a schoolmarm getting ready to chastise a rambunctious student. "Why don't you explain yourself first?"

"In what regard?"

"Don't take that fancy tone with me. You know damn well

what regard I'm referring to."

Holding up a single finger as if to number his first point, Whiteoak said, "I believe you meant in what regard to which you were referring."

The sheriff's face reddened and the muscles in his shoulders tensed. After choking down the urge to throttle the man in front of him, Willis said, "Tell me what happened the other night. Why the hell were you harassing one of this town's more reputable citizens?"

"Whatever do you mean?"

"Some of Mister Halstead's men tell me you've been giving them some trouble."

"I was merely out for a stroll . . ."

"Which, by all accounts, is something you tend to do a lot."

"Yes, actually. It's good for the constitution."

Still fighting his anger, the sheriff moved the conversation along with a quick wave.

"All I did," Whiteoak continued, "was happen upon Mister Halstead while he was talking with some other men. At least, I'm assuming that was Halstead. I ran into trouble myself, you know. Someone should really do something to clear out the unsavory element in this town."

"Maybe I should start by escorting an eyesore on four wheels right out of Barbrady?"

"Let's not be hasty, Sheriff. I'd like to cooperate any way possible."

"You can start by telling me why George Halstead is so up in arms?"

"Junior or Senior?"

Judging by the twitch in the corner of the sheriff's eye, it was entirely possible that Whiteoak didn't always know exactly when to retreat a step or two with his verbal barbs. Quickly, he said, "Senior, of course. I only saw him from a distance."

"And what happened after that?" Willis asked.

"I ran into some more of this town's unsavory element as I mentioned earlier."

"And there was shooting involved?"

"Yes," Whiteoak calmly replied. "I believe there was. Before you ask, I'm fine."

"Why didn't you come to me?"

"I thought you would have been notified of the incident."

"I was," Willis said. "But only that there was trouble in the business district. That sort of trouble, by the way, has become all too common since your arrival."

Whiteoak smirked and shrugged. "The incident was partly my fault. After all, I was the one who decided to divert my stroll through a dark alley in the middle of the night. A man in that position should expect some harassment. I defended myself, however, and that was that."

The lawman scowled at him, which was something to which Whiteoak was becoming very much accustomed. In fact, if someone in the professor's line of work didn't have a man in a badge scowling at him from time to time, he wasn't doing something right.

"Stay away from Mister Halstead," Willis told him. "Junior *and* Senior."

"Yes, sir."

"Stay away from any of the rich men in this town."

"I am a public figure," Whiteoak said while gesturing toward his wagon. "People frequently come to me and it wouldn't behoove me to turn them away."

"You know what I mean," the sheriff said, punctuating his sentence with a strong poke to Whiteoak's chest. "I get one more complaint about you, any complaint at all, and I'm running you out of this town. Got it?"

"Most indubitably."

Rolling his eyes, the sheriff turned and stomped away.

Whiteoak tugged at the bottom of his waistcoat to straighten the nearly imperceptible wrinkles that had been put in the fabric by the sheriff's hand. "Looks like I'll have to step things up," he said quietly to himself.

"What was that?"

Whiteoak turned on his heels to find Byron walking alongside the wagon toward the rear door. "Must you always sneak up on someone?"

"Wasn't sneaking. Just thought I'd pay you a visit when I saw you were already entertaining."

"Yes, well my company is gone. What do you want?"

"I've been thinking about those things you were saying," Byron said while placing one hand against the wagon and leaning against the brightly painted wood. "About there being money out there to be made. I think it'd be hard to disagree with that after everything that's happened."

"Do you, now?"

"Yes and I want in."

"In what?" Whiteoak asked.

Byron furrowed his brow and cocked his head at a confused angle. "In . . . please?"

"To what," Whiteoak said impatiently, "do you want to be included?"

"Whatever you had in mind!"

Whiteoak pulled open the door to his wagon and climbed inside. Before Byron could get overly suspicious or anxious enough to come after him, the professor emerged carrying a small metal box with both hands. Cradling the box like a newborn baby, the professor said, "Let's start with you acting as a lookout while I take a trip to the bank."

CHAPTER TWENTY-FIVE

"Ahh, Mister Whiteoak," said the same clerk who'd been there to greet him on his last visit. "So good to see you again."

"Likewise," Whiteoak replied, as if to a long lost friend. "I've got that deposit I mentioned before," he said while placing the tin box on the counter separating the two men.

Reaching out through the opening in his cage, the clerk took the box and opened it. There was a good amount of cash inside, but not enough to impress a clerk working in a town full of so many rich old men. "Very good," he said while shutting the lid. "Would you like to accompany me to the safe?"

After glancing over his shoulder through the front window to make sure Byron was standing outside the bank, he said, "I'd be delighted."

"You'll need to remove any firearms or other weapons you might be carrying."

"All I have is this," Whiteoak said as he revealed the silver-handled .38.

"On the counter, please."

Removing the pistol gingerly, Whiteoak set it on the counter where it was accepted by the clerk like he would any other offering from a customer. After that, the clerk stepped over to open the door that would grant Whiteoak access to the rooms further inside the bank.

Some small amount of chitchat passed between them as they made their way to the back of the small building. The bank's safe was tall and slightly wider than a standard door frame. The clerk and Whiteoak were greeted in there by Adam Bailey who eyed the professor cautiously.

"Mister Whiteoak has a deposit," the clerk announced.

Bailey took the box, sifted through its contents and asked, "Did you take a count?"

The clerk replied, "I thought you'd prefer to count it yourself since you need to open the safe." Turning to Whiteoak, he added, "It's bank policy. For your safety and ours."

"Of course," Whiteoak said.

The clerk excused himself from the room, leaving Whiteoak to watch Bailey count up the profits he'd made while in Barbrady.

"You get all this selling snake oil?" Bailey huffed.

"Only some. The rest came from specially prepared tonics and ointments."

"Yes, well I arrive at a sum of seven hundred and thirteen dollars. Does that sound accurate?"

"That would be my grand total over the last several months. You know, things were quite lucrative in Missouri."

Uninterested in Whiteoak's story, Bailey stepped in front of the safe so he could turn the dial of the combination lock without showing the numbers to his audience of one. In a matter of seconds, the dial had been turned the proper amount of times, allowing the heavy door to swing open.

"That's a lot of money," Whiteoak mused after having crept up close enough to watch the safe from over Bailey's shoulder.

While he wasn't happy about the other man watching from so close, the bank president was no longer as concerned about secrecy. "Yours aren't the only funds held here. As you can see, your profits will be extremely well protected."

"What are those little compartments for?"

Inside, the safe was divided roughly in half. The lower portion was open and contained neatly stacked cash. The upper portion was divided into smaller square compartments, each with its own door and its own lock. Bailey set Whiteoak's box on top of the cash. "They're for private use," he said. "There may be one or two open, but there is an additional fee if you're interested."

"Not necessary." Smirking, Whiteoak added, "Too bad I'm not a bank robber. I could take a run at that money right now."

"Yes," Bailey replied as he held open his jacket to reveal the .32-caliber pistol hanging under his left arm. "Too bad."

Whiteoak could tell by the pristine condition of Bailey's holster that it wasn't for much more than show. Even so, the bank president displayed it as though he'd stripped it off the corpse of Wild Bill himself. That proud, if unjustified, expression was wiped away by the bullet that carved a messy hole through his neck.

"Jesus!" Whiteoak yelped as he dove for the floor. As soon as he dropped, he scurried around the safe to get behind the open door. He may have looked like a cockroach running for cover that way, but at least he was a living cockroach.

Before he could collect his thoughts, Whiteoak's ears were assaulted by another trio of shots that hit the layer of metal in front of him. The iron door swung toward him and sparks flew as hot lead met cold iron. Now that he was behind the safe, Whiteoak could see that it wasn't as large as he'd imagined. More of a free-standing cabinet, the safe had enough room behind it for a man to shimmy between it and the back wall of the room. It would have been easier for a slightly skinnier man, but he wasn't about to split hairs.

"You want to hide back there forever?" asked the man who'd fired the shot that had ended Bailey's life. It didn't take more than a few words for Whiteoak to recognize the voice as belonging to the teller that had escorted him back there. Deliberate footsteps echoed through the little room, along with the metallic scraping sounds of fresh bullets being slid into a pistol's cylinder.

"I'm armed!" Whiteoak warned as he continued to scoot toward the edge of the safe.

"No you're not," the clerk replied. "Unless you managed to sneak that thirty-eight away from me when I wasn't looking."

Whiteoak's lips curled in a silent curse. He was almost to the edge of the safe when he heard those footsteps making their way around the iron box to meet him. The clerk was still reloading and taking his time. Obviously, the young man knew Whiteoak was all but pinned to the wall and felt no need to rush the job of dispatching him. Using that to his advantage, Whiteoak changed direction and began shuffling in the direction from which he'd come.

His progress was a little better this time, mostly due to all the dust and cobwebs that now coated the professor like a layer of dry grease. One side of his face was pressed against the back of the safe, causing every little imperfection in the iron surface to snag his skin and pull like tiny fishhooks. His hands worked furiously to pull him along and when they reached the edge of the safe he gripped it with his fingers for additional traction.

At that moment, the scant bit of light coming from the other side of the room was eclipsed by the teller's head and shoulders as the younger man peeked around. Whiteoak didn't need to look backward to know what was coming next. He pulled himself out of the cramped quarters, fully expecting to feel a bullet or two drill through him at any second.

Whiteoak emerged halfway from his untenable position, only to hear the first shot he'd been dreading. The bark of the gun was amplified within the tight space into which the teller had fired. Whiteoak grimaced, but felt nothing since the first round had dug into the wall with a muted *thunk*. Another shot followed quickly after that one, panging against the back of the safe to clip the professor's jacket as he plastered himself against the wall.

Once he popped out from the cramped space, Whiteoak couldn't help but count his blessings. It was no miracle that the clerk's hurried shots had missed. Considering how tight the space was, it would have taken considerable skill to line up such a straight shot without the ability to see more than a sliver of his target. The ricochet that had clipped him did more damage to Whiteoak's clothing than to his body. He didn't waste more than a second on those reflections, opting instead to scramble around the safe to get to the gun in Bailey's holster.

"Damn it," the clerk muttered as he rushed around the other end of the safe.

Whiteoak listened for the other man's steps which were quickly converging on his side of the safe. When he judged the moment to be right, he sent the safe's door moving with a mighty heave. The heavy piece of cast iron swung less than halfway shut before thumping against an obstruction. The obstruction cursed loudly, giving Whiteoak barely enough time to move around the door where he finally had some room to maneuver.

The teller staggered backward, holding his bruised face with one hand. He was already bringing his gun up to fire again as Whiteoak dove for the body of the deceased bank president. The professor landed in a less than graceful manner, hitting his stitched ribs against the floor. Not only was Bailey's pistol still holstered under his arm, but it was held there by a leather thong securing it against the hammer. Whiteoak rolled Bailey over and was about to tear the gun loose when a loud crash came from the bank's lobby.

"Are you working with the law?" the teller demanded. Lowering his hand to reveal the bloody spot where his head had met the vault door, he roared, "Tell me!"

Unable to free Bailey's pistol, Whiteoak said, "No! The law's been after me since I got here."

"Why?"

Whiteoak sensed he was quickly running out of time and made one last attempt to soothe the younger man. "Just put the gun down so we can discuss it."

"Professor?" Byron hollered from the lobby. "Where are you?"

Already on edge, the teller raised his pistol and tightened his finger on the trigger.

Whiteoak brought both legs up in a thrashing kick. One of his boot heels caught the teller's shin while the toe of his other foot knocked the pistol upward. The bullet that had been meant for Whiteoak drilled into the wall, giving the professor enough time to make his final lunge for Bailey's shoulder holster.

The instant Whiteoak closed his fingers around the pistol's grip, he pulled it free and rolled onto his back to fire a quick shot. Two more shots followed hot on the heels of that one, but didn't come from the pistol in Whiteoak's hand. After that, the room became still.

Whiteoak's heart was pounding but he didn't think he'd been hit by any of the rounds that had been fired. The teller, on the other hand, wasn't so fortunate. He stood like a marionette dangling from its strings, head drooping and arms hanging limp from his shoulders. A small hole had been punched through his upper chest and an even larger one was slightly below it. When the teller dropped, Whiteoak could see Byron standing behind him with a smoking pistol in hand.

"What the hell took you so long?" Whiteoak asked as he scrambled to his feet.

"The front door was locked," Byron said while looking down at the carnage on the floor. "The place was closed up a little while after you went in. When I heard gunshots, I tossed a rock through the window and came inside."

"Thankfully you armed yourself."

"After everything that's happened since you got to town? I'd be a fool to be anywhere near you without being armed. Who are they?" Byron asked while staring at the two bodies. "Nash's men?"

"Not as far as I know," Whiteoak replied. "One is the teller who works at the front window and the other . . ."

"Adam Bailey?" Byron gasped. "Oh my god! He was working with Nash?"

"I highly doubt it since he was the first one shot in this exchange. That other fellow was the one who killed him so if anyone was working with Nash, it'd be him."

"And he's not alone."

Picking up on Byron's nervousness, Whiteoak asked, "What makes you say that?"

"There were some men riding toward the bank before I broke that window."

"Was Nash one of them?"

"Maybe," Byron replied. "But they were all armed."

"You know something? I believe this bank is cursed!"

CHAPTER TWENTY-SIX

"We really need to get out of here," Byron said as he disappeared into the lobby, only to quickly reappear within the small room containing the bank's safe. "Did you hear me, Whiteoak?"

"Of course I heard you," the professor replied. "I'd have to be deaf not to."

"Then why are you still messing around with that damn safe?"

"I came here to get a look at it, which is precisely what I'll do. Something about this strikes me as familiar, but I can't put my finger on it."

Twitching at the sound of gunfire outside, Byron rushed to the lobby. "It's Nash, all right. And he's with one of his other men that we've seen before."

"Only one?" Whiteoak asked as he examined the interior of the vault.

"One that I recognize. Oh, Christ, here comes the sheriff."

"Good."

"Good?" Byron snapped. He stuck his head into the smaller room so he could look directly at Whiteoak. "How the hell is any of this good?"

"Because that means Nash won't be long for this world. I assume the town's protectors have taken their stations?"

"There were some men looking out through the windows, yes."

"See? That's good!"

"What are you doing, anyway?"

Whiteoak was hunched over so he could more closely examine the little square doors inside the safe. "Whatever the prize is that all these men are after, I doubt it's just this money. There's something else. Your sister mentioned some numbers."

"Numbers? Do you hear that? The sheriff's already giving his speech outside and I doubt it'll last as long as it did the first time around. We don't have time for numbers!"

"Three, four, seven, nine, twelve and sixteen," Whiteoak recited with his eyes closed as if reading the figures from the inside of his skull. "Those were the numbers Lyssa mentioned. They've got to mean something."

"You mean the numbers on the paper I was carrying?"

Wheeling around to face Byron, Whiteoak said, "Yes! Do you know what they mean?"

After letting out a pained sigh, Byron said, "I should have gone with my first instinct and taken the money that was inside that damned belt they made me wear."

Outside of the bank, voices were raised and the first couple of shots were fired. "You're right," Whiteoak said as he shifted his attention back to the safe. "The sheriff wasn't wasting any time."

Byron peeked out of the small room and through the lobby so he could catch a glimpse of what was happening through the front window. "They're headed this way," he warned.

"Who is? Nash or the law?"

"All of them!"

"Who do you think will get here first?" Whiteoak asked.

As if in response to his question, gunshots outside the bank rose to a deadly crescendo. A few stray bullets found their way into the bank through what was left of the window amid the shattering of the final shards of glass remaining in the frame.

"Get in here with me," Whiteoak said. "And keep your mind

on the task at hand."

Although he was grateful to be out of the lobby, Byron was barely able to stay on his feet. Every part of him was trembling and he was sweating hard enough to have soaked through nearly every article of clothing he wore. "What task?" he asked.

"Figuring out those numbers," Whiteoak said. "I think it's got something to do with these compartments."

The professor's finger tapped the small square doors inside the safe. There were twenty of them in all and each was locked tight.

"How do you know the numbers have anything at all to do with those doors?" Byron asked.

"Because this bank seems to be at the heart of all the trouble in this town. And at the heart of this bank is this safe. Check the pockets of the bank manager over there, will you?"

Wincing, Byron approached Bailey's body. "What am I looking for?"

"Keys to these compartments." As Byron gingerly searched the dead man's pockets, Whiteoak asked, "Did you see anyone else inside this place? Customers or maybe any other tellers?"

"No. The place was cleared out and locked up soon after you went inside. One of them looked like he might work here but I couldn't be certain. The place seemed empty except for the three of you when I came back in."

Whiteoak's attention was now focused on the stacks of money. Although he picked through them all, he didn't help himself to any of it. "Makes sense. I believe that clerk wanted no witnesses when he killed Bailey."

"Murderers are like that, so I've heard," Byron scoffed. "I'm surprised more bank tellers don't try to rob their place of work, actually."

"What he was after wasn't only to kill Mister Bailey. He needed someone to pin the death on."

"Like who?" Byron asked as he dug his hand into the inner pocket of Bailey's jacket.

"Me."

"A little self-important, aren't you?" Byron said. "Then again, we already knew that."

"Look at the gun in that teller's hand."

Byron looked at the second corpse in the room and quickly spotted the silver-plated .38 laying near him. "That looks like your gun."

"It is my gun," Whiteoak said. "He made me hand it over before taking me in here and must have pocketed it somewhere along the line. Considering the law's already low opinion of me, combined with me being here and my gun having obviously been fired recently, it wouldn't take a deductive genius to put me at the top of the list of suspects."

"And he was just waiting for you to come walking in here?" Byron asked skeptically.

"Maybe," Whiteoak replied as he examined a few smaller bundles of cash. "Or perhaps he saw an opportunity and jumped on it."

"What about Nash? You think he was waiting around for this as well?"

"He was in town and we already know he was after this safe. He and anyone else he could scrounge up were most likely poised to strike sometime very soon and me showing up here today simply sped the process along. Did you find those keys yet?"

"I did." Byron stood back up and extended his hand. "But I don't think you'll like it."

Whiteoak turned toward him and saw the keys dangling from a ring in Byron's grasp. There had to be at least two dozen of them rattling together like a collection of small, flat teeth. And no, he didn't like it very much.

"Any idea which key goes to which lock?" Byron asked.

Setting the money back down, Whiteoak rearranged some of the stacks so they were at an angle to the door. "They wouldn't happen to be marked, would they?"

Byron examined a few of them and replied, "Yes, but not one through twenty. There are at least four numbers on each one."

"Then, no. I don't know which key goes where, but I do have an idea of how I might find out."

"Good." Outside, the shooting had died to a low rumble mixed with a few shouting voices, all of which were still much too close for Byron's liking. "Wait a moment," he said. "Are you planning on robbing this place?"

"I'm planning on getting to the bottom of what these criminals, killers and crooked businessmen are after. Why have you been following me this whole time if you were suspicious of my motives?"

"Guess I've been sort of swept up in all of it. Also, there was that talk of a profit to be made."

"And there still is," Whiteoak said as he eased the safe's door shut. "Just not right now."

"Finally! It's time for us to get the hell out of here. There must be a back door to this place."

"I'm sure there is, but we're not taking it."

His body deflating like a sail on windless seas, Byron asked, "What now, then?"

"Now, we become heroes."

CHAPTER TWENTY-SEVEN

The dirt on Trader Avenue was slick with blood. Bodies were strewn like discarded toys, most of them near the bank but a few directly beneath the windows from which they'd fallen. Having survived the town's onslaught once, Nash had a good idea of what to expect the second time around. He'd landed some well-placed shots which sent a few of the elderly riflemen toppling from their high ground. While his deadly accuracy helped his cause, it wasn't enough to give him the clear shot at the bank he'd been hoping for.

But the outlaw wasn't the only one with the advantage of being forewarned. Sheriff Willis also had some of the cards stacked in his favor since his men and the town's shooters were already on their guard and ready for war. When both forces collided, the talking was kept to a minimum and tempers flared almost immediately. The first casualties were two of Nash's men. Yance and a bearded fellow that Whiteoak didn't recognize were gunned down within seconds of each other since neither one knew how to back away from a fight. In an impressive display of marksmanship, Yance had hit one of the local men while lying on the ground. The old man fell from the window, inciting even more violence from the rest of Barbrady's protectors.

Nash had backed toward the bank, only to be stopped by a hailstorm of lead that tore into the front of the building. The outlaw found some measure of refuge laying on his side behind a water trough. Occasionally, he glanced around the wooden box to fire at the encroaching lawmen.

Sheriff Willis and his deputy took their time closing in on Nash. There was nowhere for the outlaw to run and the longer Nash kept pulling his trigger, the fewer rounds he would have when he was finally taken down. Willis shot the trough in hopes of getting a lucky hit while the local men looking down on the street were content to keep firing at everything. Somewhere along the way, one of the town's younger residents got overzealous and decided to charge into the street. He wound up joining the rest of the bodies stretched out in the dirt, adding another charge to the growing list of Nash's offenses.

"Give it up, Nash!" Whiteoak shouted from within the bank. "There's nothing for you in this whole town!"

Nash looked over his shoulder at the broken building behind him. Although he was unable to see Whiteoak's face, he fired a round through the shattered front window anyhow. "If you think you can catch me in a crossfire, I'll have you know I can kill you just as good as I can kill these cowards out here!"

"There's no reason for me to kill you," Whiteoak said in a rasping voice that was just loud enough to be heard by someone in close proximity. To anyone farther than that, it would be nothing but a whisper lost in the wind. "I've already opened the safe and gotten my reward. Or, I should say, my part of the reward."

Hearing that seemed to upset Nash more than any of the gunshots being fired in his direction. "What're you talking about?"

"The bank teller is in here with me," Whiteoak replied. "He told me which doors to open inside the safe and what to do once they were all unlocked."

"Prove it."

"You want proof? Go ask your friend George Halstead."

Nash started to stand up, which drew a few more shots.

Quickly dropping down again, he roared, "You're full of shit!"

"Am I?" It may have been a risk to show his face amid all of that gunfire, but Whiteoak leaned to peek out the window. From his angle, he could see Nash laying on the ground behind the water trough like a very angry worm. "Michael Davis and I ran some jobs in Oregon when he was setting up one of his lumber camps. Meeting him here was a fluke, but it worked out in my favor. Mike recommended me to Mister Halstead and we decided to work together."

"Why the hell would they do that?" Nash asked.

"Because I'm not nearly as unpredictably violent as you. Take a look around and I think even you'd have to agree he made a good point."

Although Nash didn't say anything right away, Whiteoak could hear the wheels turning inside the bank robber's head. Those weren't the only minds racing. Sensing the tension coming from further across the street, the professor looked to Sheriff Willis and gave him a subtle shake of the head. Willis picked up on the signal and motioned for his deputy and everyone else behind him to hold steady.

"How about we work out something between the two of us?" Whiteoak said.

"You think I need to work with you?" Nash replied, spitting every word back toward the bank.

"It seems you're in quite the pickle," Whiteoak pointed out. "Whatever backup you've arranged is most likely miles away from here, or they might as well be. Otherwise they would have asserted themselves by now. Am I correct?"

Nash ground his teeth together so hard that his frustration practically echoed through town.

Soft footsteps could be heard approaching Whiteoak from behind. When the professor turned to wave Byron away, the younger man made it clear that he would not be so easily dismissed.

"What are you doing?" Byron asked.

Leaning slightly back so he could be seen from the street but not heard, Whiteoak said, "We don't have much time before the shooting commences and when it does, it won't stop until one side is done for. It's fairly obvious which side that will be."

"But what are you saying to him? The teller is . . ."

"I know," Whiteoak snapped. "I'm saying whatever I can to get him to part with some bit of information that will be useful. Already, I've confirmed a great many things." Counting off his points on his fingers, he added, "We know he's working with Halstead to rob this place and we also know Michael Davis is involved."

"We do?"

"When I mentioned Davis, he took it in stride. Read him like you're sitting across a card table from him instead of watching him fight a losing gun battle in the street and you'll see it as well."

Byron looked outside, uncomfortably shifting from one foot to another. "What else have you learned?"

"That there is, or was, backup planned to come to his aid. That means there are still cohorts somewhere nearby who are either biding their time or writing off their hotheaded partner. My money is on the latter."

"Otherwise they would have been here by now," Byron said, reciting the professor's own words.

"Exactly." Whiteoak was bold enough to take a full step outside. Where all of the nervous tension had been crackling between the two fighting parties in the street, it now shifted toward the well-dressed figure. By Whiteoak's estimation, he'd bought himself maybe another minute or two. Dropping the .38 he'd taken from the bank's president caused some of the ferocity in Nash's eyes to fade. Perhaps that would buy him more time.

"I got the safe open," Whiteoak announced.

That caught Nash's attention and held it. "What about the other compartment?"

"I know which compartments to open."

"That's enough of this," Sheriff Willis said. "Nothing inside that safe is going anywhere!"

"He doesn't know about it, does he?" Whiteoak continued, holding a hand up to the lawman as though he was taming an animal from afar. "There's more than money in there."

Nash scowled at him, blinking like someone who'd realized where they were after waking from a dream. "Of course there is. What the hell are you thinking?"

"Perhaps we should call Jeremy Christian in here."

"What the hell for?" Nash roared as his scowl deepened into hard lines cutting his face into jagged portions. "Shut yer damn mouth!" he roared while swinging his gun around to aim at the professor.

Whiteoak snapped one arm forward, causing a snub-nosed pistol to fall from a pocket sewn into his sleeve and into his hand. He pointed in the outlaw's general direction and pulled his trigger. Before the scent of burnt gunpowder could reach Whiteoak's nose, Nash rolled away from the trough so he could line up a better shot. Gunfire erupted from the street as men standing on the ground and looking down from second-floor windows responded to the shots that had already been fired.

When he ducked back into the bank, Whiteoak was grinning.

"What are you so happy about?" Byron asked from the spot where he cowered with his arms wrapped around his head.

The professor moved over to him. Before he lowered himself to the floor, a stray bullet punched through the frame of the bank's decimated window and hissed above their heads. Both men kept low and waddled deeper into the building, taking cover behind the counter in the lobby.

"Now we know there truly is more inside that safe than what can plainly be seen," Whiteoak said, ticking off his next point. "Also, we know that Jeremy Christian isn't involved in the scheme with Davis and Halstead."

"He looked like he thought you were crazy!"

"Precisely!" Whiteoak said over the crackling roar of gunshots outside the bank. "Isn't it wonderful?"

"And when you fired at him just now," Byron said, "you didn't intend on hitting him?"

"If I had, it would have been a welcome bonus."

"You wanted to get the shooting started?"

"That's right. And now, all we need to do is survive!"

"You're a damn lunatic!"

"What?" Whiteoak hollered over the growing wave of rifles and pistols barking like a pack of mad dogs outside.

"I said you're out of your goddamn mind!"

"Oh. Right. Hand me that pistol, will you?"

Byron had to look down at his hand to verify that he was holding the silver-handled .38 he'd picked up from the dead bank teller's grasp. Befuddled by the fact that he was the only one in the room showing the first hint of strain in the midst of a raging battle, he gave the professor's weapon back to him.

Taking his pistol, Whiteoak calmly thumbed its hammer back and pointed it at the gaping hole where the bank's front window used to be. Less than a second later, Jesse Nash appeared in the opening. Rushing frantically to get inside, one of his boots landed on the glass-covered floor. Professor Whiteoak adjusted his aim and squeezed his trigger, putting a bullet into the outlaw's chest. Dropping to one knee, Nash attempted to return fire but only succeeded in putting yet another hole into the bank's interior wall. After that, he was too weak to keep hold of his gun and let it fall from his hands.

"It's done, I'm afraid," Whiteoak said as he approached the wounded bank robber.

Nash wanted to kill Whiteoak. That much could be seen in his twitching eyes and menacing snarl. Instead of the hateful words he had in mind to spew at Whiteoak, the only thing to come from his mouth was a bubbling trickle of blood.

Outside, the lawmen had stopped shooting. Willis approached the bank while shouting up at the windows where rifle barrels angled downward like so many reeds bent in the wind. Judging by the sheriff's stern admonitions and raised tone, there were still plenty of frayed nerves and anxious trigger fingers among the town's protectors.

After taking the gun Nash had dropped, Whiteoak squatted down to put himself closer to the bank robber's level. "That's a clean shot I landed," he said while nodding toward Nash's sucking chest wound. "Why the hell would you take a run at this bank again, knowing about all those guns that would be pointed at you?"

"Job's a job," Nash replied. "Them windows were supposed to be empty, anyhow."

"If I were you, I'd be mighty perturbed about being left in the street to die by the men behind this poorly executed robbery. Now's your time to make them pay."

By now, Willis had gotten his deputy and every other armed local in the vicinity under control. All that remained was to rein in the last two wild elements in his sight. "You!" he shouted to Whiteoak. "Step away from that man!"

The professor held up a hand to silence the lawman, which wasn't nearly as well received as it had been when he'd shown the same gesture to Byron.

"I'm warning you," Willis said. "Step away and toss your weapon!"

Keeping his eyes on Nash, Whiteoak said, "Tell me what I need to know and you can rest knowing that I'll do what needs to be done."

"What are you saying?" Willis asked as he marched toward Whiteoak and Nash. Looking to where Byron stood nearby, he asked, "What's he saying?"

Byron shrugged. Even though he could hear some of the professor's words, he wasn't sure what they meant.

At the gruff sound of Nash's voice, Whiteoak leaned down and turned his head so his ear was close to Nash's mouth. He nodded and stood up, raising his hands high and allowing the .38 to fall to the ground.

"You too, Nash," Willis snarled, approaching the two men with his pistol held in a rigid grasp. "Lay flat and put your hands where I can see them."

"Too late, Sheriff," Whiteoak told him. "He's gone. You should probably be more concerned with the rest of his men."

"You mean these men?" Willis asked as he nodded toward the bodies scattered in the street.

"No. I mean Michael Davis and George Halstead, Senior. They're the ones looking to rob this bank."

"That's . . . that's absurd!" Willis sputtered. "They were two of the men protecting this bank from those mad-dog killers."

"Protecting from where?" Whiteoak asked.

The sheriff turned to point at one of the windows looking down on Trader Avenue. "Right there. I saw George with my own eyes."

But that window was empty. The next window the sheriff glanced at had been similarly vacated. "Avery," Willis said to his deputy. "Go into the Wayne Hotel and find Mister Davis and Halstead."

"Yes, sir, Sheriff."

"And you," Willis said to Whiteoak as his deputy raced across the street to the building containing the second empty window that had been pointed out, "stay right where you are." Turning his attention to some of the wrinkled faces looking down at the street, he added, "If either of these men move from where they're standing, gun them down!"

All of the rifle barrels that were still protruding from nearby windows came to attention and stared straight down at White-oak and Byron.

"I'd remain still if I were you," Whiteoak said to Byron.

The younger man's voice was shakier than the legs of a newborn colt. "I wasn't considering anything else."

CHAPTER TWENTY-EIGHT

By most anyone's standards, the rest of the day was slow and tedious. By the standards of two men who'd spent some of that day shooting and being shot at, the crawling pace was a welcome change. Professor Whiteoak and Byron Keag weren't allowed to move from the front of the bank until the sheriff was able to examine the wreckage left behind by the second failed robbery attempt and he couldn't do that until he found the missing members of the Founding Four. That last part turned out to be more difficult than anticipated.

The entire town streamed out of various buildings where they'd either been hiding or taking part in Barbrady's firing line. Locals emerged from the buildings surrounding the bank, walked down the street, or simply wandered in to get a look at what all the fuss had been about. After the dead were carried away, there was nothing left to do by those still lingering on the street but to chat among themselves, calm their nerves and try to make themselves useful after the recent ordeal. As time wore on, neighbors started to come together again. Robert helped the cleanup effort by feeding those who threw their backs into the job by bringing beer from the Dove Tail Saloon to serve with the ham sandwiches that were handed out by Mrs. Cassaday and some of the other women.

All the while, Whiteoak sat on the steps of the Second Bank of Barbrady. Idly, he looked up at the broken building behind him and asked, "Where's the First Bank?"

"What?" Byron asked warily.

"I just noticed this is the Second Bank of Barbrady. Where's the First Bank of Barbrady?"

"It burnt down three years ago."

"Oh," Whiteoak said. "Interesting."

"Not really."

Such was the extent of their conversation until someone else finally decided to acknowledge the men's existence. That person wasn't a peace officer, but a certain woman with a strained smile and soft, light brown hair.

"I brought you some lunch," Lyssa said while sitting down between Whiteoak and her brother.

Taking the food that he was given, Whiteoak said, "You managed to wrestle some of those sandwiches away from the others, did you?"

"Yes," she replied. "But it wasn't easy."

Byron's face was pale and his eyes were those of a soldier who'd been too close to cannon fire for too many battles. He took the food and began stuffing it into his mouth.

Noticing the other man's dazed countenance, Whiteoak said, "Looks like Byron's sandwiches were made with horse manure and dog meat."

Byron kept eating.

"He's been through a lot," the professor said to Lyssa. "It does my heart some good to see so many folks come together to help each other after the robbery."

Gathering her legs up close to her chest, Lyssa sat with her arms wrapped around her knees and her skirts collected into a neat bundle around her. "You both have been through a lot. This town's been through a lot as well. I didn't see much of it, but I heard the shooting. It was terrible."

"Were you worried about me?" Whiteoak asked as he scooted a bit closer to her.

"I was worried for my brother," she conceded.

"And?"

"And . . . I was concerned that you might be killed."

Whiteoak smiled confidently. "You'd miss me if I was gone."

"I'd probably be the one who'd have to bother with all the junk you left behind, since you spent so much time under my roof while here in Barbrady."

"There's more to it than that."

"True."

"I knew it!" Whiteoak beamed.

Lyssa plucked at a loose thread in her dress, rolled it between her fingers and allowed the wind to carry it away. "You also owe me money."

"I what?"

"You promised to compensate me for the meals I fed you," she told him dispassionately. "If you died, I wouldn't see a cent of that."

"Ahh. Have you seen the sheriff? He was supposed to talk to me after examining the inside of the bank. He went in some time ago and came out again a short while later. Haven't seen him since. I fear he might have forgotten about us."

"Please, lord," Byron muttered. "Say he forgot about us."

Lyssa reached out to rub her brother's back. "I saw the sheriff and Avery discussing something behind the bank when I was on my way over here."

"Oh, Lord."

"Your brother seems to find his religion at peculiar moments," Whiteoak mused.

"And you," Lyssa replied, "tend to take being shot at and involved with the law in stride."

Whiteoak shrugged. "No need in getting upset. What happens will happen. All I want is the opportunity to show my gratitude to my new friends."

"Gratitude?" Byron gasped as he looked directly at Whiteoak. "What the hell are you grateful for?"

"We weren't shot!" Whiteoak said. "We weren't arrested."

"Not *yet*."

"Oh, calm yourself. If we were going to be arrested, we'd be sitting behind bars right now. I'd say the sheriff is merely trying to figure out what to do with us. Isn't that right, Sheriff?"

Willis and his deputy strode forward and approached them. The two lawmen had circled around the bank, talking to excited locals and calming the nerves of a few men in suits who frantically waved their hands toward the bank. Close enough to hear the professor's voice, Willis said, "I have a few options where you two are concerned. Which one I choose depends on how you answer my questions."

Hearing that his fate was again tied to Whiteoak's, Byron hung his head low.

"Ask your questions," the professor said.

Standing with a hand propped on his gun and his deputy right behind him, Willis asked, "What happened to Mister Bailey?"

"The bank teller shot him."

"Why would he do that?"

"My guess would be that he was in league with whoever was behind these robberies," Whiteoak told him. "Right before Nash made his move, he took it upon himself to clear the place out. Ask any of the other customers who were in there."

All Sheriff Willis had to do was look over at one of the old women standing nearby to get a quick answer. The gray-haired lady had been desperate to overhear anything she could and was all too eager to reply, "It's true! Benson couldn't get me out of there fast enough. All of a sudden, he pushed me and Mister Lyme straight out the front door and locked it behind us. So rude!"

"I never caught the teller's name, but that sounds about right to me," Whiteoak said.

Whatever method Sheriff Willis used to catch a man in a lie, he used it then and studied his two subjects intently. While the conclusion at which he arrived didn't bring him to arrest Whiteoak or Byron, it also didn't seem to please him very much. "What were they after, Professor?"

"Money, I would assume."

"And why weren't you shooed out of there as well when the teller cleaned the place out?" Avery asked.

"I wouldn't presume to guess at the motives of a madman."

Becoming more flustered by the second, Willis asked, "How can you be so damn certain that Bailey wasn't in on this grand scheme?"

Whiteoak stood up and stretched his back. "If Bailey wanted to rob his own bank, I imagine he could have done so at his convenience. As for any other speculations . . ."

"Right, right," the sheriff grunted. "Motives of a madman."

"Well put, sir."

The lawmen were already jumpy by the professor getting to his feet without permission. When Lyssa stepped forward to insert herself into the conversation, both Willis and Avery visibly tensed.

"Ma'am," the deputy snapped, "please step back."

"Do you think my brother or Professor Whiteoak had any part of this other than as witnesses?"

"Well . . . I can't prove such a thing," Willis admitted.

"And did either of them do anything to hinder you when you and the others were shooting those thieving animals in the street?"

"Not exactly."

"In fact," Lyssa said while tapping her chin, "I heard the professor did a fairly good job of distracting Nash before he could shoot anyone else from their window."

Whiteoak hadn't been expecting that, but was quick enough to nod enthusiastically when the lawmen looked at him.

"Are you going to charge them with a crime?" she asked.

Avery looked at the elder lawman expectantly. All Sheriff Willis could do, however, was shake his head. "There doesn't seem to be a need for that," Willis said. "But you're not to leave town," he added. "Any of you."

"I wasn't planning on going anywhere," Whiteoak said in a voice that carried all the way down Trader Avenue and past the corner where it intersected with Second Street. "What I was planning was to lift a glass to toast Barbrady's valiant protectors."

"That won't be necessary," Willis said.

"On the contrary, good sir. I have seen these brave men fight back the tide of violence not once but twice since my arrival and I feel the need to thank them for saving my life. Considering they've protected the bank where I was depositing my personal funds, they protected my livelihood as well. Tonight, drinks at the Dove Tail Saloon are on me! Everyone is invited, but attendance by Barbrady's heroic committee or anyone else who put their lives on the line today is absolutely mandatory!"

The lawmen both seemed flustered by the announcement; a condition which only grew worse as Whiteoak's offer for free drinks was met by applause. After waving to his audience, the professor closed the distance between himself and the sheriff so he could ask, "What became of Misters Davis and Halstead?"

"Halstead got away," Willis said.

Livid, Avery groused, "You don't have to tell this peacock anything!"

"With all the flapping gums in this town, he'll hear about it soon enough as is," Willis replied. "Besides, I was hoping the professor might have something to say on the matter himself.

He was the one to have last words with Mister Bailey and Jesse Nash and Benson as well." Reading the question on Whiteoak's face, Willis added, "The bank teller."

For a moment, Whiteoak was silent. When he finally did speak, there was a tremor in his voice that had the flavor of fear or conscience. For a man like Whiteoak, one almost certainly led to the other.

"Mister Bailey's last words," Whiteoak explained, "as they are with most men who are surprised by their own end, weren't noteworthy. The teller revealed himself to be a murderer and his words were as spiteful as one might expect."

"And Nash?"

"He said that me and all the other rich sons of bitches could shove it up their asses." When he saw the consternation that brought to the sheriff's face, Whiteoak added, "You asked. Were you expecting a psalm?"

"No," Willis said. "I guess not. I won't toss you into jail for now, but you're not to leave town."

"Understood."

Recoiling as if his lineage had been insulted, Willis told him, "You step one foot out of Barbrady and I'll hunt you down."

"Of course."

"To make certain you stay put, I'll be taking your wagon."

Whiteoak bristled, which he quickly got under control with a few skilled shifting facial muscles. "That wagon is my life, sir."

"I know that, which is why I'll be taking it with me and putting it under lock and key until this matter is resolved."

"How long will that be?"

"Depends on how it goes. If there's to be a trial in relation to these killings and attempted robberies, you'll put on your finest suit and do your part. When this is done, if what you've told me is proven to be the truth, I'll turn your wagon over to you and send you off."

"What about my demonstrations? My work?"

"You can go inside your wagon and mix your tonics," the sheriff said. "But that wagon won't be moving unless you want to get on my bad side real quick."

"I guess that's fair," Whiteoak said stiffly.

"Yes," Lyssa said as she entwined her arm around the professor's. "That is more than fair and he appreciates it very much. Isn't that right, Henry?"

Whiteoak may have been a magnificent orator, but his acting skills weren't quite up to the task of putting on a convincing smile. He nodded once and allowed himself to be led away. Before he could get very far, a voice called out after him.

"And don't go sulking for too long," Avery said. "You promised all of these folks free drinks and you'll provide them."

"Yes, sir," Whiteoak replied in a mildly respectful tone that the deputy ate up like a plate of biscuits.

CHAPTER TWENTY-NINE

"These people love you," Byron mused. "How on earth do you manage it?"

Byron stood next to Whiteoak at the bar of the Dove Tail Saloon. Most everybody in town was there as well, thanks in no small part to Deputy Avery's diligent advertising campaign intended to hit the professor's wallet as hard as possible. The locals who weren't present at the time had made their presence known earlier that evening to collect their free drink.

Professor Whiteoak was dressed in a suit that was the color of lightly spoiled cream. A gold watch chain crossed his stomach and a diamond stickpin decorated the silk tie wrapped around his neck. His hair was slicked down in a smooth wave and his eyes positively sparkled as he met the smiling faces around him with heartfelt salutations. "Why are you surprised?" he asked. "I'm a delightful fellow."

"Sure. A delightful fellow paying for drinks. You might want to keep a closer eye on the barkeep. I don't think Robert is keeping track of which of these folks are coming back for seconds."

"It's a small price to pay for the goodwill of your fellow man."

"And?"

Whiteoak looked over to him after waving to an old man he didn't recognize. "What do you mean?"

"There's always an 'and' with you, Henry."

For a moment, the professor looked offended. Once Byron

waited him out for a few more seconds, Whiteoak nodded slightly and leaned in to confide, "Robert is giving me a bulk discount and he's also working off a debt."

"What debt?"

"You think this liquor tasted so good before I arrived?"

"Oh, right," Byron said. "I'd forgotten about that tonic you sold him after convincing him to purchase those tin cups."

"It's more of a spiced mixture, but yes. He bought an awful lot of it and wasn't able to pay when I made my delivery earlier this evening. Now, we're square."

"So you got all of this for free?"

"Not quite," Whiteoak said, "but almost. I did have to part with a good deal of my special mixture, but I can always make more. Such is the boon of being a professional craftsman."

Byron shook his head while tapping the glass of free whiskey that had been placed in front of him. "Always an angle."

"Life is full of angles. You either learn how to ride along their edges or get speared by them."

"That's one way of putting it."

"Did anyone catch up to those two swindlers, Davis and Halstead?" Whiteoak asked.

"I don't think so. Why don't we ask my sister?"

Perking up noticeably, Whiteoak asked, "Is she here?"

"She was to meet me. Ah, I see her over there with Mrs. Cassiday." Byron stuck his hand in the air and waved it wildly until Lyssa looked up from where she'd been sitting. Whiteoak tugged at his jacket to make sure everything was in order and picked up his hat which had been placed on the bar near him. He put the wide-brimmed hat on his head long enough to tip it to her and place it right back onto the bar.

"Have you finished those spectacles yet?" Lyssa asked once she was close enough to be heard. "Mrs. Cassaday is very anxious about them."

"I have them right here," Whiteoak said while patting his vest pocket. "If I'd known the two of you were there, I would have delivered them personally."

Lyssa rolled her eyes. "She's spent a good deal of her time trying to get this and every other saloon in town closed up. Says they're dens of sin."

"How very true," Whiteoak said. "Bless every last morally rotten plank within them."

"For someone who's so self-righteous," Byron chuckled, "the old bitty doesn't have any trouble knocking back her share of free liquor."

Responding to the smile on Byron's face instead of the words she couldn't hear, Mrs. Cassiday lifted the teacup she held between dainty fingers.

"It's tea," Whiteoak said while also raising his glass. "My own special blend. The most expensive one, no less. Brewed from leaves and spices clipped from foliage sprouting in every corner of the globe."

"Yeah, whatever," Byron said tiredly.

"I've been meaning to ask you something," Whiteoak said to Lyssa.

She sighed and walked around her brother so she could lean against the bar on the professor's other side. "I can answer your question right now," she said. "I will not accompany you to dinner until you are free from involvement with the law for at least two days. And even after that, you'd have to take me somewhere other than the cheapest chophouse in town."

Whiteoak's eyebrows lifted, right along with the corners of his mouth. "I wasn't going to ask anything of the sort, but it's nice to know where your thoughts are dwelling."

Color flushed through her face, and her mouth formed a straight, tight line beneath her rounded little nose. "What did you want to ask?"

"Since you have such a good relationship with the sheriff, I was wondering if you knew what became of the search for Michael Davis and George Halstead."

Lyssa's expression showed a hint of disappointment before she straightened her posture in a way that erected a thin barrier between herself and Whiteoak. "Michael Davis was cornered in the back of his lumber store by Deputy Avery," she reported. "He was so panicked that he fired a shot at Avery before being asked a single question."

"A guilty conscience can be a very powerful instrument," Whiteoak mused.

"Yes, well Davis's conscience landed him in jail. George Halstead, Senior, on the other hand, is a different story," Lyssa added, looking as if she'd found a piece of candy hidden in her pocket.

"Do tell."

She leaned on the bar again, this time so she could close in on Whiteoak. "He's still hiding somewhere. Two of his horses are missing from the stable at his home along with one of the men he'd hired on recently."

"Fellow by the name of Chuck Monroe?" Whiteoak asked.

Savoring her gossip like that piece of recently discovered candy, Lyssa placed her hand on the professor's arm and said, "Yes! I'd bet he's some sort of gunman."

"And you'd win that bet," Whiteoak said as he covered Lyssa's hand with his.

"I thought you said he was a bounty hunter," Byron said.

"Same difference," Whiteoak replied while wearing a distasteful look on his face. He gambled that anyone with aspirations to become any sort of peace officer would share that opinion. Judging by the sour look that Lyssa wore, he was correct.

"Sheriff Willis is convinced that those two had something to do with the bank robberies," she said. "Once they're found, both Halstead and his hired gun will wind up in the same cage as Davis."

"And good riddance to them," Whiteoak said. "So that means Willis and his deputy are out searching for them right now?"

"Avery is watching things here while Sheriff Willis takes a posse out to hunt for Halstead."

Whiteoak scratched his clean-shaven chin. "I didn't hear anything about a posse."

"You wouldn't," she replied. "On the few occasions when it was necessary to form a posse, Willis has gone one town over to Pacer Junction. Younger men around there are more than willing to sign on and collect their fee."

Looking around at all the gray hair, silver beards and wrinkled faces gathered in the Dove Tail, Whiteoak mused, "That makes perfect sense." He checked his pocket watch, put the timepiece away and knocked on the bar to catch Robert's attention. "A drink for the beautiful young lady!"

"No, I shouldn't," Lyssa said.

"Please. I'm required by the law of this town to provide at least one free drink to everyone here."

"I don't like whiskey or beer."

"Then try the tea," Whiteoak said. "It's my own brew!"

"She doesn't want to drink," Byron said. "Why don't you have one?"

"Don't mind if I do." With that, Whiteoak picked up the little glass that had been set out by Robert for Lyssa and downed the whiskey in one gulp.

Byron scowled at him. "What about the tea? You've been going on and on about it, but haven't tried a sip."

"You sound like one of the skeptics at my medicinal demonstrations," Whiteoak said through a wide smile. "I've had so much of that tea throughout the brewing and testing process that the taste is permanently on my tongue."

"I'll bet."

"Why are you being so rude?" Lyssa scolded.

Byron propped one hand against the bar and the other on his hip. "He's a professor of questionable integrity, specializing in making tonics that intoxicate in any number of ways and he's intent on getting my sister to drink something he made. Pardon me for being slightly suspicious."

"Byron!"

"It's all right," Whiteoak said as he patted her shoulder. "He's only protecting you. What sort of tonic are you worried about, exactly? A love potion?"

"Well . . . ," Byron said in a strained tone. "It's possible."

Lyssa hung her head and placed her fingertips against her temples. "Good Lord," she sighed.

Wincing at being trapped between the squabbling siblings, Whiteoak took the teacup that Robert brought over and slid it away from the Keags. When he turned back around, Lyssa stood less than an inch away from him. Being so close to her soft face and bright eyes caught him off-balance, a predicament that was only compounded when she took hold of his face in her hands and planted a magnificent kiss on his lips.

Shoving past a very pleasantly surprised Henry Whiteoak, Lyssa stood up to her brother and barked, "There! See?" before snatching up the teacup and drinking from it. Slamming the delicate little cup down hard enough to spill most of the remaining tea on the bar, she said, "There doesn't need to be any love potion, even if there was such a thing!"

"I . . . I . . . I don't," Byron stammered.

"Idiot." To Whiteoak, she said, "If you'd like to see me under more pleasant circumstances, perhaps we can arrange something."

"I'd like that very much," Whiteoak replied.

"So would I." Lyssa turned away from the two men standing

by her, only to find a good portion of the rest of the saloon staring at her in astonished disbelief. Dreadful embarrassment
soaked through her body like cold water.

"Come on," Whiteoak said as he gently took her hand. "Let's
go somewhere quieter."

He escorted her out of the saloon so they could stand on Wilcoe Avenue. There were a few others outside, but they were
either on their way in or still tipsy from the free spirits they'd
consumed. When one of the latter waved at Whiteoak, Lyssa
shied away from him and hid her face from everyone in the
vicinity.

"I can't believe I did that," she muttered.

"I know," Whiteoak replied. "What on earth took you so long?
After all the opportunities we've had and we still allow ourselves
to be sidetracked."

"Sidetracked?"

"Yes. From this." Whiteoak placed one hand on her hip and
used his other hand to brush some of Lyssa's hair behind one
ear. He then leaned in, lingering to feel one expectant breath
escape from her lips, and touched his mouth to hers.

Even after the kiss was finished, neither one of them wanted
to let more than a quarter of an inch of space grow between
them. "I thought you'd lost interest," she whispered.

"Like I said," Whiteoak told her. "Sidetracked."

"Well I'm not sidetracked anymore," she said while taking his
hand. "I know exactly where I want to go."

"You do?"

Lyssa nodded. "And you're coming with me."

"I am?"

"Oh, yes."

She held Whiteoak's hand in a gentle, yet unbreakable grip.
While leading him back to her home, she shared little stories
with him about certain people they passed and all the gossip

that was sure to flow once they arrived at their destination.

"And that doesn't bother you?" Whiteoak asked. "The gossip?"

"People have always talked about me one way to my face and another to my back. It's been like that ever since I dared to utter the words that I might like to do something other than bake or sew for a living."

"Yes, but surely being a peace officer is something quite extraordinary."

"It is," she replied simply. "That's why I want to do it! It started as a tribute to my late husband, but it feels right for me."

Whiteoak removed the watch from his vest pocket, opened it and checked its face. "Well, then," he said as he snapped the watch shut and put it away, "here we are."

"Yes," Lyssa replied while opening her front door. "Here we are."

"Are you feeling all right?"

"Why do you ask?"

"Because you look a little weary."

"It's been a long couple of days," she admitted. "But nothing would keep me from missing this."

"And what is this, exactly?"

"You're a worldly fellow," she said, pulling him inside the house by the front of his jacket. "I'd think you could come up with several ways for us to pass the time."

Following her inside and shutting the door behind him, Whiteoak said, "I sure can and I've been thinking about them for quite a while."

Lyssa leaned her head back and closed her eyes. "Let your imagination run wild," she said through a slight giggle.

"You seem a bit drunk."

"I feel like it, but I haven't had anything to drink."

Whiteoak moved in close and wrapped his arms around her. "Oh, I don't think that's quite true."

Laughing harder now, Lyssa reached around to grab the professor's wrists and move his hands onto her backside. "That's better! For an educated man, you sure need a lot of hints."

"You're definitely drunk."

"No! All I had was . . ."

Lyssa wasn't going to finish that sentence anytime soon. She was too distracted by collapsing into an unconscious heap. Fortunately, Whiteoak already had her in his arms so he prevented her from hitting the floor.

"When I considered sweeping you off your feet," he said to himself while doing that very thing and carrying her to her bedroom, "I admittedly had something else in mind."

Laying her on the bed, he looked down at her and let out a frustrated sigh. Once again, he checked his watch. "Damn my impeccable timing."

CHAPTER THIRTY

Minutes later, the Dove Tail Saloon was eerily quiet. Bodies were strewn on the floor, slumped over in their chairs or propped against the bar. Outside the saloon, the scene was very similar. A few mildly confused horses milled about in the street, nudging the snoring body of a nearby local or merely plodding over to the nearest water trough.

Professor Whiteoak took one of his strolls, viewing the figures laying on the ground while taking notes on a little piece of folded paper in his hand. After surveying the saloon district, he made his way to the row of stores on Third Street. They were quiet as well.

"Hello?" Whiteoak said as a way to announce himself when he stuck his nose into a dress shop.

Something stirred within the place, causing the professor to cautiously step inside. "Is someone there?" he asked.

The sound he'd heard was a scraping against the wooden floorboards. As he spoke and stepped inside, that sound became louder and faster. By the time Whiteoak was standing next to the shop's cash register, an old woman scurried down one of the shop's wide aisles.

"I'm here!" she said breathlessly. When she saw who'd entered the store, she picked up her feet to move even quicker toward him. "Oh, Professor Whiteoak! I'm so glad to see you!"

"What happened, Miss Tackett?" he asked, recognizing the old woman as one of his customers.

"I surely don't know! My husband and nephew came in to fix some loose shelves when they dropped right over! It was horrible."

"Are they ill?"

The more she tried to think of how to answer him, the more confused Miss Tackett became. Finally, she said, "They seem to be . . . sleeping."

"Goodness," Whiteoak said as he approached a set of feet he'd just spotted. The feet were attached to legs protruding from the back room. Before stepping into what looked to be a private office, he turned to Miss Tackett and asked, "May I?"

"Oh, please do!"

Whiteoak knelt beside the form of a younger man with thinning black hair and a pencil-line mustache. His eyes were half closed and his breaths came in long, shuddering gulps. After feeling for a pulse, Whiteoak put the back of his hand against the man's forehead. "He doesn't seem to have a fever. Do you think he might have caught this ailment from someone else?"

"You know something, I think he did! I went out the back door to try and fetch someone to help, but I could only find Mister Graves and Mister Pegg in a similar state. They were in the store next door."

"Strange. Have you seen anyone who isn't sleeping?"

"Come to think of it, no. Of course, almost everyone in town went to partake in the little party you were throwing."

"Let me guess," Whiteoak said. "You didn't partake in a thing."

"I was too busy. Also, I don't drink. Not with the spells I've been having. But you know all about those."

From the very first time he'd set up his wagon in Barbrady, Whiteoak had been selling one elixir after another to cure Miss Tackett's spells. As far as he could tell, she was simply suffering through the raised temperatures and memory lapses that many

219

women her age so often had. She did, however, enjoy the thought that one of the professor's many bottled miracles could bring her back to the vigor of her youth.

"Yes," he told her soothingly. "I certainly do know all about those."

"Can you help these men?"

"Of course I can. In fact, the reason I came along at this time was to see if there were any such cases in the area."

"So there are others like them?"

"I saw many poor souls in the saloon, sleeping like babes on their mothers' laps. Unfortunately, they were further along and had developed much worse symptoms."

More than willing to believe that something terrible was headed in her direction, Miss Tackett placed her hand over her mouth and waited for more. The professor was all too happy to give it to her.

"Fever, faint pulse, and worse I'm afraid," Whiteoak reported.

"How much worse? Has anyone died?"

"Oh, no! Not yet. Thankfully I was able to tend to them personally. Here," he said as he reached for a flask within his jacket. "Take a drink of this and you'll be spared."

"What is it?"

"Something to steel your system. Since you haven't shown any symptoms yet, this will keep you from feeling even the slightest bit of discomfort."

Miss Tackett drank from his flask and nodded while handing it back. "I feel better already," she told him.

"Good."

"That's very tasty. Is it some kind of tea?"

"Why, yes it is. The same kind of tea I was offering at the Dove Tail. A bit stronger, though."

"Oh?" The old woman's eyelids fluttered and she began to swoon. At the first hint of instability, Professor Whiteoak reached out to pull her toward him. That way, when she fell over, he could gently lower her to the floor.

"Actually, much stronger," he told the sleeping old woman. "But you'll be fine when you awake."

Since the method of offering his tonic as a cure or protection against the strange affliction gripping the town worked so well, he used it on the next several other locals he found who had avoided drinking the mixture that had been slipped into the Dove Tail's refreshments. Most of the folks he discovered were anxious and frightened at the predicament that had befallen Barbrady and were all too eager to grab on to any helping hand that was offered. Being the one to offer that hand at the right time was one of Whiteoak's greatest secrets to success.

The closer he got to the saloon district, the more sleeping figures Whiteoak found. Nodding as his theory was confirmed, he strolled past the drunken sleepers and nodded to a pair of wrinkled faces staring out at him through a small glass window. Since the faces were even more shriveled than dried apple dolls, he kept moving.

Whiteoak turned the next corner and walked north up Third Street. The businesses there were mostly stables, horse traders and a few stores catering to the needs of four-legged customers. The only movement to be found in those places was the shuffling of hooves against straw-covered floors. When he heard some whispering voices coming from one of the stables, he stopped and cautiously approached the drafty structure.

"Anyone there?" he called out.

The voices fell silent for a few moments and then resumed chattering to themselves in excited, high-pitched whispers.

Whiteoak approached the stable wearing an easy smile on his face. "It's all right. Don't you recognize me? I'm Professor Whiteoak. I'm a doctor."

That last statement wasn't entirely true, but the children hiding inside the stable were too frightened to question him. The sounds of their voices and the quickness of their movements were all Whiteoak needed to assume that's who he was dealing with. That prediction was confirmed when the pair of youths stepped from the shadows.

"You're the medicine man," said a boy who looked to be no more than nine years old.

"That's right," Whiteoak said as he squatted down to the kid's level. "Who else is in there with you?"

"My friend. James. He's scared."

"I am *not*," insisted a voice that was only slightly deeper than the first boy's.

Hooking a thumb over his shoulder, the first boy said, "He's afraid of the dark."

"What's your name?" Whiteoak asked.

"Michael."

"And have you seen any of my demonstrations?"

"You mean your medicine shows?"

"That's right. Do you know what I do?"

Michael nodded. "My pa says you're a salesman, but you know how to brew a few good drinks. You made his headaches go away, though."

"That's right," Whiteoak told him. "I helped your father and now I can help you. Do you know what's happening to these folks?"

Whatever bravery might have been in Michael's small round face quickly dissipated as he looked up and down the street. Taking a step back toward the stable's comforting shadows, he said, "No. All I saw was a bunch of men fall over like they was sick."

"Well, they are sick, but don't worry. You and your friend James aren't sick yet. Do you know how to keep it that way?"

"How?"

Whiteoak reached into his jacket and withdrew his hand with a flourish. The young boy jumped back, startled, but was fascinated by what he saw. "Take this," the professor said while handing over a small coin engraved with exotic markings, "and sit with James for a while."

"How long?" Michael asked as he turned the coin over in his little hands.

"Until you hear familiar voices outside. That will mean that I've done my job and folks in town are getting up again."

"So, they're not dead?"

"No."

"I told you!" James called out from the stable.

"Go on, now," Whiteoak ordered. To hurry Michael on his way, the professor turned the boy's head so he was facing in the other direction.

Like a little toy that had been wound up and set on its course, Michael went back to the stable and disappeared inside.

Whiteoak watched him go, making certain neither of the boys could be detected from outside. Sure enough, apart from a few bits of faint whispering between them, Michael and James had all but vanished. Although his business was on the western half of town, Whiteoak turned toward the north and the rest of Third Street. While there were plenty of storefronts and homes to be found that way, he was more interested in the solitary figure standing at the mouth of an alley twenty paces away.

Byron Keag stood with a pistol in his hand, watching the professor with narrowed eyes. Before he could say anything, he was silenced by Whiteoak who touched the tip of his finger to his pursed lips. Byron waited for the other man to draw closer, but held his gun at the ready.

CHAPTER THIRTY-ONE

The two men walked down the street a ways, one man strolling while at gunpoint and another armed with the weight of heaven and hell on his shoulders. Once they'd gotten far enough, Whiteoak stopped and turned to face the other man.

"I should kill you," Byron snarled.

"Keep your voice down."

"Why? Everyone in town is either dead or dying!"

"That's not true. They're sleeping. So kindly speak in a civilized tone so I can explain myself."

"Yeah, that's right you'll explain yourself," Byron said in a softer voice. "Why don't you start with what you gave to that child?"

"A coin I picked up in San Francisco. I believe it's from somewhere in Asia. Worthless, but intriguing. Someone passed it to me in lieu of genuine currency. It is genuine, but not here. The tonic I mixed was too strong a dosage for a child."

"So you didn't poison them?"

"Of course not," Whiteoak snapped. "What kind of a monster do you think I am?"

"That's what I'm trying to determine. Wait, where are you going?"

The professor had turned a corner to head toward First Street. "Come along and you'll see."

"You'll go where I say or you'll be shot where you stand."

"You won't fire," Whiteoak said with a backhanded wave.

"And even if you did, I've been shot before and one more time won't stop me now. Not unless you kill me, and I highly doubt you'd do anything of the sort."

"How do you know?"

"Because you could have done it already. If you were so concerned about those children, you certainly would have pulled your trigger back there."

"I was watching you," Byron explained halfheartedly. "Carefully."

"I know. I could feel your gaze. Quite chilling."

Hurrying to catch up with the professor whose strides had grown longer and faster, Byron lowered his pistol. "What the hell is going on around here? And where's my sister?"

"She's at home, in her bed."

Byron's pistol came up again. This time, however, its hammer was snapped back without the slightest hesitation. "If you sullied her in any way . . ."

"Now why on earth would I do that?" Whiteoak asked, his hands propped defiantly upon his hips.

"Wh . . . why would you do any of *this*?" Byron shot back as he waved a frantic hand at the entire town surrounding him.

Within a few seconds, the fire in Whiteoak's eyes died down. "All right," he said. "I know how this looks, but these people aren't dead. They're sleeping."

"They look dead."

"They're not. I checked a good number of them and I know exactly what I'm doing. The dosage they were given wasn't enough to kill. At the most, it would only make them sleep a couple of hours. Most will be awake before that."

"I *knew* you were the one behind it!"

"That's what I'm trying to tell you. Good Lord above, you're a trial to talk to when you're rattled."

Byron holstered his pistol. The gesture wasn't one of peace so

225

much as a show of exasperated surrender. "You drugged the whiskey you were giving away, didn't you?"

"Actually, I drugged the flavoring I gave to Robert at the Dove Tail and he drugged the whiskey. The tea, however, was all my doing. I presume you suspected something," Whiteoak added. "That's why you didn't drink either of them."

"You're damn right. Also, it seemed too peculiar for you to give away anything at all. You paying for drinks, even you parting with some of your tonics in exchange for drinks that would be handed out for free just seemed mighty strange. But you drank some of that whiskey! I saw it with my own eyes!"

Pride exploded from Whiteoak's face like beams of sunlight through a bank of clouds. "I did and after all the years I've spent working with and testing my own mixtures, I can ingest quite a lot of them without feeling any of their effects."

"Well I wasn't going to let Lyssa have any of it," Byron said. "Until she downed some just to spite me."

"Couldn't have done it better myself."

Byron's fist cracked against the professor's jaw, snapping his head to one side and sending a few drops of spittle through the air. Recovering from the blow, Whiteoak rubbed his chin before dabbing at his mouth with a handkerchief. "I had that one coming," he said.

"Damn right you did, especially with what you did to my sister."

"I already told you, she's sleeping like all the others."

"You didn't do anything . . . else . . . to her? Or with her?"

"No," Whiteoak said regretfully. "The compound is something I've been working on for some time. I perfected it after months of work and even tested it out on other men right here in town to make sure it was just right. Naturally, it was."

"Who did you test it on?" Byron asked.

"Remember how those fellows at our poker game passed out

after that round of drinks I bought?"

"Yeah."

"There you go," Whiteoak said as if he'd pulled a rose from his sleeve in front of an adoring crowd.

"What's this compound made from?"

"That would be too complicated to explain and I doubt you'd understand. No offense, but you're not a chemist."

Although Byron clearly wanted to argue the point, he couldn't exactly prove his credentials.

"Whoever drank that whiskey or my tea will be asleep for some time. Enough time," Whiteoak added while checking his watch, "for me to finish the business that brought me here in the first place."

"You put the whole town to sleep?" Byron asked incredulously.

"Not the whole town. That would be preposterous. I was only hoping to tuck the committee away so they wouldn't be around to turn the streets into a shooting gallery when I took my leave of this place. It turned out that a lot more folks accepted my invitation for a drink than I'd expected. Chalk that up to my charming personality, I suppose."

"And what brought you here in the first place?"

"The bank, of course."

"Damn," Byron grunted. "I knew you were a thief."

"My good fellow, was that ever in question?"

"No. No, it wasn't."

"I'd heard there was something valuable in that safe, but the trick was getting into it. I have many friends in various lines of work and they mentioned this prize in passing. When I asked why none of them or their associates went after it themselves, they said it was far more trouble than it was worth and getting into the safe was only half of the chore. The other half was getting out of town alive."

"So you came in under the guise of a snake oil salesman."

"How many times do I have to tell people?" Whiteoak said. "I do not sell snake oil. And my profession is not a guise or any sort of ruse, per se. I am as all of my credentials portray me."

"Uh-huh. Where on your wagon does it say you're a bank robber?"

"What I propose in this instance isn't robbery insomuch as a marvelously plotted scheme with vaguely illegal undertones." Upon feeling the thick air of disgust roll off of Byron, Whiteoak added, "Highly illegal. But nobody will get hurt and if anyone knew the lengths I went to make certain of that, they'd let me walk out of this town with naught but a pat on the back for a job well done."

"This is . . . insanity."

"Oh, come now. You must have had some sort of suspicion that something grand was taking place and even if you didn't know what it was, you wanted to be a part of it."

"Why would I want to take part in a swindler's insanity?"

"Because you're tired of being a messenger. Otherwise," Whiteoak said slyly, "why would you wait until now to see what I was up to?"

"How was I to know you were up to anything at all?"

"Why didn't you drink any of that whiskey?"

Byron didn't have a quick answer to that one. He found it even harder to speak once he saw the Second Bank of Barbrady drawing closer with every step. "I did know you were up to something," he said quietly.

"My point, exactly," Whiteoak replied. "Admitting something is the first step to overcoming it."

"I didn't think you'd do something that would hurt the entire town."

Raising a finger, Whiteoak said, "Nobody is hurt. Just sleeping."

"Yes, but I walked a good distance before finding you and I only saw one or two people on their feet and they were too old to do much of anything!"

"I appreciate that. Your observations, combined with all of the checking I did, tell me that most of the town is slumbering nicely. Now if you'll take a few deep breaths and calm yourself, you might be of some use to me."

Byron looked at Whiteoak as if the other man had sprouted a set of udders and strapped a bell around his neck. "Some *use* to you? I don't even know if my sister is truly breathing and you offer me some sort of job to do?"

"If it'll make you feel better, go check on Lyssa and confirm what I've already told you numerous times. I'll be inside the bank when you're through, but be quick about it. We don't have all day."

Like a dog that had been cut loose after being cooped up its entire life, Byron didn't know what to do with his newfound freedom. Then his expression hardened and he stabbed a finger at the professor. "You better not go anywhere!"

"I won't."

"Come to think of it, I want you to come along with me while I see Lyssa for myself."

They were directly in front of the bank by now and if there had been a bit in Whiteoak's mouth, he would have bitten clean through it already. "I'm not going anywhere but inside that bank."

Byron drew his pistol and pointed it at him. "You're coming with me."

Already on his way into the bank, Whiteoak waved off the command, bypassed the door altogether and kicked in a few of the boards that had been used to repair the large hole which had once been the bank's front window.

"Hey!" Byron shouted. When Whiteoak didn't respond to

that, Byron sent a round into the air. The sound of that single shot echoed through town, bouncing off of walls where it was apparently heard by no one, because that's who responded to it.

He considered going to find Sheriff Willis until he remembered the lawman was out hunting for George Halstead. Byron considered dragging Deputy Avery to the bank until he recalled all the times he'd seen the junior lawman at the Dove Tail. The odds of him passing up a free drink, no matter who was responsible for it being there, were slim at best.

All he had to do was consider his sister and Byron couldn't run to her house quickly enough.

CHAPTER THIRTY-TWO

It wasn't long before Byron returned to the building which seemed to be at the center of all of Barbrady's recent problems. "Henry!" he shouted while stepping in through the broken window. "Answer me, damn it!"

"In here," came the professor's reply.

Byron followed the sound of the other man's voice to the back of the lobby, which was where he'd been headed in the first place. When he got there, his hand was already resting on the grip of his holstered pistol. Although he had plenty of things he wanted to say to Whiteoak, the first thing that popped out was, "How'd you get that safe open?"

Hunched in front of the safe, Whiteoak took a quick glance over his shoulder and said, "Bailey tried to hide the combination from me when he was opening it, but he didn't do a very good job of it."

Byron looked into the lobby and saw the cash drawers near the tellers' windows were open and emptied. "Just once, I'd like to see a time when things don't go your way," he sighed.

"What was that?"

"Nothing."

"How was your sister?"

"She's fine," Byron said as he stepped into the back room so he could get a better look at what the professor was doing. "Couldn't wake her up, but she seemed fine."

"Give her another hour or so and she'll be plucky as ever.

Hopefully we'll be done with this in that time."

"We?"

"Of course! Since you're providing assistance, you're entitled to a cut of the profits. I'm certain there'll be plenty to go around."

His interest sparked, Byron huddled next to Whiteoak so he could look into the safe at the rows of small square doors. "What's in there, exactly?"

"I don't know yet, but we need to get to it quickly if we're to pull this off. Do me a favor and take a look behind that desk."

"Desk?" Byron turned around and spotted a small writing desk in the corner of the room near the door. The piece of furniture was barely large enough for two pieces of paper to be set on top of it side by side, which explained why he'd overlooked it earlier. It slid away from the wall with a single shove, exposing a dusty corner filled with cobwebs, some of which had been recently torn by a ring of keys that had been dropped on the floor.

"You find them?" Whiteoak asked. "They should be right there."

Reaching into the grimy corner, Byron picked up the keys and carried them over to Whiteoak. "Are these the ones Mister Bailey was holding?"

"The same. They got kicked somewhere during the tussle between me and that teller. Only problem now is figuring out which ones to use in which locks."

"Keep trying until one fits."

"It won't be that easy," Whiteoak replied.

Having been drawn into what now seemed to be more of an oversized puzzle box than a safe, Byron asked, "Why not? It shouldn't take too long to get most of those doors open."

"To answer that, I have one word for you. It also happened to be the same word that was the last one to pass from Jesse Nash's dying lips."

"You mean, after he said all those things about the Founding Four and who was behind the robberies?"

"He never said any of that," Whiteoak confessed.

"What?"

"Do you honestly think a dying man in that much pain could go on for that long on any subject?" Whiteoak thought back proudly to the tale he'd spun on the matter in front of his audience cloaked in swirling gun smoke. "I saw an opportunity to set some wheels in motion and being the sole recipient of Nash's final words was the perfect device. I aired some dirty laundry, espoused some of my own suspicions and generally poked the bear until it came trundling out of its cave. Considering how Davis and Halstead wound up, I'd say my display worked rather well."

"So that was a bluff?" Byron said incredulously. "With everything that happened, all the times we could have been killed, with all the guns pointed at you, you still found time to bluff?"

"The more audacious, the better where such matters are concerned."

"So what did Nash really tell you?"

"I asked him the one thing I needed to know and he answered."

"Yeah?"

Whiteoak turned around so he could look Byron straight in the eyes when he said, "Colfax."

"Colfax?"

"That's right."

"And what the hell is that supposed to mean?"

"Not a lot on its own," Whiteoak said, slipping into the melodic tone he used when pitching a new elixir outside of his wagon. "But considering this job pivots around this particular safe, it means quite a lot."

Since the professor had turned back around to carefully flip through the bundles of cash stacked beneath the square doors, Byron hastily said, "Keep talking."

"Myron Colfax is a designer of safes and lockboxes known for his sense of intricate eccentricity. He started his career building music boxes and the occasional timepiece, but found he could make more of a living crafting specialized items for a different set of clients."

"You mean building safes for rich men."

"Exactly. In one of my earlier careers, I stumbled across a few Colfax originals and found them to be quite infuriating. You see, they're designed specifically to guard against robbers."

"Aren't all safes made for that reason?" Byron asked. While he wouldn't admit as much to Whiteoak, he found himself drawn into the story. As he listened, the professor studied each individual bill in the bundles of money he was handling rather than pocketing them straight away.

"Yes," Whiteoak said, "but a Colfax safe is made to protect valuables even after it's been opened. His genius was in not underestimating the wits or tenacity of a desperate man's efforts to bust open an iron door. Any Colfax is strong in that regard. The real treasures to be found, however, lay within the compartments that aren't so easy to crack."

Byron was now crouching so he could gaze directly along Whiteoak's line of sight. Wearing the smile of a student that had just figured out the arithmetic problem that had been stumping him for so long, he said, "You mean those little compartments right there."

"Partly." Whiteoak removed one of the bills from the thin bundle he'd been examining and set it on top of the rest. He then sifted through the keys on the ring Byron had handed to him. His breathing took on a quicker pace as he excitedly held one key up to Byron's face. It was too close for Byron to see anything but a metal blur and before he could pull back far enough to get a clearer look, the key was stuck into the door of the third square compartment within the safe.

Whiteoak turned the key and, with the enthusiasm of someone who'd discovered a vein of gold on his property, opened the little door. When he turned to gloat to the man beside him, he was met only with a bland stare.

"So?" Byron asked.

"Remember those bundles of money you brought in that satchel you were hired to deliver?"

"Yes."

"You mentioned earlier that you were never hired to deliver money on any other occasion. And since there are much better ways to send that amount of money besides giving them to a nearly helpless courier . . ."

"Hey!" Byron snapped. "I wasn't helpless!"

"My point is that sending cash is such a standard practice that there's no good reason to assume your employers would choose to hire you instead of sending it along any of the other many routes and means they use for such transactions. I mean, this isn't even a lot of money for men like Halstead."

By now, Byron knew he had to break down what the professor said and find its meaning like he was crushing a boulder into smaller chunks that could be sifted for flecks of gold. Like those boulders, the amount of gold to be found in Whiteoak's abundance of words was usually fairly small. "So you think there's something special about these bills in particular?" Byron asked.

"I've been sure of it since the moment I heard what you were carrying."

"You knew I was coming to Barbrady and you knew I was

carrying an important parcel for my employer?"

Already busy sifting through the next bundle of cash, White-oak said, "How could I know such a thing?"

"Jesus," Byron sighed. "I knew you had some agenda of your own and I knew you were a swindler, but this is more than I could have imagined."

"Oh, don't play the innocent."

"What's that supposed to mean?"

"Don't try to act with me," Whiteoak chuckled. "It doesn't suit you."

"I'll admit, I thought staying close to you might prove to bring me some measure of profit that I couldn't get as a courier, but it wasn't much more than that."

Whiteoak turned to look at Byron. Unlike the previous times he'd done so, the professor's face was cold as steel and twice as sharp as a tempered blade. "Tell me that you haven't enjoyed this."

"Enjoyed what?"

"This! The excitement. The freedom. Making a fortune using your wits and gall like the men who carved this great country from a savage land."

"All right," Byron said, knowing full well he wouldn't be able to float anything less than the truth past those sharp eyes and sharper ears. "Perhaps it was a little . . . exciting."

"I knew it," Whiteoak replied as he found a bill within the stack and pulled it out. He set that bundle down and picked up another. "We are two of a kind, you and I."

"Is that why you served me a drink of that whiskey as well?"

Whiteoak shrugged and continued examining the money.

"I'm certain you wanted to put me out as well," Byron said smugly, "considering what a potential threat I might be."

A smirk flickered across Whiteoak's face before he twisted back around to face the safe. "Sure. Right. That's it."

Gritting his teeth, Byron decided not to press the matter and instead focus on whatever was capturing so much of the professor's attention. The square compartment was open, but appeared to be empty. "Looks like that theory of yours didn't pan out," he said.

Whiteoak immediately shifted his attention to the second bill he'd removed from its bundle. "Shouldn't you be more worried about watching the front of the bank for any stray killers?"

"What stray killers?"

"There were some key figures missing from my little celebration. Namely, Chuck Monroe himself. He's been laying low for a spell, but I doubt he simply pulled up stakes and left town."

"All right. I'll go take a look. But don't run off on me."

"For Christ's sake," Whiteoak snarled. "If I took more than two steps in here, it'd echo all the way outside. Just take a peek out the damn window."

Whiteoak's claim about the acoustics within the empty bank proved to be correct when Byron walked back to the lobby. His steps knocked throughout the entire building with the special kind of reverberation that was only found in unnatural desolation. Outside the bank, Trader Avenue was quiet as well. Further down the street, however, some dust was being kicked up by at least two horses.

Byron stepped outside, careful not to make too much noise. Knowing the town well enough to guess where that noise was coming from, he cut across a few empty lots until he was closer to the sheriff's office. Sure enough, the horses were being brought there by one man leading them to the little building. There were other men already there and they weren't deputies.

Pressing his back against a wall, Byron shimmied closer so he could hear some of what was going on.

". . . don't know what the hell is goin' on around here," said a man Byron recognized as Chuck Monroe. "With them law dogs out of the way, we got us a chance to bust Mister Davis outta jail without any fuss. Hell without that damned committee to fire at us from the windows, we can just shoot the locks and just stroll on out of there."

"Are we moving on that bank again?" asked someone who only sounded vaguely familiar.

"Damn right we are. Whiteoak and that courier fella are probably already there. We can put them down easy."

"No witnesses," snarled the man Byron couldn't place. "I like it."

Byron's heart clenched and his throat went dry. He then leaned around the side of the building next to the sheriff's office to get a look at who was having the conversation. With Chuck Monroe was the slender dark-haired fellow who'd attacked Byron and Whiteoak some time ago. Seeing his face also brought the man's name to mind. Eastman.

"Soon as Davis is free, we'll go to the bank and clean it out," a third man said as he strode out of the sheriff's office. Byron didn't have any problem recognizing George Halstead, even from a distance. "He's pulling himself together now," Halstead said. "You'd think he never sat on a damn cot before. We also got us some extra help as well."

"Anyone we can trust?"

"He's got a love of money and none for Whiteoak, which is good enough for now. There's plenty of guns and ammunition inside as well, so stock up before we head on up to Trader Avenue."

Easing away from the wall, Byron put some distance between himself and the other men. After that, he broke into a run.

CHAPTER THIRTY-THREE

"They're coming!" Byron said breathlessly as he hurried into the room where Whiteoak was still working.

Still hunched over as Byron had left him, the professor asked, "Who's coming?"

"Chuck Monroe and some of the other gunmen hired on by Halstead and Davis."

"How many are there?"

"I don't know for certain. I just heard Monroe talking to Mister Halstead near the sheriff's office. They were going to break Davis and someone else out of jail and then they're headed here."

"Do they still think you're working for them?"

"Doesn't matter," Byron replied. "They intend on killing both of us."

Whiteoak looked up from what he was doing. "Hmmm. We'd better hurry, then. I've only got one more door to open and then we can get whatever is in here."

"Forget that! We need to leave!"

"If we get the prize locked in this safe, we'll have something with which to bargain. Otherwise, we'll have to take our chances running from experienced killers and trackers. You think you're up to that?"

Reluctantly, Byron said, "Probably not, but you have experience too, right?"

"Not in that arena, unless you count being the target and

that usually doesn't end well. Now help me find the key to get this last door open."

Having reached his limit, Byron snatched the keys from Whiteoak's hand and shoved him away from the safe. "I suppose it makes some kind of sense to empty out this safe," he said while looking at the keys, "but why do you have to make everything so damn difficult?"

"Give me that!" Whiteoak demanded.

Byron drew his pistol with his free hand and pointed it at the professor. "Back the hell away from me!"

Whiteoak did as he was ordered, glaring at Byron like a tiger eyeing its next meal.

"You're right in what you said before. I actually thought working with you might be a good idea. You know why?"

"Please. Enlighten me."

"Because you're a blowhard and a cheat, but you're a smart businessman and at least you're not a killer. I thought I could stand to make some money. Then I found out you're a damn *lunatic*!"

"I'm not crazy."

"No," Byron said as he flipped to the key next to the last one Whiteoak had used, "but you're also not as smart as you think you are." That key didn't fit, so he tried the next one and the next. "In the time it would take you to decipher whatever clues you think you'd found, I could've gotten this damn thing open by process of elimination."

"Stop," Whiteoak said. "You don't know what you're doing."

The fourth key Byron tried slid into the lock all the way. "Don't I?" he said as he turned it. The locking mechanism clicked smoothly within the little door, as did a similar mechanism that rattled behind the rest of the doors like a series of falling metal dominoes to shut them all tightly. "What was that?" Byron wondered out loud.

"That," Whiteoak replied, "was all of the doors being shut and locked again because the keys were turned out of sequence."

"How does that happen?"

"Same principle as the tumblers of a lock, but on a different scale."

"I've never heard of a safe like that!"

"Didn't I mention Myron Colfax safes were *rare* and *exotic*?" Whiteoak fumed. "Wait a moment, I believe I *did* mention that!"

"Yes, but . . . aw, hell."

Whiteoak snatched the keys from Byron's hand. "Give me those! You're damn lucky I have such an excellent memory." The professor then proceeded to flip through the keys until he found the one he wanted. That key fit into the lock of the third door and opened it. The next key he selected opened the door beside it.

"How do you know what doors to open?" Byron asked.

"There was a note in the satchel you delivered with the numbers three, four, seven, nine, twelve and sixteen written on it. I surmised those were the doors that needed to be opened and I was correct."

"But the markings on those keys are all numbers, and none of the numbers are less than three digits long so they can't be matched to numbers on the door."

Working furiously, Whiteoak spoke as though he was trying to explain scientific theory to a pinecone. "There are six numbers in that note. In your money belt, there were also six bundles of cash. The cash wasn't a remarkable amount, but you had it deposited into this safe."

"No," Byron said. "I dropped the whole belt off and it was picked up by someone else."

Whiteoak looked up and scrunched his face into a thoughtful grimace. "Oh, right. It was. Well, I saw it was in here when the safe was opened by Mister Halstead. Six little bundles, wrapped up in twine. Because they were delivered with the note, I figured the bundles also had something to do with opening the grander scheme of cracking the safe. Upon closer examination of the money, I discovered this."

Whiteoak handed over one of the bills he'd separated from the rest and Byron took it. His hands were trembling and his heart was thumping an irregular drumbeat within his chest. "What am I looking for?" he asked.

"Look at the writing on that bill," Whiteoak told him.

The bill in Byron's hand was for twenty dollars. More used to spending them than studying them, it took a moment for him to find the writing to which Whiteoak was referring. On the note was the number three and then another string of four numbers after it. "So what?" Byron said. "I've seen things written on paper money before. Is this supposed to help?"

"One bill in each stack is similarly marked," Whiteoak said. "Numbers one through six and the other sequences correspond to six keys."

"The keys that open the compartments you need?"

"Yes!"

"How the hell did you know about that?"

"It's a puzzle," Whiteoak said. "The pieces are there and the goal is to open this safe. Once I got to the safe to see what needed to be done, the pieces started making sense. When I saw that a key matched that number which, in turn, opened a compartment, I knew I was on to something."

"So you didn't know exactly what you were doing until you got here?"

"Partly."

Looking at the professor with open astonishment, Byron asked, "You poisoned an entire town to give you some time to try and figure out your puzzle? What if you couldn't figure it out?"

Whiteoak started laughing so hard that he almost lost track of the keys in his hands. "I admit to working on a constricted schedule, but I don't need much time to figure out what goes where. Just do me a favor and get some horses ready. We'll need to ride out of here as quickly as possible once I open this secret compartment."

"Shouldn't we stand and fight?"

"You can if you'd like. Myself, I'd prefer to keep the number of holes in my head at the original number."

Whiteoak had opened the seventh and ninth compartments by the time Byron started feeling really nervous. He'd been watching the street outside as the professor worked, feeling every second tick by as though it was being dragged through a sea of tar.

"I see horses coming down the street," Byron reported. "How much longer?"

The twelfth door had been opened and Whiteoak inserted the key into door sixteen. "Almost there," he said as he turned the key. When the door came open, he let out a short victorious yelp.

"What's inside that's so special?"

"Don't know yet."

"You've got about a minute to find it, so hurry up!"

"The other compartments looked empty," Whiteoak said. "So does this last one."

Byron rushed into the room and gawked at the safe. "For Christ's sake. This is a waste of time. I should never have tried to throw in with you. I should've stuck to being a courier."

Whiteoak stood up to his full height and wheeled around in a rustle of expensive tailored fabric. "No! You're your own man, like myself. You follow your gut and travel wherever it takes you. That's why you threw in with me and seen it through for so long that we're nearly done with this heist."

"Heist? Good lord, we're criminals."

"At this moment, I'm a criminal. At best, you're an accomplice. At worst, we'll both be dead if we don't put an end to this real quick."

Without waiting to see what effect his words had on Byron, Whiteoak turned back around and dropped to his knees so he could reach desperately into a pair of the safe's compartments.

"Well?" Byron asked.

"There's something in the back. Feels like it's attached. A ring of some kind."

"A diamond ring? Gold?"

"No. Copper, maybe. Or brass. Could be tin, I suppose."

"Copper or tin?" Byron moaned. "That's great. We're dead."

"Where are Monroe and the others?"

Leaning out of the room to look through the lobby and the front window, Byron turned pale as a frog's belly and said, "They're almost here. Jesus, Mary and Joseph."

"Save the gospel for Sunday. Right now, hide." As he spoke, Whiteoak collected the bills that he'd separated from the bundles and started stacking the cash back into neat piles the way it had originally been arranged.

"What the hell was I thinking? I'm not an outlaw or bank robber or anything else but someone who takes satchels from one spot to another."

"You through?" Whiteoak asked.

"I guess so."

The professor grabbed the younger man's sleeve and dragged him toward the tellers' windows. Shoving Byron to the floor behind the low counter, Whiteoak peered between the bars separating the tellers from their customers and then dropped to the floor.

"All right," Whiteoak hissed. "Keep quiet. If they find us, we're dead."

CHAPTER THIRTY-FOUR

They were discovered almost immediately.

"Lookee what we have here!" Chuck Monroe said as he came around the tellers' counter. "The medicine man and his assistant."

"I'm not an assistant," Byron announced.

The gunman dragged him to his feet and stepped back so Whiteoak could be forced to his. "Whatever you say," Monroe grunted.

There were two other men accompanying Monroe. One was Eastman and the other was a skinny, scruffy fellow with sunken cheeks and a dirty face. He was the one who dragged the professor into the open. As he was pulled up from his paltry hiding spot, Whiteoak asked, "Where's the sheriff? Surely he'll be arriving soon. Best if you let us go and worry about making your escape."

"Not until we get what we're after," said one of the others who'd stepped into the bank. George Halstead spoke with calm assurance as though he'd glimpsed into the future and was satisfied with how everything turned out. "I'm guessing you already got the safe open."

"It's open," Whiteoak replied. "But you won't have time to do much about it. Even if you empty that safe, you won't get far before the sheriff hauls you all back. He's forming a posse, you know."

Being the one who'd been so recently locked in a cage, Davis stomped forward angrily and punched Whiteoak in the face. It was a weak blow thrown with all the force an old businessman could muster, which barely turned the professor's head. "That incompetent sheriff is dead!" he said. "And you will be too in about three seconds."

Whiteoak reached out to pat Davis's shoulder and give him a playful swat on the ribs. "Now I see why you can't do your own dirty work," he said smugly. "Feels like you've barely got the muscle to lift your own arm, let alone a pistol. Or perhaps you intend on using a derringer. Those are favored by women, after all, so—"

The next punch that Davis delivered was stronger than the first, but not by much. It succeeded in shutting Whiteoak's mouth, however, which was enough to satisfy the older man. He was even more satisfied when he motioned over his shoulder for the skinny gunman to step forward. The sunken-faced man now had a shotgun in his hands which he jammed into Whiteoak's stomach. Before cutting the professor in half with a close-range blast, Monroe spoke up.

"Hold on," Monroe said. "Let's make sure we got what we want before killing this snake. Odds are, he's got something up his sleeve."

"I do," Whiteoak said. "And it's something you'll definitely want."

"Just shut your damn mouth until you're spoken to," the skinny shotgunner said.

"Now I remember you!" Whiteoak said. "You're the bank robber who was wearing the mask when Nash and all those others were cut down."

"Yeah," the outlaw replied. "Now shut the hell up!"

Whiteoak did as he was told, watching silently as Halstead went into the room containing the safe. "Looks like the money is here," Halstead called out.

All of the gunmen smiled, but Davis was reluctant to join in. "What about the rest of it?" he shouted.

Halstead grumbled to himself in the next room as a familiar metallic jangling drifted through the air. After a few seconds, he stormed back into the lobby carrying the keys in one hand and one of the bundles of cash wrapped in twine in the other. "They're missing," he snarled.

"What's missing?" Davis asked.

"The notes that were supposed to be sent to the safe so we could open it."

"Can't open the safe?" Whiteoak chuckled. "That is a predicament."

"Shut up!" Davis roared. Speaking in a somewhat more subdued tone, he looked back to Halstead. "You told me you arranged to have everything we needed waiting here for us."

"It was sent, like I told you," Halstead replied. "I was told exactly where to look for the numbers and I'm telling you, they aren't there."

"Did you check every bundle?"

"You want me to take these two out of here so you can talk?" Monroe asked as he glanced at Whiteoak and Byron.

Dismissing the two prisoners with an impatient wave, Davis said, "They'll be dead soon."

"You like that, don't you?" Whiteoak said.

"Yes," Davis said through gritted teeth. "I do."

"That way I can't tell your partners here what I saw."

Monroe brought his pistol up and took aim at Whiteoak. His thumb was on the gun's hammer when Halstead barked, "Wait." Monroe refrained from pulling his trigger, but kept the pistol aimed at the spot he'd chosen between Whiteoak's eyes.

"What did you see?" Halstead asked.

Davis stomped into the next room and returned with a few more bundles of cash. "What the hell does it matter?" he said as he flipped through the money. "He's a bullshitter and a cheat."

"Spare me the righteousness!" Whiteoak said. "You're all cheats. Which one of you told Nash that there wouldn't be anyone firing at him from the windows the second time he made his run at this bank?"

"You should thank me for that," Halstead replied. "How else were we going to get that mad dog out of the picture?"

"Bullshit," the professor laughed. "You were covering him, hoping he'd succeed in his second attempt. And once it looked like he wouldn't, you cut him loose to be killed."

Halstead shrugged. "The man was good at his job. He had a better-than-average chance at success."

"More like there was *no* chance of him taking it well when you used him up and tried to cast him aside. Let me guess. You tried working with him, realized what an enormously bad idea it was and then wanted him gone."

"You're a smart man, Professor," Davis said. "It seems you've skulked around with trash like those robbers long enough to pick up a thing or two."

"I've also been around Barbrady long enough," Whiteoak said, "to witness you do some skulking about yourself, Mister Davis."

Shaking his head, Davis tossed one of the bundles aside so he could look through the other.

"What are you talking about?" Halstead asked.

Even while surrounded and held at gunpoint, the professor couldn't resist pausing for dramatic effect. After the appropriate number of seconds had ticked by, he locked eyes with Halstead and told him, "Mister Davis intends on keeping the contents of that safe for himself."

Halstead's eyes narrowed.

Byron drew a nervous breath. He'd been too frightened to say much of anything so far and wasn't about to draw attention to himself now.

"He doesn't even know what we're after," Davis said. "Shoot the lying son of a bitch."

Keeping his focus on Halstead, Whiteoak spoke in a voice that was as cool and steady as Monroe's gun hand. "He wants you to kill me so I don't finish talking."

"So finish," Halstead said.

"Clearly, I intended on robbing this bank as well," Whiteoak explained. "While I wasn't ultimately successful, I did plenty of scouting beforehand. During that time, I saw Mister Davis enter that room and remove something from that safe. I questioned one of the tellers and he told me that what Mister Davis took was crucial and had only just arrived when my friend Mister Keag came to Barbrady."

Some of the sharp edge disappeared from Halstead's face. When he glanced in Byron's direction, he nodded as if confirming something he already knew.

"I believe it was only a few dollars," Whiteoak said. "At least, that's what the teller told me."

"Bullshit," Davis spat. "I already told you, he's a liar. There was no teller who knew anything."

"Actually," Monroe said after clearing his throat, "there was one fella working here who was working for me."

Slowly turning his head to look at the bounty hunter, Halstead asked, "Worked for you . . . how?"

"I paid him to keep an eye on Mister Bailey and if things got too far ahead of schedule, he'd kill him."

Davis puffed out his chest like a frog drawing air into its throat, but Halstead jumped in before he had a chance to unleash the hell he was surely preparing. "We all knew Bailey might get wise to what was about to happen, Mike. We were going to kill him sooner or later and this way, he never got a chance to clean out the safe himself."

Davis's eyes flicked back and forth between Monroe and Whiteoak. "But what he said about the teller seeing me do anything is preposterous! I just got out of jail, for Christ's sake!"

"And you had plenty of time to do plenty of things before you landed there," Whiteoak pointed out.

"We've been in this together long enough," Davis said to Halstead. "You're going to trust a known swindler trying to save his own hide over me?"

To Whiteoak, Halstead said, "You'd better come up with something more convincing than that and I'm not about to waste much time on waiting for it. I'm guessing whatever you did to the folks in this town won't last all day." Furrowing his brow, he added, "Will it?"

"No," Whiteoak told him. "And it doesn't have to. Mister Davis clearly intended on following through on his own plans right here and now, so it stands to reason that he'd have any incriminating articles on his person."

"This is asinine," Davis snapped.

"Search him," Whiteoak said. "That's all I ask."

Davis stormed up to the professor and punched him in the gut. His fist succeeded in doubling Whiteoak over, but only because it had surprised him. "You don't get to ask for a god-damn thing and if you say one more word, I'll knock your teeth out. Monroe, kill this prick and be done with it."

"Monroe," Halstead snarled, displaying more power over the gunman with one word than Davis had done with an entire tirade. "Search Mister Davis."

"What?" Davis gasped.

"There's no harm in it," Halstead said. "If there's nothing to be found, I'll step aside and let you kill him any way you like. So humor me and let's move on."

Shaking his head, Davis threw up his hands. "Whatever you say, George."

Eastman and the skinny fellow stood by, both of them adopting Byron's policy of keeping their mouths shut while the others argued. They did, however, shuffle a few steps closer to Byron and Whiteoak in case one of them tried anything unexpected.

"Too bad this snake oil salesman's going to die," Davis mused as Monroe stuck his hands into his pockets one at a time. "He can talk anyone into damn near anything. I'll give him this much, though. He managed to buy himself a few extra seconds on this earth. I can guarantee you one thing, Professor Whiteoak, you will most certainly not enjoy those seconds."

Monroe pulled something from the pocket of Davis's jacket. He examined it for a moment before handing it over to Halstead.

A few seconds was all Halstead needed to study what had been found. "What the hell is this?" he asked in a voice that was more of a predator's snarl.

Still laughing at the paces he was being forced to go through, Davis asked, "What's what?"

"This," Halstead replied as he held out a small wad of folded twenty-dollar bills. "These were in your pocket."

"So?"

The rage on Halstead's face grew like a fire ripping through a warehouse stocked with kerosene. As he held the money closer to Davis's eyes, his hand clenched tight enough to turn his knuckles white. "*Look at them!* They're the marked bills we've been looking for!"

"That's . . . why would I have them in my pocket?"

"Now that's the real question, isn't it?"

Byron looked at the professor, but could read nothing on Whiteoak's face.

"They weren't in the bundles," Halstead fumed, "and here they are with you."

"They must've been planted on me," Davis said. "That god-

251

damn medicine man must've done it.'"

"To hell with that," was Halstead's reply. "Nobody's that slick. You meant to keep us from opening that safe now so you could do it yourself later! Ain't that right?"

Davis's voice became calm and steady when he said, "You know better than that, George. We've been in this together from the start of this town and we're together now."

"Not anymore. Monroe, shoot this backstabbing prick and then shoot the professor and his friend. I've had enough of this."

Still steady, Davis's voice became sharper when he said, "Mister Monroe, I'll double your fee once you ignore whatever comes out of that man's mouth."

"Shoot him!" Halstead commanded.

"Triple your fee," Davis countered, "after you put a bullet in his mouth instead."

Eastman and the skinny fellow next to him didn't know which way to turn. Their hands gripped their weapons tightly, but their eyes couldn't decide where to look.

Whiteoak's expression was unreadable as he simply waited to see what would happen next.

Chuck Monroe, on the other hand, was perfectly clear in his purpose as he raised his pistol and fired a single shot through Halstead's forehead.

Michael Davis let out a breath and nodded solemnly. "Good choice. I'll have your money for you once we're out of town."

"Keep it," Monroe said as he shifted his aim and pulled the trigger again.

The second bullet caught Davis in the chest, spun him around and sent him flopping to the ground. Eastman and the other gunman reacted instinctually, swinging their pistols toward Monroe and opening fire on him. Monroe responded by dropping to one knee and squeezing his trigger as though he was knocking empty cans from a fence rail on a warm summer day.

The skinny outlaw was the next one to catch a piece of hot lead. He buckled as a bullet drilled into his chest, but didn't go down until the next one punched through his lung. As soon as that fellow could no longer hold his gun, Monroe fired on Eastman.

Monroe had shots fired at him as well, but they were fired in a panic. It didn't matter how close he was to his target when Eastman barely kept enough wits about him to make use of the short range. Eastman was still sending lead into the walls when Monroe's next shot entered his right eye and exploded out the back of his head. His body hit the floor, followed by the sharp clatter of empty casings being dumped from a warm cylinder.

Calmly reloading his pistol, Monroe said, "When assholes like that start turning on each other, it's only a matter of time before they shoot at other folks around them. Usually, the next people on the list are them that might pose a threat."

"Umm, well, yes," Whiteoak said. "That makes sense."

Dropping the pistol into his holster, Monroe strode into the next room. Whiteoak and Byron barely had a chance to exchange cautious glances before Monroe returned carrying the bundles of cash cradled in one arm. He rooted around for a few seconds, finding some more cash stuffed beneath the teller's counter in a strongbox. "I'll take this as my payment. Whatever else is in there, I don't want any part of it, of you, or of this town. Too much damn trouble."

"Very fair."

After searching the bodies of Davis and Halstead for a few more dollars, Monroe walked toward the front door, stopped and turned back around. "We're parting on amicable terms this time, Whiteoak. If I hear one word that you bore witness against me to the shootings in this bank today, I'll come back for you and it won't be quick like it was for these sons of bitches.

Understand?"

While some men preferred to lace their threats with colorful grotesqueries, or obscene details, Monroe made a succinct point well enough to shut Whiteoak's mouth for the moment. He stuffed his payment into his jacket and left the bank.

The professor straightened his clothes and marched back into the room containing the safe. "After this ordeal, I'm not leaving without the contents of that safe."

Byron wiped the sweat from his brow. "I've been through the same ordeal, so we're splitting it."

CHAPTER THIRTY-FIVE

Having gone through the motions once already, Whiteoak had the safe's inner compartments unlocked and open in a fraction of the amount of time it had taken before. Whiteoak was reaching inside compartment number seven when Byron asked, "How much longer is this going to take?"

"Hard to tell. Colfax is said to be a genius, but more than a little crazy."

"Hmm. Sounds like you two have something in common."

"Really? Thank you!"

Although he was referring to the crazy part of that equation, Byron didn't correct him. "How much longer will the locals be sleeping?"

"At least another half hour, I'd imagine. Although some of the people who didn't get a dose might be wandering about sooner than that. Aha!"

"What?" Byron asked as he crouched down to get a look inside the safe. "What did you find?"

Whiteoak slowly pulled a small ring out of the compartment. It looked to be cast in an unremarkable metal or possibly even carved from wood. It was difficult to tell since it was painted black to match the interior of the space in which it had been found. "Just as I thought," the professor said. "There's even more that remains unseen."

There was a cord attached to the ring which was so thin that it took Byron a few moments to spot it. "What happens when you pull it?"

After giving it a tentative tug, Whiteoak said, "Don't know."

Growing impatient, Byron reached into compartment number sixteen and found the ring laying beneath a few scraps of folded paper. "Here's another one!"

"Yes, but—"

Byron pulled the ring to get a better look. Immediately after the thread attached to it drew taut, it snapped. Holding it so the ring and thread fragment dangled from his finger, he said, "Must be old. Let's get out of here."

"Idiot!" Whiteoak bellowed. "This is a delicate work of art. Eccentric, yes, but there is a purpose."

"Safes lock and unlock," Byron grunted. "That's it."

"And thinking like that is what keeps the contents of a Colfax safe out of the hands of simpletons like you."

"I beg your pardon!"

"Don't worry," Whiteoak said as he gently pulled the ring from compartment three as far as it would go. "Most people in this world are simpletons."

Being the one with the broken string dangling from his finger, Byron wasn't in much of a position to argue.

The professor had already moved on and was easing the ring out of the fourth compartment. "I heard something when you pulled that ring, however. It was a little creak of metal. I'd say it's a latch, which is what I would have guessed anyway."

"Naturally," Byron said sarcastically.

Looping his finger through both rings, Whiteoak held them taut which placed them a few inches outside of their compartments. "What I want you to do is . . . carefully this time . . . take the rings from nine and twelve and hold them out like so." Whiteoak reached into compartment seven with his free hand and extended that ring out as well. "I'd do it myself, but this is clearly designed to be opened by no fewer than three men.

Since you so deftly knocked one compartment out of the picture, we'll see if we can make up for it with some steady hands."

Byron reached into the compartments, slipped a finger through each ring, and eased them out. When he'd taken the slack from the threads, he waited for a signal from Whiteoak.

Intense concentration was etched into the professor's face. Ever so slowly, he moved the rings out a bit more. "Something's definitely moving," he whispered as though his voice alone might be enough to snap the threads. "It's a matter of tensile strength. One thread is too weak to lift the latch on its own, but if the weight is distributed . . . pull yours out a bit more."

Byron did as instructed. After exposing less than half an inch more of thread, he could feel it straining against his finger. Closing his eyes, he thought he could hear individual strands within his threads give way.

"If the weight is distributed among many threads," the professor continued, "the latch can be lifted. It must have taken exacting measurements and craftsmanship, but the true wonder lies in the idea itself. Genius."

"Can this still be opened after one of those threads was broken?"

"If it is a matter of weight distribution, then there's a chance. If not, then we'll soon find out. Either way, it's worth a shot."

The two men eased the rings out bit by bit, each one wincing at any and every sound that came from within the safe. Although Byron thought the threads might snap at any moment, Whiteoak seemed pleased with the progress that was made.

"There's a bit more tension here," the professor said excitedly. "Can you feel it?"

"Yes," Byron lied. "What should we do?"

"When I count to three, I want you to pull slowly but consistently."

"What if another thread breaks?"

"Let's not think about that," Whiteoak replied. "Ready? One . . . two . . . three."

Byron did as he'd been told, matching the professor's motions while tugging on the delicate threads attached to the rings. At once, all of the threads seemed to be snagged on something.

Whiteoak nodded and urged Byron to keep at it. "One more good pull," he said.

Closing his eyes, Byron kept pulling until something within the safe gave way. The sound he heard wasn't what he'd expected, but was instead a metallic clank as a panel at the bottom of the safe's interior popped up. A fraction of a second later, four of the five remaining threads snapped loose and came free.

"That was exhilarating!" Whiteoak exclaimed. Flicking the rings off his fingers, he lifted the panel up and out of the safe. Although there were papers stacked inside the hidden compartment, he turned his attention first to the mechanism that had kept the panel shut. "It's a latch all right. Just like I'd hypothesized. The strings were attached and with enough counterweight applied, they pulled the latch open which freed the panel."

"Great. What's inside?"

Whiteoak removed the papers. "Documents of some kind," he muttered while sifting through them. "They're deeds. Mining rights. Stock certificates." Whiteoak slowly looked up from the papers as his mouth hung open. "Good Lord. These papers represent the bulk of the companies owned by the Founding Four. Bailey must have been holding them here for safekeeping."

"No wonder they were all fighting over them. Those papers are worth a fortune. Three fortunes!"

"Son of a bitch."

"I know," Byron said as he took the papers so he could have a look for himself. "It's really something."

"No," Whiteoak said with fire in his eyes and venom in his tone. Turning around, he stomped back a step so he could pivot and kick the safe with every bit of strength he had. "Son of a *bitch!*"

"Are you angry?"

"Yes, I'm bloody well pissed! This couldn't be worse!"

"But . . ." At a loss for words, Byron held up the papers so Whiteoak could once again see the collected legacies of the richest men in Kansas and many of the surrounding states. "How much more were you expecting?"

"Diamonds! Gold! Stacks of cash in larger denominations! Anything I can spend, dammit! What the hell am I supposed to do with this?"

Byron smiled. For once, he was the one with the answer.

CHAPTER THIRTY-SIX

Jeremy Christian's house wasn't hard to find. Everyone who'd lived in town for any length of time knew about it because the sprawling yellow colonial with the wraparound porch had been there since Barbrady was established. As they took the short walk from the bank to the Christian spread, Byron and Whiteoak spotted a few more people out. They were confused and concerned with locating their close acquaintances, which allowed the two men to get past them without much fuss. All in all, however, those that drank the doctored beverages were still asleep.

"What are we doing here?" Whiteoak grumbled once they arrived at the rich man's house.

"To prove a point and to show you that a good deed can be its own reward."

The professor's laugh was spat upon the ground like a wad of tobacco juice. "And where did you get this sudden change of spirit? Surely not from the scoundrel snake oil salesman you threw in with for so brief a time."

"No," Byron said while climbing the steps of Christian's front porch. "But trying to make a few quick dollars by straying from the work ethic instilled by my parents only got me shot at, chased, lied to, robbed, involved in two bank robberies, chased down alleys and hounded by the law. Also, I doubt my sister will trust me anytime soon and rightfully so."

"Let's get this straight. Your situation is far from dire. You being robbed had nothing to do with any bad decisions on your part and your sister will forgive you. She's a good woman."

"She is a good woman. Good enough to make any man into a better one."

"I'm sure," Whiteoak said heavily. "But some of us are beyond repair."

"You may be a swindler, but I have full confidence that you're not half as bad as some people say you are." With that, Byron knocked on the front door. There was no response from inside at first, so he knocked again. Eventually, a haggard, grating voice came to them like claws tearing through linens.

"Is that my medicine?" the voice screeched.

"Mister Christian?" Byron said to the door.

"Did you bring my medicine?"

"No, sir, but I have something important to discuss with you. It's about your partners."

"Come in!"

Byron tried the door and found it to be unlocked so he pushed it open. The interior of the house was modest considering the outer shell, but very comfortable. Walls were covered with faded paper. Shelves were filled with books. Vases held blooming flowers and the air smelled of freshly baked bread. The foyer opened into a staircase with a room branching off on the left and right. The only sign of life came from the room on the left.

"Who the hell are you?" growled a withered old man propped in a padded chair with a blanket cocooning his lower half. Spectacles were clipped to his nose and held in place by a string that wrapped around the back of his spotted head. His mouth waggled open even after he spoke like a feeble attempt to echo his own words.

"Mister Christian, I'm Byron Keag."

"Lyssa's brother?"

"That's right and this is my associate, Professor Henry Whiteoak."

"Professor?" the old man snorted. "That's a hoot. He's the idiot who parked that wagon in town everyone's talking about?"

"Right again."

Whiteoak acknowledged the introduction with a wave.

"Where's my medicine? My nurse was supposed to bring it to me, but she hasn't been back. Said something about a commotion."

Byron cleared his throat uncomfortably. "Yes, well that's still going on. I came to tell you something about your partners. You may find it difficult to believe."

Over the next several minutes, Byron told the old man about what had happened at the bank and what had almost been stolen by Davis and Halstead. He topped off his tale by presenting the old man with the bundle of papers that had been in the safe's hidden compartment.

Despite the shaking in the old man's hands, Christian went through the papers and nodded while skimming each one. "You say it should be difficult to believe? Not hardly. Michael and George had been after my seat in this town for years."

"Seat?" Whiteoak asked.

"Yes. Me, those two and the president of the bank . . . Adam Bailey run this town. We get a cut of the taxes, we control trade with other towns, we negotiate deals with railroad companies that want to build on nearby land. There's a lot of money to be made if a man knows how to run the system properly. Then when you put this into the mix," Christian added while waving the papers, "you're talking plenty more."

"I'm sure."

"And you said the other three are dead?" the old man asked.

Whiteoak stepped forward and asked, "And you didn't know that Adam Bailey had been killed?"

Christian dismissed that impatiently. "I never leave this house. I'm too old to get around very well and not interested enough to bother looking out the window. In here I have my books and my nurses. They cook damn good, tend to my health and every other thing a man needs if you know what I mean."

Shuddering, Whiteoak stepped back again.

"You don't seem very upset, sir," Byron pointed out.

"They were greedy sons of bitches. Good partners, but bastards all the same. They were gonna come to bad ends sooner or later. Me? I still got my books and my women."

Whiteoak settled into one of the other chairs in the parlor. "It does sound like a good arrangement."

"Well, we thought you should have these papers," Byron said. "Some of them do belong to you and the rest to your partners. Being a member of this town's ruling body, it only seemed proper to bring them to you. A lot of good people's jobs are at stake, no matter how unscrupulous their employers might have been. Also, those companies provide much needed supplies and products across this part of the country. We are both aware of what a tremendous civil responsibility it is to keep those things running smoothly."

It was difficult to tell if Christian was nodding or if his shakes were increasing in severity. Either way, he seemed rather pleased when he reached out to pat Byron's hand. "You are a noble young fellow."

"Thank you, sir," Byron replied while turning to Whiteoak to give him a curt nod.

The professor was still agitated enough to roll his eyes at the morality lesson he was supposed to be learning.

"I appreciate this," Christian said. "And I doubt you could take this over to the Davis or Halstead places, since they both tried to kill you. I did hear tell about some gunmen robbing a courier on his way into town so he could acquire some important documents."

"Halstead hired those two?" Byron asked.

The old man shrugged. "I suppose so. It's rare that Halstead ain't up to some kind of dirty deed. I found it best to only concern myself with that nonsense when it's absolutely necessary. Maybe you should keep to yourself for a while too, now. No telling who else might be gunning for ya, huh?"

"Actually," Byron said as his smile melted away, "I hadn't thought of that."

"Well I know how to take care of my friends, son. Don't you worry. You and your sister will be well cared for."

"I do appreciate that, but that's not why I came over here."

"And there'll be a reward, naturally."

It had likely been several years since anything in that house had moved as quickly as Whiteoak when he sat up straight and leaned forward with both hands propped on his knees. "Reward?" he inquired.

"Naturally," Christian replied. "Any man who does this kind of service for me or my company would be paid. How's five thousand each strike you?"

"Very well indeed, my dear sir," Whiteoak said, slipping easily back into his scholarly tone.

"No," Byron said. "Everything that had anything to do with that bank or those men or any idea that came out of your head," he declared while pointing an accusing finger at Whiteoak, "has gone horribly wrong! Any money connected to this affair is bloody and tainted. No offence, Mister Christian."

"None taken," the old man replied. "I've spilled enough blood to fill a few wells to gain the prominence I have now."

Byron rubbed his eyes and sighed, "Oh, God."

Whiteoak checked his pocket watch. "That's fascinating, but I really need to be going. That celebration is almost over and I'd hate to overstay my welcome. I sincerely appreciate the reward, sir. Is there any chance I could get it now?"

It took some doing, but Mister Christian managed to stand up from his chair and walk over to a large painting on the wall. He swung the adequately drawn landscape away to reveal a much smaller and less complicated safe than the one that had occupied so much of the professor's recent time. "Of course. Some of it might be in gold," Christian said. "Will that suit you?"

"Like a feather suits a mallard."

"No!" Byron declared. "Keep your money, sir. I thank you for looking out for my sister and me while we're here, but keep your money. I'll only take what I earn from this day forward."

"I can put you to work whenever you like," the old man said, securing the future of the Keag family for decades to come in one sentence.

"Oh. Well . . . I appreciate that. I think we should go now. Thank you, Mister Christian. It's been a pleasure." Byron shook the old man's hand, straightened proudly and strode out of the largest house in Barbrady with his dignity and moral compass properly aligned.

Whiteoak stood up, tugged at his lapels to straighten his collar and shot his cuffs. "It has certainly been delightful meeting you, sir. I can see this town is in very good hands."

Scowling beneath a deeply wrinkled forehead and bushy eyebrows, Mister Christian asked, "Are you taking the reward?"

"Most definitely! And, since he's spiritually opposed to the wickedness of wealth, I'll gladly accept Mister Keag's as well."

ABOUT THE AUTHOR

Marcus Galloway is the author of several novels and short stories in the western genre. His previous series includes *The Man from Boot Hill* (HarperCollins), *The Accomplice* (Berkley) and *Sathow's Sinners* (Berkley). He currently resides in a small West Virginia town with one perfect dog and a whole lot of books.

The employees of Five Star Publishing hope you have enjoyed this book.

Our Five Star novels explore little-known chapters from America's history, stories told from unique perspectives that will entertain a broad range of readers.

Other Five Star books are available at your local library, bookstore, all major book distributors, and directly from Five Star/Gale.

Connect with Five Star Publishing

Visit us on Facebook:
  https://www.facebook.com/FiveStarCengage

Email:
  FiveStar@cengage.com

For information about titles and placing orders:
  (800) 223-1244
  gale.orders@cengage.com

To share your comments, write to us:
  Five Star Publishing
  Attn: Publisher
  10 Water St., Suite 310
  Waterville, ME 04901